BROKEN
Redemption

To my readers. Thank you so much for all of the encouragement and support. Without all of you this book wouldn't be here. Thank you for not giving up on me.

Editor: Amy Briggs, Briggs Consulting

Proofreader: Virginia Tesi Carey

Cover Model: Bryan T. Snell

Cover Photographer: Reggie Deanching, RplusMphoto

Author Photographer: Cassy Roop, Pink Ink Designs

OTHER BOOKS BY MELISSA HUIE

The Broken Road Series *(should be read in order)*
  The Broken Road
  Broken Promises
  Broken Rules
  Broken Redemption
  Untitled – to be released in late 2022/early 2023

PLAYLIST

Broken Redemption Playlist
https://spoti.fi/3Lf9S3F

Maddness - Ruelle
In My Zone - Rittz, Mike Posner, B.o.B
I Don't Mind - FNKHOUSER
Wicked Games - RAIGN
Hurricane - I Prevail
Humble - Kendrick Lamar
Sober - KC Makes Music, Jordan Meyer
My Drug - Anthony Mossburg
About Damn Time - Lizzo
Drunk (And I Don't Want To Go Home) - Elle King & Miranda Lambert
It Was a Good Day - Ice Cube
You Should See Me in a Crown - Billie Eilish
When I get Home -Fieldhouse, Clever
Adrenaline - Zero 9:36
Solid - Young Stoner Life, Drake
Sinner - DEZI

Kissin' On My Tattoos – August Alsina
Smells Like Teen Spirit - Malia J.
Church - Chasing Atlantic
Breathe - sKitz Kraven
In The End - Tommee Proffitt, Fleurie, Jung Youth
Angel - Theory of a Deadman

1

SKETCH

"CATCH ME, SETHIE!"

Her musical laughter echoed in my ears as she ran from me, her blonde pigtails swinging in the breeze. I chased after her, making sure I was just far enough away to not trample her. The sun shone on her golden skin, and the ocean nearby fragranced the air. She started to get further away, and I quickened my pace to keep up. My fingers stretched, but she remained out of reach. The panic started to build in my chest as I struggled to keep her in my sights.

"Jennie, wait for me!" My demand was lost in the wind. Her small frame disappeared over the horizon, and I dug deep to push myself to go faster. I crested the sand dune, and looked around the vast, empty beach. "Jennie!" I shouted.

"You should have been there, Seth. You should have saved us." The deep, angry tone of adult Jennie came behind me. I turned and gasped in shock. Gone was the light in her blue eyes, and healthy glow of her skin. Gone was the five-year-old innocence. In her place was a twenty-three-year-old addict, with needle-prick marred skin that practically hung off her bones, limp dirty hair, and the scowl on her face. A little girl with her back facing me held her hand.

"Jennie, I'm sorry. I tried! I swear!" I pleaded with her, to make her believe me, even though I knew I could have done more. I should have done more.

"Bullshit," she spat. "You could have done more! You were so concerned about helping everyone else out and going out to play hero overseas, you didn't give a rat's ass about me! This is your fault!"

"Jennie no, I'm sorry! Please, let me help you." I walked toward her, but the beach fell away. Suddenly, we were on a wooden stage, surrounded by gunfire. Her drugged-up body had impaired her senses so much she didn't even flinch when a man in black put the muzzle of his gun to her head. Her eyes barely registered the impact of the bullet into her skull, and I could see whatever life was left drain from her eyes as she collapsed onto the stage.

"*No!*" My eyes popped open, and I shot up, gasping for air. I breathed deeply, trying to calm my racing heart and unclenched the gun I had drawn under my pillow. My hands shook as I rubbed them over my face, damp with sweat. I glanced over at the clock on the wall.

Five o'clock on a Friday morning—you've got to be fucking kidding me.

I groaned at the time. Sleep was a fickle bitch. My fucked-up mind constantly replayed my past sins, but Jennie wasn't the only one haunting my dreams at night. Another innocent life was interwoven in my spiral down into the darkness. I don't often see the face of my humanity, but I know she's there. The nightmares. The terrors all reminding me those I loved weren't safe around me. How I destroy everything good. I didn't just toe the line between heaven and hell. I danced with the devil across it.

I knew trying to go back to sleep would be useless. I threw

off the black comforter and swung my legs over, letting my feet hit the floor. I heaved myself off the bed and shuffled into the bathroom, trying to get the cobwebs out of my head. After throwing on some clothes, I grabbed my phone and trudged down the stairs to get the day started. Murray, my Bullmastiff, begrudgingly followed, his displeasure at the time quite evident as he lumbered outside into the cool, early spring air.

After I put the coffee on, I made my way on to the back deck, cupping my hands as I lit the first cigarette of the day. I inhaled deeply and tried to clear the remnants of the dream from my memory. I knew it would be hopeless. I closed my eyes and listened to the quiet noise of nature waking up. Isolated amid urban sprawl on the outskirts of Baltimore, I had managed to find my fortress of solitude. My own personal Bat Cave up on a hill, surrounded by trees and an acre of land. Too bad this wasn't Wayne Manor and I sure as hell wasn't as rich as Bruce Wayne or as powerful as Superman. Like the dark knight, I stayed in the shadows as much as possible. But that's where our differences ended. I had no problem with exacting justice in my own personal way. I was more deadly. And I found peace in destroying those who did me wrong.

It was all a matter of time before I found the bastards who ended Jennie's life. I just hoped that when I did, I'd finally find peace.

After throwing together my meals for the day, I grabbed the cooler, then whistled for Murray's fat ass to follow as I headed for my Challenger. The training center I co-owned with my teammate Cole Turner was only ten miles away, so I made the trek in minimal time. Cole wouldn't be around until closer to eight, so I had the place to myself for a bit. I unloaded my gear into the space I called an office for the administrative nonsense and turned the warehouse speakers on high. The sounds of I Prevail came through the speakers and I let the music drown out the demons. Anything to help me get the rage out. For the next hour, my feet pounded the treadmill. I ran. I ran from the demons chasing me, from the terror of witnessing my baby sister falling to the ground dead and not being able to stop it. I ran so I didn't have to think. I ran to become numb.

Once the machine slowed to a halt, I hit the weights. One by one, I hit my maximum, pushing my limit as much as I could, harder and faster than yesterday. I dropped the last bar with a roar, my voice echoing off the empty walls.

"That good, huh?" Cole's voice penetrated my thoughts. I glanced over at him strolling into the weight room and gave a grunt. He paid my lack of response no mind and threw me the hand tape.

He knew the drill.

I quickly wrapped my hands and followed him into the open training area. We got into our fighting stances. Cole threw out a smirk. "Let's go, Beast."

I threw myself into the sparring match. At first, each hit was more strategic, planning both my offensive and defensive moves. But today, Cole was better. He ended up blocking everything I gave him. I threw a punch, aiming for his gut, and ended up pinned beneath him.

"You're not focused," Cole gritted out.

Fuck this. The beast took over. I leveraged my legs and pushed up, throwing him off me. My adrenaline from the nightmare and the rage that had been simmering in my blood erupted. I grabbed him and slammed him against the rails.

"Hit me!" I roared.

Cole shoved me back. "I'm not going to be the one to beat you down. You're doing it all on your own." His voice, rough with emotion, cut me in shame.

"Fuck you, Cole," I seethed. I ripped off the tape and let the rags flutter to the ground as I stalked off toward the locker room.

There were very few people who knew me. But Cole, he knew me better than I knew myself.

I slammed my bare fist against the wooden door, throwing it open with a bang. I turned on the shower full blast and stepped into the freezing enclosure. I ignored the cold, only to relish the stinging-like drops onto my overheated skin. I scrubbed my ink covered skin, looking to take off the reminders of the past, then turned off the water, and quickly dried off.

After throwing on another set of clothes, I pushed out of the locker room and headed up the metal stairs to the room we used as an office. My mood hadn't changed at all, but I was good at putting on a façade. My true self only shown when absolutely needed. Until then, I would continue to be the same numb, cynical bastard everyone knew me to be.

We need a fucking secretary. Are they even called that anymore?

Despite my animosity toward everything administrative, shit needed to get done. Thanks to the warmer weather, groups wanted to book the outdoor tactical training portion of our program. We ran local and federal law enforcement and military groups through a variety of rigorous courses—everything from active shooter, high intensity hostage negotiation, clearing of facilities as well as combat and artillery tactics to sniper targets and hand to hand maneuvers. We were certified by the DOD, and despite my misgivings and basic lack of trust for any government agency, we ran one of the best training courses out there for a team of ten men. Well, ten men and one female.

I threw one of my prepared meals into the microwave sitting on my filing cabinet to heat up while my computer booted up. Thanks to my fellow teammate Zeke, my computer system would make any computer nerd jizz themselves. I don't know or hell, even want to, understand the mumbo-jumbo behind it. Just make it work; that's all I asked for.

I sat and ate my chicken, eggs, and broccoli while I answered emails. Who would have thought after ten years being in the swamps and deserts killing bastards for money, with six of those years after being with the most elite force there was, I would be sitting behind a fucking desk? *Yeah, well, who would have thought you were about to lose your fucking humanity while you were out there?* I pushed the nagging voice aside. The voice eerily resembled my father, a ghost who died three years ago of the same addiction which addled my family. I had to get out of the Special Forces when I did. If I hadn't... the darkness would have consumed me.

"You good?"

I didn't have to look up to see who was shadowing my doorway. Her normally no-nonsense voice was gentle. Filled with pity. It made me sick. I didn't want her pity. I didn't need her pity.

I barely passed her a glance as I ignored her. She took it as her mistaken cue to come further into the office and stood in my line of sight.

"What?" I asked, my gaze finally moving away from the screen and taking her in. The blonde tresses and tight muscular body would have done any man in. And while she was hot as hell in the eyes of every other man, I was immune. I looked at Kate like I used to look at my own sister. Her take-no-prisoners attitude, her low tolerance for bullshit, and her general badass nature made her tolerable. The fact she was Cole's sister and a damn good teammate, made her part of the family.

"When was the last time you went out?" she asked, crossing her arms over her chest.

"Does it matter?" I grumbled. With Kate now shacking up with my best bud Noah, and Cole still hooking up with his girl, Traci on the regular, I had pretty much abandoned them and started hanging out more with the rest of the guys. That way I wouldn't feel like the single fifth wheel at the parties. Toren, Zeke, Benji, and I never had a problem getting the women.

There were a couple of spots we would go to on the regular where women who liked the same type of play we enjoyed were, and they knew the rules. No talking, no kissing, and definitely no relationships.

Granted, I hadn't been up to the spot in over a month or so. And no matter who I fucked, I always pictured a voluptuous, tattooed nerd with strawberry blonde hair and green eyes I could get lost in.

"We're planning to have a BBQ next weekend. It's going to be warm enough so you should come."

"I see you all week. Why am I going to come hangout with you people on the weekends too?" I groused. She saw through my bullshit.

"Sorry, I was trying to help your grumpy ass actually be social and enjoy the company of others." Her eyebrow lifted. "Charlie will be there."

My cock twitched and I was thankful my lap was covered by my desk. I held my gaze steady on her blue eyes. "And your point is what exactly?"

"Whatever. I've seen the way you look at her when you don't think anyone is watching. You're looking at her like she's your last meal and you're on death row."

"Get the hell out of here with that shit. I am not into your sister," I grumbled, rolling my eyes. *Liar.*

"Don't bullshit me. I remember how you two were at the bonfire after Megan and Shane's wedding," she teased. Of course, she remembered. That memory was burned into my brain and was the focus of my spank bank material.

"You were drunk as fuck at the wedding. You're imaging shit," I grumbled, turning back to the screen, and trying not to remember the feeling of Charlie's back pressed against my chest, with my dick grinding into her ass, with only two thin layers of cotton between us, as we danced in the shadows of the barn. Her throat was grasped in my left hand while the fingers on my right slipped in her yoga pants. The feel of her skin when I found she didn't have on any panties...

Fuck. All of my blood ran south, and my cock swelled at the memory. That's not what I needed right now. I could only image Kate gloating if she knew the effect her sister had on me.

Thank God a response popped through our secure mail server; a response I had been waiting on from Zeke down in Florida. "Hey, do something worthwhile and grab your brother for me. We got a hit from Zeke."

She gave me the one finger salute and sauntered off, bellowing for Cole. I was happy for the little reprieve. I adjusted my cock and willed it to go down, thinking of anything but the curve of Charlie's hips, and the gasp as my fingers slipped inside her...

Cole's leaded footsteps came thundering up the stairs. I shook the waves of lust out of my head and turned my monitor toward him as he walked through the doorway. Kate lingered in the doorway.

"What's up?" He pulled up the other lone chair I had in the office and started reading the message. I could hear his thoughts without having him speak. I read the message again, feeling my blood begin to boil.

"The shipment drops at twenty-one-fifty tonight. If we hop on a flight by noon and get down there, we may have a chance to knock some heads together," I surmised, pulling up the list of the flights available to us. Thanks to our contacts with some ex-federal agents, we had access to a private plane if situations like those arose.

"Toren and Zeke are already down there. They have the rest of Alpha team standing by. And I need to head to New Orleans with Benji tomorrow morning. They have a potential lead Rick Sims told us about," Cole said, rubbing his hands over his beard.

"Fuck the Alpha team. I'll take care of it. You know I'm looking for a smackdown," I growled.

While we weren't technically with Triton's Edge, we maintained a connection with the Alpha unit of the team. Even after their commander sold his soul to the devil, otherwise known as the Syndicate. Ten men, all well-trained, who I thought would have covered my six in the field. But it all came to a crashing halt in Vegas after they let Sebastian Cruz shoot my sister in the head. Half of the fools left and the ones that stuck around seemed legit, but I didn't trust those bastards to wipe the shit from their ass, let alone take care of a situation for us when we're not around.

"Yeah, I get it. But there's no reason to Hulk out now when we have Toren and Zeke already watching over them," Kate replied stoically.

"I'd trust your kid with an AK before I'd trust those fuckwads." But I knew we had no choice. Our resources were stretched thin as it was and we were currently still under contract to work with the Department of Defense, despite the clusterfuck that happened in Vegas.

"Preaching to the choir, bro." Cole checked his watch and nodded to Kate. "I need to get going. Dinner at Mom's tonight?"

"Yeah. Noah's going to meet me here with Aubrey, so we'll see you there." Cole nodded and left the room.

I turned my attention back to the emails at hand, making notes on the upcoming shipment of women destined for the shipping port in Florida. My methods may not have been orthodox, but my memory was sharp as a tack. I jotted down some notes onto our encrypted site, with thoughts and suggestions for Zeke and Toren to take into consideration. After everything was done, we'd do our after-action report. Go over all the players, the situation, the dirty and the ugly. Every pattern, every detail was critical. We knew from experience the Syndicate didn't allow for complacency, so we had to watch for the minute details. Any deviation, someone else driving, an off-pattern phone call, or new car, was one more detail which could possibly help in our case. Zeke would catalog it and use some sort of computer algorithm magic to pull up the potential scenarios we'd look into.

I ignored Kate's gaze until I couldn't take it anymore. "Either spit out whatever the fuck has you all up in my business or get the hell out of my office," I growled.

"Dude, chill out. Don't get your pecker twisted. Man, you really need to get laid." She moved as if she were about to walk away, but then she turned back to me.

Fuck. I figured she wouldn't let me off the hook that easily. "Seriously, Sketch. You have been doing everything you can for everyone else. You barely leave this facility and when you do, it's to sleep, shower, and shave. She may have died, Sketch. But you're living. You need to live for her. Do better for her. Wasting away in here or in the field, isn't living. You should make the most of the downtime we have right now, because it sure as shit won't last long."

"You done?" I seethed, finally looking into her blue eyes.

"Yeah, asshole. I'm done. Class is about to start, so I'll leave you to your sulking and brooding." She rolled her eyes and headed down to the gun range where we had a class coming in.

I shook my head. I wished it were easy. I wished I could say the words, and everything would be magically better. But with my humanity barely in check—and the rage of the monster inside me—I didn't think being around those who have joy and light in their lives was something I could handle.

I threw myself into paperwork, losing myself while the faint sounds of rock music and weights being lifted faded into the background. Before I realized it, the sun had faded behind the trees and the shadows danced across my monitor. I sat back and rubbed my eyes. I had been at it for hours, and finally our summer training schedule had been completed. With everything going on, I wanted to ensure the team wasn't stretched so thin we couldn't focus on the business. Thankfully, we had a few more recruits in the pipeline. Good guys, men we had worked with before. We expected and demanded the best of our crew, and thankfully we would be able to get it with the crew we were putting together.

"I'm rolling to my folks. Why don't you come with us?" Kate said, popping her head in. She had changed from her work out shorts and blue tank to a black t-shirt and jeans.

"Nah, I'm good." I stretched my arms over my head and leaned back in my chair.

"Shut up and come with us. You haven't seen Aubrey in forever and you could use a decent home-cooked meal and not that low carb stuff you stuff your face with."

Oh, low blow. She used my only and favorite niece as a bargaining chip.

I narrowed my eyes at her. "Seriously? You tried to bribe me with my niece. And you insult my cooking? Tell me again why I should come out with you?"

Kate's smile widened. "Hell yeah I did. That little girl is the key to getting you to say yes to anything. Plus, you'll come because you know you're sick of the health food."

Fuck. She had me there. I heaved a sigh. "Yeah. It's been a while since I have seen the rug rat. Let's go." I logged out of my network and secured the system while Kate went around the office locking up. The smell of bleach filled my nose as I went down the metal stairs. Kate had already gone through the cleaning portion of the night. I appreciated it, as that was one of the chores I dreaded most. I even tried hiring a cleaning crew, but my anal retentiveness and OCD about keeping a facility like this sparkling. . . let's just say I went through a couple before I figured out the best thing to was to do it ourselves. That way I knew it was clean.

I grabbed a small bag of food for Murray and followed her

out of the warehouse we used as the training center. I climbed into the truck, with Murray riding shotgun, and jutted my chin, when Kate waved as Noah pulled out of the gravel parking lot. Knowing Kate's mom, the meal would be huge and something Southern, so I knew my work outs tomorrow will be hell trying to compensate for all the carbs I was about to inhale.

The trip to Essex from Odenton was about thirty miles, but as soon as we got onto the Baltimore beltway, the clouds opened, and rain drenched the roads. As usual, people seemed to have lost their damn minds. Traffic came to a screeching halt, and we sat for what felt like forever. I debated taking the Challenger off-roading and going around the clusterfuck, but I didn't feel like dealing with Baltimore's finest. After a while, I was able to get around the traffic and made my way to Kate and Cole's parents' house.

It had been a minute since I had spent any time with them. And with Kate being Aubrey's mother now, you would think I would make an effort to spend more time with them. And don't get me wrong. Kate's parental instincts were much more than Jennie's ever were. But... part of me wished it were Jennie who was being the mom Aubrey deserved. That she chose her family over the high.

Jennie was consumed by drugs to the point she never told Noah or anyone, including me, she was pregnant. How Aubrey was born without the effects of heroin or meth in her system is beyond our understanding. We hoped that Jennie was wise enough to not use anything during her pregnancy. But it was not like she was around for us to monitor, either.

The pattern of disappearing for days and weeks on end was a common one. We didn't know she even delivered the baby until child protective services called my mom. Jennie had gotten busted in a house raid, and poor Aubrey was found in a back room, dirty, barely dressed, dehydrated, and hungry. Mom took one look at Aubrey and called Noah, who rushed home from his mission early. We barely saw Jennie after her arrest, and when we did, she was never fully lucid. She was constantly high, and rehab did shit for her. She didn't want to get clean, and we came to find out why. She had gotten involved in a world that wouldn't let go.

The Cruz Cartel got to her. They wrapped their hands around the throats of Jennie and anyone else who was susceptible to drugs. They used her. They used her body for their sick pleasure. They used her body for testing of their products and left her to die. We eventually found her and after a scary and tense standoff between her and Norah about the baby, we managed to get her into an off-the-books rehab facility. But the cartel was one step ahead of us. They removed her from the facility and brought her to Las Vegas, where we were taking down a human trafficking operation. That's when Sebastian Cruz put the gun to her head and pulled the trigger. I can only be thankful she was high, too high to even understand what was going on.

Sadly, addiction ran in the family. My father was a raging alcoholic and died in a boating accident three years ago. This was around the time I returned home from my own hell, and I fell down the rabbit hole of hard-core drugs. Popping pills, injecting shit into my veins, and drinking until I was numb. Anything to get rid of the memories. It took me almost dying from an overdose before I got the help I needed. It was a struggle at best, and at worst, the hardest I've ever fought. I was grateful for my mom. With her and Cole's help, I was able to get clean. She was our rock. She fought for us. She fought against the temptation of what the rest of her family was dependent on. Until she lost her daughter.

Everything had changed since Jennie died. Our mother blamed me for her death before blaming herself. Which was worse. I would take the blame a thousand times over rather than for her to feel guilt. She spiraled down, retreated into a bare shell of someone she used to be. Gone was the smile and laughter in her eyes. All I could see was the pain and guilt. Guilt for not doing more. Resentment at me for not doing enough to save her in Vegas.

Her spiral into the darkness took her down the same path Jennie took, using alcohol and sedatives to numb her conscience. Like with all troubled souls, she had to hit rock bottom before she took her mental health and depression seriously. With the help of Noah's and Kate's mothers, we were able to get her into a top-notch rehabilitation clinic, one that specialized in mental illness. One with better security than the one Jennie went to and was later taken from. Unfortunately, the facility was in upstate New York, and she refused visitors. I hadn't seen her in four months. It killed me that she was in there and I wasn't there to take her pain away. Her doctor said her healing took time and our family had to temper our expectations. She refused to communicate with anyone, the only exception being a letter she mailed to Aubrey. In it she apologized for not seeing the signs of Jennie's drug use sooner. She laid out all her heartache on paper and I felt every single word like a stab to the heart.

MURRAY'S WHINE shook my focus. "Yeah, bud, we're going." I opened the door to the pouring rain, and the big lug of a dog bounded out and up the driveway to the front door. I hurried after him and let us into the warm house.

"You look like you need this," Kat said as she came down the stairs with Aubrey on her hip and two beach towels folded over her arm.

I took the towels gratefully and dried my face. Murray decided to shake off the excess water and drool, causing a mess everywhere and Aubrey to shriek in delight.

"Of course it's funny to you, kiddo. I get to clean up the

mess." I smiled and reached to tickle her under her chin. Her big blue eyes and blonde curls reminded me so much of my sister, it made my heart ache.

I caught Kate's gaze and looked away, reaching for Murray. I couldn't handle the pity or sadness filling her eyes. She quickly changed the mood and went into the kitchen, talking excitedly to Aubrey about all the food she was going to make a mess of.

"You're getting a bath later, dude. You stink," I grumbled, rubbing him vigorously with the towel. After a minute he had had enough and bounded away when he heard the telltale noise of food being banged around in the kitchen.

"Sketch. Good to see you." Cole's dad came walking down the stairs.

"What's going on, Pops?" We hugged quickly. The Parker family took me in when I first met Cole six years ago after we served together. They always treated me like I was part of the clan, even going as far as including my mom and sister in their holiday plans. After hearing how they treated Shane, I knew this was part of their genuine nature. And after all the bullshit with my sister and my mom retreating into her mind after losing her daughter, they helped maintain the shred of humanity I had left.

"Nothing much. Glad you made it. We're waiting for Charlie and then we're ready to eat."

"Sounds good, need any help with anything?"

"Nope, Cole is grabbing the extra chairs from the basement. Dry off because Cathy doesn't like water on her floors. Charlie shouldn't be too far behind you."

I chuckled. "Duly noted, sir." I grabbed the extra towel and started drying off my arms. Nonchalant and cool on the outside, but inside my stomach dropped. The one I'm not supposed to be dreaming about, the one I'm not supposed to jerking off to, the one who was one million percent off-limits, would be there. Of course. *Why the fuck wouldn't she be, asshole?*

This is her folks' place. Just play it cool, man. Mind over matter. I'm good.

Until a thump at the door had me turn around and a tiny, five-foot two frame with curves for days popped through the door.

Fuck, I'm screwed.

2

CHARLIE

Ruelle's "Madness" played through the Bluetooth speakers as I worked on the cell analysis from the latest test I ran in the lab. Something was off with the purity level, and I was frustrated I couldn't figure it out. I mindlessly reached for my ever-present baggie of gummy worms and chewed thoughtfully.

"Don't you think you're a little too old for children's candy?"

I glanced up from my laptop and blinked to get my eyes to focus on the person speaking to me. I rolled my eyes at the obnoxious jerk who sat across the table from me.

"Fuck off, Michael." The words barely slipped from my lips before my eyes were back on the formula in front of me. Out of the corner of my eye, I saw what he was reaching for and immediately smacked his hand from reaching his target.

"Don't even fucking think about it. You can't insult me then try to steal the only thing keeping me from not going batshit crazy right now."

"Like you need any more sugar." The snide comment slid off my back as I knew he was bitter as fuck. The bag of gummy worms wasn't the only sugar I wouldn't share with him. "Whatever. Let me see what you're working on." He walked around to my side and tried to peer over my shoulder.

My brow furrowed. "So you can take credit for it again? No. We're working on two different sections. I'm working on this fentanyl molecule. You're supposed to be looking at the cocaine library."

Michael Van Buren's grin faltered but came back as quickly as it had left. "I finished it. I can give you some hints and see where you went wrong."

Of course, you did, you ass. I bit my tongue. The boy was a genius and never failed to let anyone else know it.

"I didn't say I got anything wrong. I said I don't need your help because I'm taking my time with this." The no-bullshit tone I had normally worked with people. But of course, Michael was oblivious. I checked the clock on the wall in front of me.

"If you were finished with the library, why the hell are you still here?" I questioned.

"I knew you wouldn't be able to figure this out, so I stayed behind to help you." He ventured closer to me and grazed my hip bone with his hand. My face twisted in disgust, and I shrugged him away.

"And now you can see I don't, so go ahead and run along."

"Come on, Charlotte. Why don't you be a nice girl and let me correct some of those errors." His hot nasty breath infiltrated my personal space and I almost gagged.

"You may be book smart, but you sure as hell ain't smart enough to read the room. Get the fuck out of here." I nudged him back, glaring at him with disgust.

"Come on Charlotte, don't be like that." He stepped into my personal space again. It always pissed me off when he refused to call me Charlie. He hated nicknames and said Charlotte was more fitting for a woman in this profession. Or for someone whose future would have entailed a life of being on the arm of a pompous asshole at society and community events. A future I never had interest in. I would love nothing more than to never see this asshole again. Unfortunately, his family's name was on the program. And he was one of the three top competitors in this internship so of course I had to work with him.

"You need to back the hell up, Michael. I really don't want to have to get your blood on the floor. That would be a pain to clean up." I elbowed him hard in the gut, and he finally moved back a step.

"Charlotte, you know if we worked together, we would be the power couple in Pharmacodynamics. The research journals and exposure alone would be worth millions, shit probably even billions. Don't you want your degree to actually be worth something?"

"Um, we are working together. What you're really saying is you want me to do all the work while you take credit. You can have that with Nessa, but not me," I replied dryly, my patience dwindling with each second he stood by.

"Please. You act like it would be detrimental to your own reputation if you were seen with me in public, when we both know it would be the other way around. If anything, I would be taking the hit."

I saved the document I had been working on and closed my laptop. I pushed my stool back and turned sharply. Michael took a step back at the disgust on my face.

"Oh, for fuck's sake, Michael. Even if I had a modicum of attraction to you, I would still say no. I'm not interested in sharing any sort of STIs you probably have. And don't forget we all walked in on your little show in the lounge with the student aide, Maria, so I know what you're working with. Your dick is so damn small, I would have to buy stock in Duracell." I sneered.

"Back off, Mike. I have made it abundantly clear I want nothing to do with you. It's bad enough we are in this damn internship together, but if I see you outside the lab, you can be damn sure I won't be polite. You need to leave me alone."

"Do you really think you could get further in this world without me? You need me, my name, and my money to even get your foot in the door. I know you went to public school, but I didn't realize the schools were that bad," he spat, his face reddening with fury.

Oh, little boy, you're so radiating the small-dick energy. I chuckled without any humor. Yet another reminder I don't fit the typical stereotype of a scientist because I spent my formative years as a commoner in a working-class neighborhood and had a public education instead of pricey private schools and having a butler and maid in a house overlooking the bay.

"Looks like that private school education made you think you were a bigger deal than you really are. Hopefully, you didn't have to pay for the air they inflated your ego with," I replied with a false, saccharine sweet smile on my face.

His eyes narrowed and jaw clenched. I knew I was getting under his skin.

"Okay fine. Apparently, we got off on the wrong foot. Let me start over. We have some developments that require discussion, and it would be best outside the lab. I have a standing reservation at this club downtown. Nessa will be joining us, but only if you have something decent to wear," he placated. His arrogance grated on my nerves, because I knew it must be killing his ego to need my assistance.

Ah yes. The typical dig at my appearance. Michael wasn't a fan of curvy women with piercings and tattoos. But then again, what the fuck did a typical twenty-six-year-old scientist look like? Were they supposed to dress like Michael, with chinos and a white button-down? Did my nose stud and forearm tattoos make me less of a scientist? Did my strawberry blonde colored hair, thick thighs, chubby waist, and booty make me less smart? Of course not. And if the board of directors didn't have an issue with my appearance, than he shouldn't either.

"Aw. Are you afraid someone may think you're slumming if you show up at your prestigious club with me?" I smirked. "For someone who is hell-bent on getting me to be part of a 'power' couple, you seem to have a tough time with my appearance. Do you honestly think you could bend me to your perceived notion of a scientist's wife? What's even funnier is that you have the audacity to even think I would lower my standards to be seen with a high-brow, limp dick pissant like you. I like my men like how I like my coffee, hot and strong." I crossed my arms and let my gaze scan his lanky frame. "Not weak and watered-down."

"You fucking cu—" The anger stormed in his brown eyes, and I knew he wanted to take me down a peg. I almost wished he would so I could justifiably knee him in his nuts and be done with his bullshit.

"You're lucky there are cameras in here," he said menacingly.

"Again, with the lack of common sense. Take the hint, Michael. I'm not scared of you. I'm not interested in being your anything. I'm not interested in talking with you. I can barely stand to work with you. So, take your temper tantrum over to someone else who will kiss your butt-hurt feelings." I lifted my chin and glared him in the eyes as my jaw clenched.

"You know what? You're nothing but a carpetbagging whore who probably fucked everyone on the board to get this spot. Remember this when you're a two-bit chemist working in a drugstore." Michael shoved the entire stack of notes and books off my table. "I don't need some stale pussy in my bed anyway," he sneered, stalking through the automatic sliding doors.

"Oh, and Michael?" I called before the doors closed behind

him. "Next time you make a threatening move toward me, I will file a complaint with the board. Because like you said, there are cameras everywhere."

"Go fuck yourself, Charlie."

"Instead of you? Gladly!" I cheered gleefully to his retreating back. I turned back toward my station and sighed.

"Oh, for fuck's sake," I muttered, as I gathered the mess of notes littering the ground. Michael had always been a pain but for some reason he was worse lately. I didn't know if it was because he wasn't getting laid or if the program was getting to him. But he was getting on my last nerve and further comments like these were going to get him punched in the junk.

There were two types of people in the world. One type who wanted to do the good work to help people; to actually make an impact on the lives we're supposed to be helping. The other type was those who wanted the notoriety of doing the work of other people. One guess which type Michael represented. He was cute in an average sort of way, but that and his bank account were pretty much the only things going for him. His off-the-cuff comments about women at the school, his lack of respect for anyone on campus, and his arrogance were major turn-offs.

I knew all of this going into my line of work. I was a woman in a male dominated world. Science—chemistry, physics, pharmacodynamics, and genomics—it's my thing. I didn't get where I was in the community by being shy or weak. I sure as hell didn't get where I was by sleeping with my professors or sponsors. I may not have had the financial backing of doctor parents, but I had the brain power. I didn't sleep where I worked. I learned that lesson by watching others fail and I've always kept my social circle separate from my internship and work life. Sure, I dated other students when I was in college. There may have even been with a teacher's aide a time or two. But they were temporary. Something to scratch the itch so to speak. Because when the guy you're crushing on is someone who only sees you as his buddy's little sister, you're bound to look elsewhere to take care of those physical needs. At least until he got his head out of his ass.

The bright light from my monitor against the dimness of the rest of the office had my eyes crying for relief. I jotted down the rest of my notes, the formula matching the sample almost exactly, then closed the lid to my laptop. I loved my program, but it drained me.

The war on drugs was a multi-billion-dollar industry. From pharmacies developing anti-OD drugs like Narcan for heroin users, to the pesticides used to destroy the poppy crops in Afghanistan, everyone had their hands in the cookie jar. Obviously, Bowen Biotech was not an exception. Thanks to a major grant and a partnership with the National Institute of Health, and the DEA, Dr. Weber was using his vast array of resources to recreate the formulas that were better than the crap found on the streets. The program developed by Dr. Weber would allow us to tailor the drug to specific genes and it would help treat patients quicker and more thoroughly. Of course, it wasn't an exact replica. Various conditions would ultimately determine the drug's success rate, such as compromised immunity, other narcotics, the purity of the drugs, or other behavioral or physical disabilities. We were on the breakthrough of making a synthetic replica without using the lethal ingredients and with less harmful addictive properties and matching it to the patients' DNA to ensure they received the right medication, at the right dosage in the first place.

My current project was to create a replica of heroin using the purest form, to see how well it could be used for the world's nastiest and terminal of aliments. Fascinating, but also extremely dangerous. The internship program was extremely selective, with only three students a year selected to participate. The rounds of qualifications, along with background and psychology tests, took a full year to complete. My four-point nine GPA, along with recommendations from my professors and sponsors in my master's program, helped me snag a spot. And I'm not ashamed to admit I pulled the "My sister is a kickass FBI agent" card either. This program was the pinnacle of my graduate studies and my dream job. I may not sleep my way to the top, but I sure as hell can name drop like the best of them.

Unfortunately, Michael and our other partner, Nessa Bradshaw, were part of the equation. Despite the lack of common ground and the fact we may not get along, there was a slight consensus of respect. The three of us were making serious strides but we weren't the ones in charge. We were the worker bees behind the formula process. It still had to go through the review sequence, analysis, and needed further testing, but I was confident we were on the right track for something amazing.

I rubbed my eyes and checked the time.

"Ah crap." I was already running late, and I still needed to clean up. I finished up at my station, then hurried back into the lab to make sure my supplies were locked up. Once I set the alarms, I headed into the locker room. Despite all the precautions we took with the drugs and traces, no one wanted the drug sniffing dogs to positively alert on a scent they may find. I quickly stripped out of my lab coat and scrubs and threw my strawberry blonde hair into a messy knot. I pulled on my beat-up pink Chuck Taylors, a pair of black leggings, and gray hoodie bearing the logo from my brother's training center over a white t-shirt.

I gathered up my bag, then headed to the parking lot. My small, white SUV waited for me all by her lonesome in the darkened parking lot. As usual, I was the last to leave the facility. The temperature had dropped about twenty degrees since this morning, and dark clouds had moved in. Rain lingered in the air. Pretty much a typical spring day in Maryland. It could feel like summer one day and be freezing cold the next.

I climbed into my Escape and sent my mom a quick text to let her know I was on my way. I turned on my playlist and let FNKHOUSER's "I Don't Mind" be the soundtrack for the drive back to Essex. As always, I was running late for our monthly dinner with the family. Even though our family was close, getting together was always difficult, especially with Cole and Kate's schedules. Mom insisted, *well actually demanded,* we set aside one Friday night a month. I tossed my phone into my bag when thunder cracked. *Shit.* I despised driving in the rain. I pulled out of the parking lot and hit the road, hoping the twenty-mile drive wouldn't have any major issues. But, of course, the heavens opened and as usual, people forgot how to drive when there was precipitation in the air. What should have only taken me twenty minutes, took twice as long.

My stomach turned into a loud, grumbling monster and my patience was shot to hell by the time I pulled up to the Cape Cod style home we grew up in. The house that brought together two families. My dad, Frank, met Kate's mom, Cathy, when she was a single mom working at a diner and he was the widowed father of a two- and seven-year-old. He was a hard-as-nails dock foreman, who worked from sunup to sundown. He was often too tired to cook, or it was too late, so we ate a lot of dinners at that diner. And it didn't take long for Kate to join us. She would push aside her book of the day and would eat dinner with us. Soon after, Kate and her mom were moving in, and we instantly became a family. They both worked odd hours to accommodate us kids being home, as well as all our extracurriculars. The house was small and sharing one shower between the five of us wasn't always the greatest, but we were loved and well taken care of.

I heaved a deep sigh, bracing myself for the deluge of water that would hit me as soon as I opened my car door. I opened the door and put my foot right into a puddle.

"Of course," I gritted out. I grabbed my bag, chirped my car, and ran for the front door. It didn't matter. The ferocity of the rain had me soaked by the time I made it to the front porch. Needless to say, I was not in a good mood by the time I pushed my way into the house.

"For fuck's sake, you'd think people would learn to put on their damn blinker when it rains. Or at the very least, turn on their worthless headlights. But I guess that's asking way too much for Baltimore's finest citizens," I ranted, shucking off my soggy sneakers. I pulled my soaked hoodie over my head and my t-shirt almost came up with it. "Oh, and I'm going to have to borrow a pair of your sneakers because mine are..." I finally got my clothing situated and I finally looked up. The first pair of eyes caught mine were molten and silver. "Soaked." Suddenly, I was wet for reasons other than the rain. Sketch Davis, with his massively inked build and sexy as hell smirk, sat on the couch right in front of me. His thick, corded arms were resting on his thighs and his silver eyes gazed at me intently. I flushed with embarrassed heat and raised my hand to flatten the mess on my head.

"Oh, hey there, Sketch. How's it going?" I said with a quick smile. Of course, he had to be present for my impromptu clumsy striptease. Because why would I not want to embarrass myself in front of the guy I masturbate to? I cursed myself for being a complete idiot when it came to this man. There was something about him that made me trip over my own words.

"Pretty good, Charlie. How about you?" And there it was. The slow grin crossed his face. His smiles were rare and only with purpose, so my heart sung a little. And... so did my stomach. A loud rumble answered for me.

"I'm starved. Excuse me." I quickly sidestepped him and

walked through the living room into the kitchen, my face flaming with embarrassment.

"Hey there, sweets. You're just in time for dinner," Mom said with a smile, as she put my father's favorite fried chicken onto a platter. Kate put the last plates around the table, while her fiancé, Noah, placed his daughter into her bright yellow highchair. My brother's girlfriend, Tracie, rounded the table with bowls of grilled corn and fried okra.

"Yeah. I meant to be here earlier, but people have lost their damn minds out there." I brought the bottle of white wine resting on the counter over to the table and poured myself a healthy portion. Kate looked over at me with a smirk and reached for her own glass. I gave her a mock scowl and blocked her before she could touch it.

"Nope. You failed the sister code. No wine for you," I hissed.

A mask of fake innocence came over her face. "Why, whatever do you mean, dear sister of mine?"

I raised my eyebrows. "Really? You're going to play that game?" I muttered, as Sketch, Cole, and my father walked in, their conversation about the upcoming Oriole's season masking my own distress.

"Don't know what you're talking about, Charlie. But you know, maybe it's time to pull up your big girl panties and go after what you want," Katie hissed back, her ice blue eyes sparkling mischievously. She maneuvered around me and took her place on the opposite side of Aubrey.

"I got my big girl panties on," I retorted. *Annnnd that was when all other conversation in the room had paused. Of course.*

"What's this about panties? Kate's got some Wonder Woman ones. Did you get some too?" Noah joked. Kate reached around the back of Aubrey and smacked him on the shoulder. "What? I thought we were talking about panties!"

"I don't need to hear about my sister's panties," Cole grumbled.

"At least she's wearing them," Traci quipped, giving Cole a wink.

"Can we please have one meal without discussing anyone's undergarment choices at the dinner table? Charlie, grab a seat. We're ready to eat," Mom said, bringing the homemade biscuits to the table. My dad took his position at the head and my mother to the opposite side with Noah and Tracie. Which left me in between Cole . . . and Sketch. Great.

I gingerly sat in my seat, careful not to look at him, I didn't want to make this situation any more awkward than it already was. Noah sat across from me and tried his best not to laugh at my embarrassment. I subtly gave him the finger while my parents' attention was diverted. The platters of food made the rounds and soon the conversation turned to topics other than my underwear. *Thank God.*

I surveyed the table. Despite my awkward as hell predicament, I missed this. We had been so spread out sometimes, coming home was a way to press pause in our lives. Even growing up, we made it a point to have dinner together at least three times a week. In between Cole's sports, Kate's dance lessons, and my afterschool clubs, we always seemed to be on the road. Add in Mom's shifts at the diner and Dad working at the shipping docks, dinner was a way to reconnect as a family.

As the meal wound down and everyone was stuffed, we sat with either booze or coffee and caught up with each other.

"Seth, do you have any plans for the summer? Taking any trips?" Mom asked, refilling her glass of wine. That's one thing I loved about my parents, they included everyone. Once you met them, you were a part of the family. Cathy and Frank were parents for everyone. While it was impressive in most instances, she'd be up in your business before you could say no. When Cole brought Sketch over the first time six years ago, my mother refused to call him anything but Seth. Whether he liked it or not. And she finally wore him down, and now my folks are the only ones who can call him by his given name.

"No, ma'am. The center is in its busy season, so it's all hands-on deck for the next month or so. We close everything down the last week in August to give the trainers a summer break with their families, but I don't have anything planned," Sketch said, reaching for his water glass. We were so close I could feel the heat of his thigh next to mine. I slowly drew in a deep breath as he shifted, and our thighs grazed each other. I kept my gaze straight forward trying not to give any reaction. But Noah, the observant asshat that he was, smirked in my direction.

"Actually, we're going to change that," Kate said with a smile on her face. She looked over expectantly at Noah, who gave her a nod. "Because it's the only week we'd be able to get away, we decided we're going to get married in August, the Friday before we close down for the week. We're not going to do anything huge, just something small at City Hall in Annapolis. Afterward, we'll have a party at our house on the beach for everyone who wants to come down and celebrate with us. Then we'll go on a quick honeymoon. That way, we won't have to take away any resources from the center."

"Wait, hold up. Do not worry about TR. You know we have more than enough coverage for anything we have going on," Sketch interjected.

"And what about all our other obligations?" Kate asked pointedly, raising her eyebrow. Other obligations meaning taking down the Syndicate and Cruz Cartel. They purposely don't tell us anything, only when they're leaving and when they're coming home. Seeing as how we were at risk because we're their family, they wanted to keep as much information separate from the family as possible.

"We got it handled," Sketch argued, putting his fork down.

"No, we don't. You said not three hours ago we were

stretched thin when it came to resources." She held up her hand when he opened his mouth to protest. "It's done, Sketch. We don't want a big fancy wedding. That's not who we are," Kate said firmly. "This is what we want to do. This way, everyone we want to be there can be. They won't be taking any time away from their families."

"You're going to deny your old man the chance to walk you down the aisle?" Dad asked softly. I melted a little. Frank Parker may not be Kate's father by blood, but he was the only daddy she knew.

"Of course not. You're going to walk me down the aisle at City Hall and who knows, maybe we'll even dance on the beach," Kate said with a soft grin.

"Okay, good. That's settled then," Dad said gruffly. The old man may have had the façade of a crusty-old dock worker, but he was a softy at heart.

"Well, it means we need to jumpstart the planning," Mom said with a twinkle in her eye. "It's already the beginning of April. That leaves us with only four months."

"Mom, it's not necessary. Seriously, it's not going to be a big to-do," Kate protested. The planning wheels were already in motion, and I could see our mother scheming.

"And this is where my opinion is no longer required," Noah said jokingly. He picked up an extremely messy Aubrey out of her highchair and held her out with his outstretched arms. "I'm going to give this one a bath. Remember, we're not taking out a second mortgage for this." He bent down and softly kissed Kate on the lips.

I wanted to swoon, but I inwardly sighed. I was so grateful Noah came into our lives. He's changed her for the better. He broke down her walls, allowed her to love and trust again. That's what couples are supposed to do. Finding the love of your life means breaking all the rules and tearing down any obstacles holding you back. Someone for the good days and to make the bad days better. Everyone deserved that. I know I did.

"Yeah, don't forget about Pinterest. There are tons of ideas on there," I piped in, my lips in a smug smile. I chuckled as Kate's eyes widened in panic.

"Oh! That's right. Let's check out my Pinterest board. I have a few ideas already picked out," Mom said as she pushed back her chair.

"Me and Trace will leave you to it. We'll clean up and then we need to roll out. I have a flight in the morning," Cole said with a devilish smile.

"Sounds good. Be safe, love you." With a quick peck on their cheeks, Mom hustled out of the kitchen.

"Charlie, you need to save me," Kate pleaded.

My chuckle turned into a full-belly laugh. "Oh no, sister dear. This is pure karma, coming back and kicking your ass."

Ever since Mom found Pinterest, no party has been simple. Take Aubrey's first birthday for example. Mom completely took over all aspects of the planning. Noah and Katie were going to have a few friends and some family over with their kiddos, but apparently it wasn't enough for Cathy Parker. Oh no. Not by a long shot. Mom doesn't do anything half-assed. Not only did we have someone bring a miniature pony, dressed as a unicorn no less, for the three toddlers to ride, but there was also a petting zoo with bunnies, baby chicks, and ducklings. The house was decked out to the nines with pink and purple streamers and balloons.

Kate was screwed.

I laughed even harder, holding my stomach as Mom hollered for Kate to join her in the spare bedroom where the computer was.

"I got your karma right here," she snarked, giving me the double finger. I hooted louder, loving this cosmic switch. Sketch shook his head and got up, taking his dishes to the sink.

I wiped away the tears and sighed happily. It felt great to laugh that hard. I took his lead and brought the rest of the dishes to the counter. The four of us fell into a rhythm, with Cole and Tracie putting away the food and Sketch and I washing the dishes. Well, he washed, and I dried the pots and pans.

"All right, ladies. It's been real," Cole said, as he put away the rest of the food. "It's time for me to take this woman home and break in our new bed."

"What happened to your old one?" Dad asked, as he came back in from taking out the trash. He paused, realizing who he was talking to. "Nope. Never mind. Forget I asked."

Cole chuckled and gave Dad and Sketch one of those half hug – back slap things guys do and came over to me. "See you later, Shortcake," he said, giving me a hug.

"Be safe, dork," I muttered, saying our standard goodbyes. I may not know what he does on the day to day, but I know it keeps both of our parents up at night. They worry constantly, and I hate when he goes on his missions.

"Always." His standard reply. He took Tracie's hand and led her out through the front, hollering his goodbyes at Mom. Murray shuffled out of the kitchen now that any chance of scraps was gone. Knowing him, he'd make his way to the dog bed in the family room, right next to Dad's recliner.

I reached for a platter and stood on my tiptoes to place it in the cabinet. I felt his heat against my back, as his fingers pushed the dish onto the top shelf. My eyes closed for a brief second. As I inhaled his scent engulfed me. Opening my eyes, I gave him an awkward smile and shimmied around him, wanting to but trying desperately not to touch. We've been alone only one time before—at the bonfire at Megan and Shane Turner's wedding and I had had a lot of liquid courage then. We had a moment then, a moment where I had pulled up my big girl panties and pulled him into the shadows to dance. The feel of his large body against mine, the way his hips moved in time with mine... The heat of the memories from that night floated up and I instantly clenched my legs together. I didn't need him to know how he affected me. I cleared my throat as I wiped my hands off.

"How's it going with you, Sketch?" I asked, trying to fill the silence. I leaned against the cabinet and grabbed the wine I had been nursing during dinner.

The corners of his lips turned up and I quietly melted at the sight of his small grin. "So far, so good. What about you? How's your program going?" he asked.

"So far, so good," I repeated his answer. His smile grew by the tiniest of fractions and he gave me a side nudge. "Seriously, it's good. It's complicated as hell but good lord, it's so freaking cool. I mean, we could be creating a new cancer treatment or a cure for Parkinson's. Knowing what we know now, and all the new data coming in everyday, we're taking something so vile and destructive and turning it into something useful. It's absolutely amazing, you know?" I couldn't help the pride in my voice. My birth mom died from breast cancer when I was two years old. And while I would be forever grateful Cathy Lyles and her spunky five-year-old daughter came into our lives when we needed them the most, no child should ever have to lose their parent to such a hateful and disgusting disease.

The look on his normally stoic face surprised me. He didn't smile often, but when he did, it was absolutely beautiful.

"That's great, Charlie. You're kicking ass. I'm proud of you." He turned away, putting the sponge to the wine glass. A thought flittered into my mind, about how he would stroke me. With a sponge... in the bathtub.

"Charlie?"

"Oh, I'm sorry. What did you say?" My face burned with heat, and I looked away from his amused grin.

"What were you thinking about?" he said softly, his silver

eyes dark and heavy. The tip of his tongue glided across his bottom lip as if he could tell the effect he had over me.

About how much I want to take a bath with you. But of course, I couldn't say that.

"Oh, nothing," I said sheepishly.

"I would love to know what's going on in that head of yours," he murmured, wiping his hands on the dish towel.

I pretended not to hear him, because speaking those thoughts out loud would have me in a puddle on the floor.

"How about you? How have things been?" I took another sip of my wine.

"Same ol' shit." He put the last glass into the dishwasher, then leaned against the counter. I mimicked his movements.

"Is that good or bad?" I asked.

"It is what it is," he answered vaguely. His gaze zoned in on my lips and I subconsciously licked the drop of wine from my lip. I saw his fingers clench the counter, and I so wished I could read his mind right now. We were close enough my fingers ached to reach over and pull him over to me by his belt loop.

"Sketch," I started softly and leaned in, but then Aubrey's shrill cry permeated the air. Whatever connection we had was broken in that instant. I pulled back just as Noah walked in with a sobbing Aubrey.

"We're going to get going. This one is exhausted," Noah said, sounding tired himself. He pulled me into a hug, and I kissed the tearstained cheeks of my niece. He released me, and gave Sketch a quick one-armed bro hug, then they filed out. I heard Kate making her escape as well and I had to shake my head. Using the kid as an excuse to get away from Mom's Pinterest addiction. I couldn't wait to give her hell for it.

"Yeah, I better get going too," Sketch said ruefully.

"Okay, be safe driving home," I replied nonchalantly, with a little wave. His face hardened, and he grabbed my hand, pulling me into him.

"Come here," he growled, and I swore my pussy clenched. He wrapped his arms around me, and I buried my face into his chest. I softly inhaled the scent of tobacco, clean cotton, and just him.

"Don't be a stranger," he murmured into my hair, his lips lightly grazing my ear. I shivered from the contact.

"You know I'm not good at following the rules. But really, you should take your own advice," I muttered back. His grip on me tightened.

"You're too good for me, Angel."

The words were barely louder than a whisper, but I heard them loud and clear. He released me, and coldness washed over me from the lack of contact. He gave me one last hard glance and walked out of the kitchen.

My heart pounded so loudly; I could barely hear him say goodbye to my parents. Once I heard the door slam behind him, I fell against the counter. *Holy crap.* What was that? Except for the night at Megan and Shane's wedding, we have not touched, let alone hugged. And it wasn't any hug. That was an embrace. A sexual embrace. An embrace I would love to repeat.

Snap out of it, Charlie. I scolded myself. I'm acting like a lovesick idiot. I poured out the leftover wine and grabbed a bottle of water from the fridge before I headed toward the front of the house to say goodbye. I stopped by the family room closet and found an old pair of Sketchers I had left behind. While I moved into my own place two years ago, I was constantly leaving stuff here.

"Rolling out, Charlie?" Dad said from his recliner, his attention focused on the baseball game.

"Yeah, Pops. I'm wiped. The program has me running on fumes." I slipped on the old but familiar sneakers and grabbed my jacket and bag from the hook.

He stood, his five-eleven frame slightly hunched thanks to the wear and tear of working manual labor most of his life.

"Okay, Shortcake, I love you. Be safe and call me when you get home." He wrapped his bear paws around my shoulders and squeezed. "Hurry, before your mother gets you sucked into her Pinterest planning," he said loudly.

"I heard that! Bye, sweets! I love you! Frank, come here and check this out. I think..." My mom's voice carried from the other room.

Dad gave me a conspiratorial wink. "Save yourself!" he whispered with a grin.

I laughed as I hustled out the door. Thankfully, the rain had stopped and the drive back to the home I shared with my best friend, Summer, was easy.

I pushed my way into our small, narrow row house on South Clinton Street. We lived on a busy block in Canton, an up-and-coming neighborhood in the city of Baltimore. Our two-bedroom, two-bath row house has the charm and personality these hundred-year-old homes are supposed to have. Thankfully, Summer's father is a contractor and used his limited free time and unending connections to get the house just the way we wanted. From the gorgeous walnut floors to the exposed brick interior walls, it's exactly what we wanted. Granted, it wasn't the Ritz. The water pressure sucked. The windows were drafty. We had a furry trash panda we named Edgar, named after a famous Baltimore poet. And we only had one parking spot, but the house was close to everything, we could either walk or take public transportation.

"Hey chick, how was dinner with the fam?" Summer said, looking up from her spot on the dark purple couch. Her silver and black tresses were piled on her head in a big bun, and she was dressed in a hoodie and sweats for our weekly Friday night binge fest of TV and wine.

"Completely filling, as always." I put the leftovers I had swiped from Mom and Dad's in the fridge and toed off my shoes into the overfilled closet next to the back door.

"That's good to hear." She went back to flipping through the images on her laptop. As a freelance photographer, she was in high demand. Her portfolio was impressive, she was steadily building clientele in both family and boudoir photography, but she also supplied a freelance service to the local papers. I peeked over her shoulder and saw a beautiful, voluptuous woman standing at a window, dressed in nothing but a tank top and panties, with the light hitting her exquisite features exactly right.

"Holy shit, Summer. She's gorgeous. The shot is amazing."

Summer nodded. "That's my girl, Ashley. She's rocking it."

I flopped down on the couch next to her and closed my eyes. The exhaustion from the week had overtaken me. The program was draining every ounce of my energy and it was all I could do to stay upright.

"Charlie? Earth to Charlie?"

"Shit, what did you say? I'm sorry, I totally zoned out." I blinked.

"Yeah, no shit, Sherlock. Where did you go?" Summer asked with a grin. "Was this about a certain broody, inked, bad boy with silver eyes?"

I gave a small smirk. "No. This isn't about Sketch. I wasn't daydreaming."

Summer snorted in disbelief. "He was there, wasn't he?"

"Yes, but that's not why I zoned," I said with a laugh, smacking her with one of the many throw pillows we had. "I've been going non-stop lately. I'm dead on my feet." I paused.

"You know what? I'm going to take a bath and go to bed." I got up from my corner of the couch and stretched, then walked the five feet to the stairs.

"Yeah, I was thinking the same thing. Why don't we go out to Walt's Inn tomorrow night, see what's going on? It's supposed to be beautiful this weekend, perfect for hanging out in town,"

Summer said, putting her laptop on the old steamer trunk we converted to a coffee table.

"Works for me. Good night, lady." I trudged upstairs, my body feeling heavier and heavier with each step. By the time I got to my bedroom, I was done. I took a quick shower, pulled on a tank, and slid under the cool, crisp white sheets. I was out before my head touched the pillow.

3

SKETCH

It took everything I had in me to walk out of Charlie's parents' house on Friday night. I saw her need. Hell, I could feel it. She tried to hide it from me, but I knew. Her eyes dilated as soon as I got close, and her breath quickened slightly. The artery in her neck hummed. Her everyday fragrance of honeysuckle and lavender had infiltrated my senses. Holding her in my arms like I did almost had me losing control. I had to step away, knowing if I didn't, I wouldn't be able to let her go. I ended up taking matters into my own hands and coating the walls of my shower several times through the weekend.

Three days later and I still couldn't stop thinking about her. The shallow point at the base of her throat. The way her eyes looked at me, like she could see my soul. As if she could save me if I let her. The innocence and purity were there. I wasn't talking about her virginity; I knew she wasn't a virgin. Although the thought of any other man touching her had me seeing red. No, I was talking about the darkness that lives in everyone. The darkness had consumed the best people, turning them into monsters. The very darkness which filled my soul. Her happy-go-lucky nature and genuine kindness hadn't yet been tainted by the cruel, cynical world.

Which is why I had to walk away. She's too good. Her humanity...her heart...she was still good. Too good. Because I know I'm not worth it. I'm barely hanging on to the last shred of humanity I have left, and I sure as hell don't want to ruin her.

But the thought of ruining her, corrupting her? Putting her over my knee, or tying her to my bed while I take her in deeper...

I pushed the thought of her out of my head and willed my cock to settle down. I needed to remain focused on the mission, on what needed to be done. And as much as I wanted her, I knew I couldn't have her, so I was only torturing myself.

I took another drag of my cigarette and flicked it to the gravel covered ground and opened the heavy metal door to the warehouse. Hearing it automatically lock, I sauntered inside. At five o'clock on a Monday evening, the day was winding down. Our classes were over. It was only me. Just the way I liked it. No noise, no bullshit. Just me, my messed-up thoughts, and my toys. I went over to our secured weapons rooms, a heavily secured area that required retinal and voice recognition to access it.

After I locked myself into the weapons room, I crossed over to one of the gun lockers and pressed my thumb against a hidden panel. The door slid open, and I let the beast's smile come across my face. I walked into my own personal trophy room. Once inside, the lights came on by motion and they highlighted my personal trophies in their cases. I'm not talking about my football records or the medals I received from the military. I'm talking my personal mission trophies. The kind you take with the fucked-up joy one gets from hunting a hunter. Like the hatchet that was used to kill a drug kingpin, after I found him injecting elderly women with a combination of tranquilizers and heroin. A particular nine-inch blade with a

mother-of-pearl handle that cleanly sliced open a human-traf-
ficking sheikh in Afghanistan. And my favorite, a carbon steel
fourteen-inch machete with a gold-plated handle. I used a
pedophile's own weapon against him, in the jungles of Asia. It
felt good to hold the blade to his flaccid appendage—while he
screamed like a baby, pleading for mercy. Sick fucks. Didn't give
any mercy when he was taking the innocence from children. I
sure as hell didn't give him any mercy, either.

Pride had me thinking I did the world a favor by taking the
devils in waiting. But I knew as my body count went up, my
conscience dwindled down. All those items resembled a past, a
past few know. A past that needed redemption.

After we got back from our last mission, I was in a bad way.
I gave the middle finger to everything. To my family, my future,
my life. I turned to anything which could dull the pain and
quiet the voices in my head. Heroin and cocaine became my
pleasures of choice. They kept the beast at bay, and everything
numb.

Until Cole came at me with an ultimatum, he wanted to
open Tactical Redemption, like we talked about when we were
in between missions, sitting in a straw hut. But only if I was
clean. It was as I had hit bottom, and I was jonesing for a hit so
badly, I would enter underground fights to earn enough money
to buy more. With his and Noah's help, I went into rehab. I went
to the meetings, and I did my time. I threw myself back into
getting stronger. I climbed out of the depths of hell. And
watching Jennie suffer through what I had gone through was a
double gut punch. If I had been aware of what was going on, I
could have helped her sooner.

My team believed I had changed for the better. Maybe I
had. For the most part. I still had to feed the beast his justice,
but it was hidden from the rest of the world. My team knew
about my playroom. Under my trophy room, through a hidden
door, was a secret, soundproof bunker that had everything I

needed to extract the truth out of those who sought to do harm. I had the skills and tools needed to ensure evidence would never be discovered and made sure justice was done. I knew I would never be completely redeemed, and I was okay with it. Because even the devil was once an angel.

I went back up the stairs and secured my trophy room then made quick work of packing up the necessary equipment and ammunition we would need for the upcoming mission. This crate, along with another filled with protection and communication gear, would be sent to our secure location in Florida, where Toren and Zeke were holed up. Our operation against the Syndicate and the Cruz Cartel had finally gained momentum. The raid Toren and Zeke had launched a couple weeks ago opened up doors and more questions were being asked.

The original intel was wrong. When they took control of the container bound for South America, the team found a horrific situation. Children as young as three, and pregnant women, were set to be sold for slavery. Once I read Toren's report, I about threw up. Not only were they selling these innocent souls to the depths of hell, but they were also raping the women and keeping them as incubators so they could sell the babies on the adoption black market. They were growing and cultivating their own product, like the drugs. That put the urgency back into our mission. Our team was more determined than ever to take these motherfuckers down.

"Yo, Sketch. Open the damn door!"

The voice echoed through the massive warehouse, thanks to the speaker at the front buzzer.

"Fucking Sims," I growled, using my last nail to close the crate. I tossed the mallet down onto the metal table, and stalked out, taking careful measure to secure the room behind me. Agent Sims wasn't a douche like the rest of the FBI agents we knew. In fact, he was probably one of our best sources for any information on the Syndicate and Cruz Cartel. He had been burned as badly as Kate had been, but he felt it was in his best interest to ride it out. Said he would be more useful on the inside.

"What?" I snarled, throwing open the door. Rick Sims leaned against the doorframe, his tall frame dressed casually in a pair of jeans and a green button-down shirt. "I see you aren't wearing your badge, so this must be a social visit."

"Nah, I wanted to see your smiling face," he replied, following me inside. As soon as the door shut behind him, Rick reached into his shirt.

"It must be really social then," I joked as he lifted his shirt to uncover a manila folder.

He gave me the middle finger and then handed me the folder. "Yeah, real social, fuckhead. Take a look."

My smirked flattened into a thin line as my eyes skimmed the single photo in front of me.

"You've got to be kidding me."

"Nope. Right there, is our boy Tommy Green. Aka Thomas Cruz, the heir apparent to the Cruz Cartel and notorious life-fucker." The FBI's former golden boy, Tommy Green, who fucked up everyone around him. A toxic human being, he led a double life; the son of a drug cartel kingpin while using his FBI background and badge to keep the business afloat. Kate tried everything in her power to get the upper levels of the FBI to see what a danger Tommy was, but they never took her words to heart until after he tried to take Shane Turner, my brother in arms, and kidnapped his now-wife, Megan. Their ineptitude caused all sorts of physical and mental trauma to them both.

"Who are the dickheads with him?" I growled.

"Well, you know Nicholas Santori, the owner of the infamous Ravenous nightclub down on Gay Street. The other guy, we're not sure. We're running facial recognition through Interpol, FBI, and DEA. But so far, nothing."

Nicholas Santori was a quasi-legitimate businessman. His

clubs were popular, and at first on the up and up legally. However, the clubs were private, and only the richest of the rich got to pay to play. Kate found out the clubs were funneling the girls into the sex slavery market, through the guise of an escort business run by a professional sex therapist, Madam Syn. Madam Syn was the person to get Jennie out of jail when she was arrested for solicitation and assault on a police officer after the Cartel left her drugged out of her mind. We thought Jennie would be able to get the rehab she needed, but the lure of the next high was too strong. And the cartel was three steps ahead of us. They took Jennie from the rehab facility Noah and Kate hid her in and whisked her away to Vegas to be auctioned off. That's where we found her.

Kate had gone undercover at the Ravenous club in Vegas, under the guise of an escort. We didn't know Jennie was there until Sebastian Cruz pulled her on stage, and then put a bullet in her head right in front of everyone. Thanks to a mole within our former team, they knew exactly what was going on. And they got away.

Nicholas's part in all this became known while we were in Vegas. Evidence was minimal at best, and thanks to his hot shot lawyers, he was able to get away with a misdemeanor. Of course, he pleaded ignorance, but it didn't stop the court of public opinion, and the community helped bankrupt his businesses. After three months of testimony, the charges were dropped due to some technical bullshit and Nicholas fled the area. He hadn't been seen or heard from since. But this... this was a different story.

"When and where?" I bit out.

"That was taken last night in the French Quarter, by my undercover guy. He sent them straight to me this morning, but they had to go through the proper channels."

"Cole and Benji are down there already. Did you hit them up?" I groused, more to myself than to Sims. Sims was anything but incompetent; he would have had Cole and Benji in on the set up from the beginning.

"Yeah. They've already been introduced to our asset and are currently watching them now," Sims said dryly.

"Fuck watching them, they need to make a move," I growled. "I'll fly down there and take care of the shit myself if I have to. Sitting around twiddling our dicks isn't going to get shit done."

"Hold the fuck on here, Davis. You're not going to NOLA, with a raging hard on to fuck up Tommy Green. The director wants this done by the books, so they don't get off on the same fucking technicality Santori did."

I scoffed. "Remember Playboy, we tried that before and it sure as fuck didn't work. Maybe it's time to try it my way."

Sims rubbed his head in frustration. "Sketch. I came by as a professional courtesy because we're on the same fucking side."

"Your professional courtesy is letting the bastard that killed my sister get away. So, fuck your 'courtesy'," I growled.

I didn't have to see him to know he was about to blow a gasket. Helping us on the side is one thing, it's almost an obligation for him. He was a solid dude, and he knew the bureau fucked up when they let Tommy slip out of their hands. But he also had the god-forsaken sense of patriotic duty and this whole rights and justice bullshit. We had a level of trust, as much as one could between an officer of the law and a band of mercenaries. We weren't vigilantes, but we did play in the gray area, so-to-speak.

"Come on, Sketch. I know your fucked up mind is thinking of all the ways you could have fun with the bastard, but you got to play by our rules this time. We go out there, we do recon, we get him, we get out."

"Then don't come. Stay behind, with your tail tucked between the folds of your pussy and let the big dogs do the work," I spat out, pulling up the secure messaging system on my phone and sending a text to Cole demanding an update.

Oh, if he was a cartoon, Sims would have had steam coming out of his ears.

"Listen here..." he started but was cut off by the ring of his phone.

"Looks like the boss is checking in, making sure you're doing what you're told to do," I sneered.

"We're not done talking, Sketch," he warned, then put the phone to his ear. "Agent Sims." I listened, as his body language grew more tense. Whatever it was, it didn't appear it would bode well for our little planned getaway.

"How the hell did that happen?" Pause. "Yeah, I'll be right there. Get me on a flight within the next hour. I don't care if you need to charter a damn plane, but get it done. I'm on my way in now."

He shut off his phone and glared at me angrily. "Greene was spotted getting on a private jet in New Orleans. The manifest destination is set for Columbia, but who the fuck knows where he's really going. I'm on my way to Miami to meet up with the field office."

"Should I tell you I told you so now, or do you want to kiss my ass later?"

"Yeah, yeah. I get it. Keep your phone on you, I'll call you with any details."

"Yeah, I got you." I followed him out the door and lit another cigarette. Fucking Tommy Greene. I can't wait for that asshole to see his end. He deserves nothing but the worst. He's fucked up so many lives, and the path of destruction only seems to get worse.

I finished my cigarette and headed back inside, waiting for Cole's reply. Thankfully, it didn't take too long for my phone to ring.

"I was about to call you when I got your text," Cole said, his voice tense. Whatever happened, I knew it wasn't going to be good.

"Sims got word Tommy took off on a private plane bound for Columbia," I muttered.

"Yeah, we followed him out on to the tarmac. We tried to get them to stop the plane – but we were a minute too late."

Fuck.

"Sims said he went to Columbia. How can we confirm it?"

"Zeke is waiting for a phone call from his source. He'll let us know what he finds out," Cole replied. The voices in the background faded and I knew Cole had walked away from the group.

"So basically, we're stuck twiddling our fucking thumbs, waiting?"

"Yep." His tone was clipped, and the frustration was clear. Tommy had slipped through our fingers so many times. This motherfucker was taunting us.

We disconnected after Cole confirmed our next steps. Our mission was still clear, even though Tommy was in the wind. We'd take them down. One by one.

And the amount Tommy would pay...would be priceless.

4

CHARLIE

FOR ONCE, I HAD WOKEN UP EARLIER THAN MY ALARM AND GOT out of bed on time. I was able to have a cup of coffee and my cereal and didn't have to run around like a freaking lunatic because I was late. Plus, the weather had been gearing up to be absolutely gorgeous for the weekend which was perfect because the beach BBQ at Kate's was scheduled for Saturday. And the best thing? Creeper Michael had been out of town all week, so I didn't have to deal with his bullshit. It couldn't get any better than this.

I sang along to Lizzo's "Tempo" as I got ready, the song already setting my mood for the day. I picked out a pair of destructed skinny jeans, a fitted gray button-up shirt over a deep purple tank. I had slid my feet into a pair of weathered black Chuck Taylors when my phone rang.

Knowing most people text, I glanced wearily at the device.

It was Kate.

Phone calls never brought good news, especially when it's from your former-FBI-agent sister.

The great day feeling slipped away and was slowly replaced with dread and trepidation.

"What happened?" I answered automatically.

"Why does anything have to happen in order for me to call you?" Kate's voice came through, although I could tell she was in her car.

"Because you never, ever freaking call me. And if you do, it's either bad news or you want something," I replied, grabbing the patchwork tote I carried my work life in and walked out the door.

"Okay, so you're right," Kate confirmed.

"Duh, I always am. What's going on?" I held the phone against my shoulder as I locked the door. As usual, the key in the lock stuck so I didn't hear what Kate was mumbling about until she mentioned the word lab.

"Wait, hold up. Back up," I demanded. I finally got the key out of the damn lock and walked down the sidewalk to my car.

"You're on your way into work, right?" she asked.

"Yeah. Why?" I replied cautiously. "What's going on, Kate?"

I slid into my Escape and locked the door before I started the engine.

Kate sighed. "I'll meet you there. Just do me a favor, okay? Don't freak out when you get there."

"Telling me not to freak out is a guarantee for me to actually freak the fuck out. Last time I'm asking, Kate. What the fuck is going on?" I demanded loudly, putting her on speaker and attaching my phone to the holder on the console.

"I'll explain it all when you get here. Heads up though. There is a heavy security presence here. They're scrutinizing everyone."

"So, you're telling me walking around with a baggie full of H isn't the best idea?" I trolled, rolling my eyes.

"Not unless you want to get arrested for intent to distribute and manufacturing of illegal narcotics. But then again, with your coloring, you'd look great in prison orange."

"You can't give any clue on what I'm walking into?" I asked, pulling on to the highway.

"Not really something I can or wish to discuss over the phone, Shortcake."

Great. The last thing our project needed was for some government weenie with a stick up his ass making noise about the illegal contraband we were looking at. It's happened more than once; some brown-nose rule stickler wanting to make a name for himself with the higher-ups would make a fuss because we happened to be working with heavy duty drugs like cocaine and heroin to see how they would react to certain cancer cells or someone with Alzheimer's. Or some big pharma lobbyist would try to claim patent rights.

Over my dead body. My foot pressed harder on the gas pedal, picking up speed. I'll be damned if someone put the kibosh on my project.

Thirty minutes later, I pulled onto Bowen Biotech's research campus and let out a low whistle. Kate wasn't joking about the heavy security presence. Cars with emergency lights had set up a barricade around the building and there was an extensive line of cars waiting to get into a parking lot. The fire department and hazmat vehicles were mobilized in front while vans marked with various media outlets were parked haphazardly on the side of the road. Perfectly coiffed anchors and cameramen were busy setting up for interviews, grabbing whomever they could off the streets to get their reaction.

But reaction to what exactly?

After forty-five minutes of waiting, having my car searched by drug sniffing dogs, hoofing it a mile from the nearest parking lot, and having to show my campus badge to no less than eight officers, I finally made my way into the Van Buren building, and slowly followed the crowd and voices to the wing where the project's labs were located.

My heart dropped.

Heavy metal barriers blocked the corridor that led to our wing. The heavy, hazmat protective sheeting covered the entrance to the lab my team used. A portable decontamination shower had been set up next to it. People in coats with DEA, ATF, and FBI labels were everywhere, taking photos, talking to each other, and intently looking for clues. The smell of lingering smoke and sulfur permeated the air.

"What the hell happened?" I whispered to myself. Knowing this day wouldn't be business as usual, I looked around for my program partners. My normally calm advisor, Dr. Weber, looked flustered and worried as he talked to what I assumed was a detective.

A hand clasped my wrist and I jumped. Kate's face was grim as she handed me a mask. She had her hair pulled back into a protective cap and her face was covered in her own filtered mask.

"You need this if you're going to stick around." Her voice was muffled, but I complied quickly. Her former partner, Rick, nodded his greeting and then walked away. Kate shook her head, then pulled me out into the hall.

"Well, hello to him too," I mumbled, watching as he talked to a tall, skinny man.

"He doesn't want to give any sign he could be biased or tainted," Kate replied. "Sims almost went apoplectic when I showed up."

"What the hell is going on, Kate? Why does my workplace look like a war zone?" I stressed quietly, gazing around in horror. But before she could respond, Dr. Weber caught the students' attention.

"I guess we're about to find out." Those who weren't wearing a badge followed the professor to one of the abandoned conference rooms. We gathered around him, our voices clamoring together in questions.

"All right folks, listen up. I know we're all in big shock. I don't know much, because the damn agencies who have taken over my labs are refusing to talk. But here's what I do know. Obviously, there's been a massive security breach. The lab was destroyed. Decimated. Our beloved security guard, Maurice Watkins, was shot and killed while responding."

Gasps sounded throughout the crowd as we took in the dreadful news. Maurice was the biggest teddy bear anyone had ever met. He would always have a smile on his face, no matter the situation. My heart broke for his wife and ten-year-old boy.

"This is a traumatic loss for Maurice's family. And the department will not only be fully funding the funeral expenses, but we'll also collect donations to help defray any additional costs for his family." Dr. Weber paused for a moment, to let the team take it in.

"And now on to other bad news. Our servers were hacked and wiped clean. The test samples, the replicas, the equipment, they were all destroyed or tainted. Our current supply of chemicals was combined and it's a hazmat site now. Our project is on hold until the investigation is complete, and the feds have done whatever it is they need to do. If we are even able to continue," Dr. Weber announced, his deep tenor voice rising above our collective groans of disappointment.

"Our work is important, but until we get better security protocols in place, I wouldn't feel comfortable with any one of you working on it."

"What about the research grants?" a girl from one of the other projects asked.

"Funding is frozen as well." The groans and angry shouts grew louder until the air was pierced by a shrill whistle. "I know this is horrific news, but at this point, there's nothing we are able to do. I'm going to work with the department and the Dean to ensure you all still maintain your credited hours." The murmurs from the crowd slowly died to a low buzz. "I do have to let you know that the investigators will be talking to you all, individually. Your computers and notes will be confiscated for evidence and for safekeeping."

"Are we in danger, Dr. Weber?" a male voice from the back piped up.

Dr. Weber hesitated, then heaved a sigh. "I don't suspect you would be in any particular danger. But you should remain vigilant. Be aware of your surroundings. What's the phrase? If you see something, say something? Remember that. Live by it. Does everyone understand?" A knock at the door came, and a group of people walked in wearing FBI jackets. While they were all stern-faced and serious, a tall man with a sharp chin and narrow brown eyes captured my attention. He glared around the room, as if the murderer was here with us. He and Dr. Weber had a hushed, quick discussion before the man shook his head sharply and stepped to the side. Dr. Weber turned his attention back to us.

"This group of agents will be conducting the interviews. Post interview, you're free to go." Dr. Weber nodded to the group and left the room. One by one, we were called over to chat with the agents. After about two hours, I was free to go. I texted Kate to let her know I was done, and she replied she would meet me at my place. So that's where I headed.

Thirty minutes later, Kate, Summer, and I were lounging on our miniscule back patio area with subs and other fried goodness from Jimmy's, a deli up the street. A situation like this definitely called for an afternoon of junk food.

"So aside from the 'official statement,' what's really going on?" I questioned, taking a swig of my soda.

Kate shrugged. "I honestly am at a loss. We haven't heard anything about this from our sources in the cartel so this may be someone else entirely. If this were on their radar at all, we would have done something about this already."

"What did Rick say?" Summer asked, snatching the last crab-stuffed mushroom from the dish. I glared mockingly and threatened her with my fork. She gave me the finger as she chomped away happily.

"Pretty much the same thing. This is the first they're hearing the project being an actual target. There has always been the slight possibility, but it's not like what you're doing is a secret. This is a well-known program with major potential reach. It's not like you're close to even coming up with a commercially viable product, let alone have enough produced to make a dent in the cartel's books," Kate replied.

"What did the DEA say?" I asked, thinking of other avenues.

"It's been the same from them. They're as in the dark as we are." An alert sounded and Kate quickly checked her phone. "That was Cole. I need to roll out."

"All right, go do your Wonder Woman thing. Just keep us updated." I rose and gave her a quick hug.

"I will. Are you sure you two don't want to stay with us?" The second I got home, Kate pleaded with Summer and I to stay with her and Noah. While it was fun for a night or two when we were having a good time, it's not something I'd want to do long-term.

"Um, that would be a nope. I already turned in my laptop and all my notes. I have nothing here any asshole wanna-be-drug manufacturer could want. And besides, we're already planning to come over this weekend for the BBQ." I sighed. Although I didn't feel necessarily confident in my words, the last thing I needed was to encroach on their life.

Kate rolled her eyes. "You're bullheaded. Fine. You two be safe. Keep an eye on each other and stay vigilant. Give us a call day or night. Cole and Sketch are pretty close if you find your-self in trouble." She casted a worried look at our measly security measures.

"At the very least, I'll have someone come up and update your security. And don't even try to argue with me." She held up her hand as I opened my mouth to protest. *Fine*. I looked over at Summer who shrugged. I know she wouldn't say no to my sister. In fact, if her brother heard of the incident today, he'd ship us both off to a deserted island.

"Are we still on for the BBQ this weekend?" I asked, wiping my hands with the napkin.

"I doubt it. I have a feeling we'll be working all weekend." Kate checked her phone again. "I really need to get to TR. I'll text you if any information comes up."

"Thanks, sis. Be safe out there."

"You too. Remember, be vigilant." And with that, she walked out.

"Do you really think we're in danger?" Summer questioned, pulling her hair into a ponytail.

I thought about it for a moment, then shrugged. "I don't know. If anything, Kate is trained to think of worst-case scenarios. If whoever did this had the names of all the students on the program, it wouldn't make any difference. All our laptops are now evidence and in the hands of the feds. Even when we work from home, all the info is stored on the Bowen Biotech cloud, so it's not like we have private home servers or anything. And it's not like we can memorize everything we've worked on." Okay, that was a lie. When you work on something for so long, you're bound to memorize key pieces. The formulas we had been working on were our babies.

Summer didn't look convinced, but she changed the subject to something less stressful. We finished up the food and moved inside once we felt the sprinkle of raindrops. She went off to do more photo edits and I wandered up to my bedroom. I threw myself on the bed and stared up at the ceiling.

The calming blues in my bedroom made me feel anything but. While I put on a brave face in front of Summer, the entire situation had my anxiety reaching heights I hadn't seen in a while. My mind whirled around the possible scenarios and the what-if situations. I felt myself spiraling and I wanted nothing more than to run. These were the issues Kate faced on the daily and I didn't know how she coped. I wanted desperately to call Kate back, to have her tell me everything was going to be okay. But I knew if I did, she wouldn't be able to do what she needed to do. I would feel like a weak fool in asking her to calm me down.

I selected my meditation app from my phone and let the sounds of the ocean waves wash over me. I closed my eyes and breathed deeply, concentrating on breathing through my nose and exhaling through the mouth. After about thirty minutes, my body finally let go. As sleep took hold, my last coherent thought was that I wished Sketch was there with me.

5

SKETCH

"WHAT'S THE LATEST?"

Five days later, Kate's demand filtered through the open doorway to the weapons room. I didn't need to ask what she was talking about. Once she texted me about the situation at Charlie's lab, Tactical Redemption went into defensive mode. Contacts were made to our various informants, and we mobilized them to gather as much information as possible. But so far, nothing tangible has come to light. With a power play like this, regardless of who was behind it, people tend to run scared, and the information dries up.

"You know damn well if I had any current info, you and Cole would be the first to know," I growled. My patience was barely existent, and it took everything in me to not go directly to Charlie and bring her back here. She was in danger and my prime instinct was to throw her over my shoulder and lock her in a safe space. Preferably my bedroom but I doubted her siblings would go for it. I had a sinking feeling something big was about to go down. Cole felt the same. He dispatched Trey to watch the girls while Zeke and Toren did recon in their areas.

With all this going down, we still had the cartel to contend with. As stretched thin as we were, we needed to ensure we were able to take on whatever we needed. Namely, the new shipment of drugs that were due to come in over on the Eastern shore. Because Cole knew I would be going crazy, he put me as lead for this operation. It barely satisfied my bloodthirst, but it was the only legal action I could take for now.

"I know. I know. The unknown is killing me though. Normally, I'm good. I know we have to keep going and wait for all the information to come in. But this isn't a normal case. This is personal. This is my sister they're ..." A look of horror crossed her face, and she slapped her hand over her mouth. "Oh shit, Sketch. I am so sorry. I didn't mean it like that."

"Oh, keep going, Kate. What? You didn't mean to imply my sister being killed by the Syndicate wasn't personal enough for you? That your child's biological mother, my sister, didn't make this personal? I guess because she was an addict, it didn't matter," I snapped, the venom laced in my voice.

"Sketch, that's not what I meant, I'm sorry. You're absolutely right, Jennie's death made—" Kate said softly, remorse filling her tone.

"Fuck off, Kate. I don't want your bullshit apologies." I slammed down the lid to the crate I just packed. I stalked toward her, getting toe to toe with her, having to look down at her. "Once the Syndicate even looked at Jennie, it became personal to me."

"Back away, Sketch," Noah warned me. I looked sharply at him standing behind Kate, and I narrowed my eyes, then turned back to glare at Kate.

"Your sister is my number one priority right now. Don't ever think otherwise. And don't ever question my fucking priorities." I glowered at her, and to her credit, Kate didn't back away from me. I snarled at her then turned back to the large steel table, where the rest of the weaponry needed to be packed.

This conversation was over, hell it was over before it started. I knew Kate. This was a misspoken error and she regretted even thinking it. But fuck if it didn't dig the knife in my heart a little deeper. The edge of pain I felt expanded, cracking my heart even more. I couldn't save my sister. But she could be damn sure I wouldn't let anyone else fall to the hands of the Syndicate.

Not on my watch.

I focused on the task in front of me, packing up the last case of weapons into my covered truck bed and then jumped into the cab. I swung by Cole's to pick up him and Benji, then we made our way toward the Chesapeake Bay Bridge. Noah and Kate would be arriving separately. Tactical Redemption would be taking point, then the local DEA office would be called in. Manpower wise, it wasn't ideal. But it was the best we could do with the hand we were dealt. And while Trey bitched up a storm about watching Charlie and Summer, I was out of fucks to give. Because if I knew she wasn't being watched, my focus, and that of Cole's and Kate's, would be on her. We had to stay sharp, and it meant leaving our biggest men behind to watch over two scrappy females.

The team made it to the rendezvous point in under an hour. Located back at the old bait and tackle shack that had a great line of sight to the lone pier of the abandoned marina. We stowed my truck in the woods and made the half mile trek to the shack on foot. We moved methodically. Dusk had fallen over the Choptank River and the only sound was the quack of a random mallard duck. Dressed in black, we staked out our positions throughout the marina, and waited. Three hours later, my eyes caught motion on the gravel road leading toward us.

"It's time for fireworks," I muttered into my mic. Replies of "Copy" came through my ears, and everything went radio silent. We weren't sure of the tech these assholes would be carrying, but we sure as hell didn't want to divulge our positions until it was absolutely necessary.

A medium-sized box truck rental and an older pickup came into view and backed in next to the pier. Five figures emerged from the cabs. But something didn't seem right. Why bring a moving truck to a drug shipment? It didn't make sense.

Unless they were moving something other than drugs.

"You thinking what I'm thinking?" Benji murmured next to me.

I nodded. The sound of a large boat motor came from the west. It was time. I drew my Barrett M-70 against my shoulder and watched the heavy-duty fishing boat arrive through the scope. It shouldn't take much time for them to exchange the product and we had to be ready for whatever was being moved.

A lone shadow was at the wheel as the boat pulled up to the pier. The three men hustled down the dock, taking the ropes that were thrown to tie it down. Once the boat was secure, the driver of the boat ducked under the deck only to reappear with a child, who was bound and gagged.

"Fuck," I said to myself. Benji cursed with me. This was a game changer. I nodded to Benji, who sent a quick text to Agent Sims, informing him of the change in mission. This wasn't a take-down. This was now a rescue operation.

6

SKETCH

"We take them down once the kids are secured in the moving truck," I said quietly. Benji agreed and sent a quick, secure text to the rest of the crew. While we were figuring out our next move, five more kids had been transferred from the boat to the truck. One man stood with a semi-automatic rifle in his hands, keeping an eye on his surroundings.

We crept from the shadows, the team knowing their markers, as what appeared to be the last kid was tossed into the back of the truck by one of the men. The other two and the boat captain hustled to untie the boat. We made our move.

Benji, Cole, and Noah made their way to the pier, hidden by the shadows. Kate crept around the truck holding the hostages. The goon guarding the kids didn't realize what hit him until the butt of Kate's gun hit him in the back of the head, and he fell with a thud.

The other men turned at the noise and before they could raise their guns, I had them in my sights. I pulled the trigger, firing three quick shots in rapid succession. Two men on the pier went down but the bastard in the boat ducked. He shouted in an unfamiliar language and threw the throttle. His boat surged forward, the last untied line straining against the pier. The power increased and finally the line snapped, just as Noah and Benji jumped into the boat, knocking the captain down. The three of them came to blows, and a shot rang out. With Cole engaged in a hand-to-hand fight with the last man standing, I flew into action, racing down the pier as Benji and Noah fell backwards overboard into the river with a splash. The boat revved its motor and took off down the river.

"Noah!" Kate's cry rang out.

Noah's head popped up in the dark water, sputtering.

"I'm good!"

I scanned the surrounding area in case they were expecting backup. They didn't disappoint. Two more trucks flew down the road. I raced back up the pier to the rental truck and took aim, as they slammed on their brakes. Gravel went flying. Friend or foe? It didn't matter. I shouted a command for them to get out of their vehicles with their hands in the air. Their response was to throw open their car doors and fire their pathetic pistols.

Bunch of fucking pussies.

I fired three shots with precision, taking all three of them out with bullets to their foreheads. They went down. The silence was deafening.

"Status check," Cole shouted from the pier where he had pulled up our two friends.

"Clear!" I yelled back, my eyes watching the road. The sound of tires on the dirt road drew my attention and I raised my gun to take aim.

"FBI ETA is thirty seconds. Two large SUVs are incoming. Do not fire," Kate informed me through the earpiece.

"Of course, these bastards arrive now, right as the party ends," Cole groused. Benji walked slowly up the pier, his boots echoing on the wood. He clutched his arm gingerly and looked more pissed off than hurt.

"You okay, bro?" I asked as he got closer.

"Yeah, the cocksucker couldn't get me with a solid shot. Just a graze," Benji muttered, his slow drawl more prevalent with his anger.

The SUVs Kate warned us about pulled up to the pier. Various men and women in suits and FBI emblazed jackets filed out, like clowns from the circus. And that's what it ended up being.

We tried to process the scene as much as possible, but the bullshit had already hit the fan. As we surveyed the damage before us, more vehicles arrived. Multiple bodies strewn among the shell casings. The two lucky ones that were alive were hogtied with thick zip ties. FBI agents milled around, ensuring we couldn't get anything we needed from the scene. And then more arrived.

The various alphabet agents milled around, ensuring not only they could spread the blame, but take the credit for the work they didn't do. Local child protective services had already come to whisk away the kids. Kate did a great job in keeping them calm, but it didn't mean they weren't traumatized. But they were alive. While we didn't get the drugs, we saved lives from dire straits. I called today's mission a success.

"Parker!"

Cole and Kate's heads popped up as their last name bounced over the water, causing it to echo in the night. I glared at the voice, watching Special Agent in Charge Rapoles and Agent Sims come barreling down the road.

I lifted my head in acknowledgement to Sims, then slammed the lid to the cover of the truck bed.

"Need me to stick around?" I muttered to Cole. As much as I wanted to roll out, I wasn't going to leave Cole to the wolves. I may have been point man on this operation, but Cole was the leader of our team. Whatever happened on ops, it fell on Cole's shoulders.

"Nah, we're good. Just get this dumbass to the hospital for stitching," he replied, smacking Benji on his bum shoulder.

Benji gritted his teeth against the pain. "Fuck off, dick. I'll be fine with some dry clothes."

I chuckled. "Come on pussy, let's get you checked out. Kate, you good?"

Kate nodded. "I got Noah. He's good. Bullet hit him in his vest, so we need to get him changed."

I nodded and headed toward my truck with Benji in tow. Cole would hitch a ride back with his sister and Noah, but it was high time for me to hit the road. I wasn't the best one to deal with the bureaucratic bullshit. They wouldn't like what I had to say, and they could make our lives hell if they really wanted to.

7

CHARLIE

GROWING UP, SATURDAY MORNINGS MEANT WE OPENED UP THE windows and deep cleaned the house. Music, specifically the classics like Bob Marley, Jimi Hendrix, The Doors, and Skynyrd, were played at top volume while everyone in the house worked on the chores we couldn't get to during the week. That meant the bedding was washed, the bedrooms were cleaned, the floors mopped, the bathrooms were sparkling, and windows were done. My mom worked her tail off at the diner and often told us she wasn't working when she was at home too. Dad, who worked long hours as a foreman at the shipyard, agreed and from an early age, my siblings and I were responsible for keeping the house clean. Now granted, the room Kate and I shared never stayed tidy, but for one day, it was spotless.

The habit continued once I started living on my own. I still woke up at seven on Saturdays, turned up my cleaning playlist with all the songs I grew up with and started cleaning. The routine centered me. It gave me the respite I needed, especially after a long week at work. Plus, it meant the rest of my week could be spent doing whatever I wanted.

By ten in the morning, the house was sparkling clean. I had

already showered and had my beach bag packed. As usual, Summer slept through it all, and I hadn't heard a peep from her. I was ready to get on the road. After a week of being at home thanks to the lab closure, I was going stir-crazy.

"Summer! Are you ready yet?" I called to her closed door.

I pulled my t-shirt over my head and situated it over my teal bikini top. I pulled my hair back into a messy knot on the top of my head, as I waited for Summer to respond.

"Summer?" I slid my feet into my flipflops and wandered into her bedroom next to mine. Without thinking, I walked right in.

"Summer? Come on woman, we need to get going." I shook the lump under the covers and pulled back the purple duvet. A familiar head popped out.

"Well, hello there, Casey. You're not who I was expecting." I looked over as the bathroom door opened, and steam filtered out.

"That's okay, you're welcome to jump in here with me." The deep, sleep-filled voice should have sounded sexy, but I laughed at him. At slightly under six-foot, Casey was gorgeous, and his ego knew it. Casey was an up-and-coming club promoter, so he was on everyone's radar. If I wasn't crushing on a certain six-foot-five sexy beast, I would certainly entertain Casey Rogan in my bed. But since I couldn't get Sketch out of my head, and I knew he was seriously into Summer, Casey was stuck in the friend zone.

"As much fun as it sounds, I'm going to have to pass," I teased.

He put his hand against his bare chest. "Charlie, I thought we were closer than that."

"You can barely handle me. What makes you think you would be able to handle her?" Summer came into the bedroom wrapped in a towel. "It's time for you to roll out, Rogan," she said breezily. Summer didn't look at him when she went into her closet, dropping her towel on the floor. But Casey watched every move she made with hunger in his eyes. I'd seen her naked plenty of times, so it didn't faze me one bit. Casey, on the other hand, looked like he was drooling and ready for round...whatever number they were on.

"Oh sweet Summer. I can totally handle you," Casey replied, sitting up in the bed. He flicked the duvet off his lower half and unfortunately, his boxers were tented.

Clad in only her purple bikini bottoms, she turned around and tossed his shirt and pants at him, then continued getting dressed. "It's time to go, Case."

"See, you can't even argue with that," Casey said with a smile.

"Oh shush!" Summer yanked the pillow he was laying on and smacked him upside the head with it.

"Summer, you know you were screaming your head off last night. You just can't admit it." He took his time pulling on his clothes, enjoying getting on her nerves. He gave me a wink and shoved his feet into the sneakers on the floor.

"Did you hear me screaming?" Summer asked, turning to me, and giving me a pointed look.

"Nope. And I'm a light sleeper," I lied. Yeah, she had been screaming all night and it was so freaking annoying. I was only slightly jealous since it had been a good while since I screamed like she did.

"You're such a liar, Summer. But it's cool. Don't worry, I'm sure you'll be walking funny later," he said with a smirk and headed out of the room, and down the stairs.

"Next time, I'll have to use a magnifying glass to make sure you're big enough to ride," she called after him. The door slammed and the rest of the house shook. I shook my head and had to laugh. Last night was a doozy. We had walked the two blocks to Walt's Inn, a local joint known for its karaoke and Jell-O shots. That's where we ran into Casey and his buddies.

Summer and Casey had known each other since high school, and it was always like this. Arguing with each other one minute, the next minute they're having loud, angry sex. Summer preferred it that way and feelings made a mess of things because someone always ends up being hurt.

"Since he's gone, ready to hit the beach?" Summer asked brightly, coming up the stairs.

"Must you treat him like that?" I ignored her question and asked my own with a raised eyebrow.

She bent over and ran the towel over her hair. "If I treat him nicely, he'll catch feelings."

"I think it's too late for that."

Summer sighed and pulled her hair into a messy top knot. "I know. He's too good for my bullshit. Now, come on. You ready to go?"

I rolled my eyes and laughed. "Fine, just ignore what's going on between the two of you. I've been waiting for you. Hurry up and get dressed."

"Give me ten. I'll be ready. Do we need to pick up anything else on the way?" she replied, opening her dresser.

"No, we're good. We got plenty of booze and snacks, plus Kate said they're grilling out," I replied, as I headed back into my bedroom. I grabbed my beach towel and sunscreen and stuffed them into my beach bag. Once downstairs, I pulled out two cases of our favorite spiked seltzers, and the plate of caprese salad kabobs we had made before our night out last night. Into the grocery bag went the package of pretzel rods to go with a chocolate hummus Summer picked up and the container of dark chocolate covered strawberries. We had been waiting forever for the weather to warm up, and today was gearing up to be perfect.

After twenty minutes, we loaded up the small cooler and beach gear into the back of the Escape and took off down the highway. As much as I loved living in the city, there was always a sense of peace whenever I was at Kate and Noah's place. Set on the peninsula in Mayo, the house backed to a public beach on the South River. It was a great neighborhood for my niece, and I could tell Kate was taking on her new role as a mom with ease.

We managed to pull up to the small, but cozy beach house on Bayside Drive an hour later. As soon as we cut the engine, Shane Turner, my brother from another mother, came bounding down the front porch steps.

"Hey there, Shortcake," he said warmly as I opened my door. He pulled me into his huge arms and hugged me tightly. "It's good to see you outside the lab."

I hugged him back. I hadn't seen Shane since February; thanks to all the work I've been putting in at the lab. But to be fair, he was also so busy, working with Tactical Redemption and with the auto repair shop he ran with his best friend, Adrian.

"I know, big brother. It's been a while. You remember my girl, Summer, right?" I replied warmly, stepping away. Summer came around to join us and gave Shane a quick hug.

"It's been a minute. Good to see you too, Summer," Shane replied. He walked around to the back of the Escape and pulled out the two beach chairs. "What the hell, Charlie? Are you sure you brought enough stuff?" he asked with a chuckle.

I shrugged. So, what if I had a tendency to overpack? "We wanted to make sure we didn't need to make a run to the store." I pulled out my beach bag and flung the strap over my shoulder as I reached in for the cooler.

"I got it, Angel."

I closed my eyes for a moment and let his deep, gravelly voice wash over me. I swear I could orgasm just by talking to him.

"Oh, hey Sketch, I didn't see you there."

"You should know by now I'm a ninja," Sketch said softly, a

small grin pulling at the corner of his luscious lips. "You'll never see me coming." He pulled the cooler out of the trunk and swiftly made his way up the steps.

"No, but I definitely want to feel it," I muttered under my breath, turning toward the porch steps. A barking laugh behind me had my face turning beet red. Apparently, I spoke louder than I thought. I glanced over and groaned. Shane raised his eyebrow, hearing me loud and clear. I shook my head and rolled my eyes, the universal sign to forget whatever he thought he heard.

The screen door slammed open and Shane's wife, Megan strolled out, with her daughter Katie on her hip. "Charlie! Girl, it's been forever."

"You look amazing, Megan." I kissed her cheek and reached up to tickle Katie on her tummy. "You've grown, baby girl."

"Yeah, we're growing like a beanstalk here," Megan said with a smile. "Come and get settled." She opened the door for us, as we hauled in our bags.

"Shane and Sketch, go ahead and take the cooler and chairs to the beach. Noah's getting the grill going, and as soon as I slather the baby with sunscreen, we'll be out." Megan's commands were law, and the guys dutifully did what they were supposed to do.

"Who all is coming today?" Summer asked, as she put her bag down on the foyer bench.

"Zeke's got back in town, so him and Benji are on their way. Cole and Tracie are coming over after Tracie gets off work, and Kate and Aubrey are already on the beach, with the kiddie pool," Megan replied, rubbing sunscreen on Katie's porcelain skin.

"Great, what can I help with?" I asked, dropping my beach bag by the door.

"Take this monster out and give her to Shane, so I can go get my swimsuit on." She handed me the giggly toddler and headed toward the bathroom.

"Let's go outside, Katie Bug!" I said in a sing-song voice. Summer grabbed my bag and followed me out the back door to the deck, and then onto the sand below. While the beach is part of the public park, not many people ventured down this way, so we had our own slice of privacy. The chairs had been set up near the edge of the South River. An inflatable kiddie pool sat under the shade of a pop-up tent, to protect the babies from the bright sun.

I handed Katie off to Shane and went to my beach chair set up next to Kate.

"How's it going?" she asked, gently splashing Aubrey on the legs.

"So far so good. How about you?" I replied, taking off my shirt. I adjusted the beach chair and slipped on my shades, getting comfortable in the shining sun.

"Good. This one is keeping me on my toes," she replied. "Mom's driving me nuts with her wedding planning."

I chuckled. "You knew it was bound to happen. She can't do anything on a small scale."

Kate shook her head. "Apparently not. If she had her way, it'd be a full-blown formal affair, complete with a string quartet and a ten-layer cake."

I burst out laughing because Noah and Kate were anything *but* formal.

"Yeah, laugh it up. Just wait until you get married. You're the baby of the family, she'll guilt-trip you into doing everything."

I stopped laughing and looked at her in horror. Shit. She was right. Mom wouldn't get her way with Kate, and while Cole and Tracie were tight, I doubt she'd have any influence over their potential nuptials. I was the only one left. I was the baby. It didn't matter who the lucky bastard would be, Mom would totally run the show.

"Fuck. I'm screwed," I groaned, throwing my arm over my eyes.

"Who are you screwing?" Sketch muttered, dropping down into the chair next to me. Even though his voice was low, I still jumped. Damn ninja.

"No one lately," Summer quipped. *Gee thanks, Summer.* I shot her the finger. "Oh, come on, Charlie. You know it's been like . . . months since you got some."

Oh my God, I'm going to kill her. "Summer doesn't know what she's talking about," I muttered, completely mortified.

"Really? Let's discuss this, shall we? Who was it?" Summer retorted, sitting up from her chair.

"Yeah, give the name, Angel," Sketch growled softly.

My face was hot, and not from the sun. "We're not discussing my sex life," I retorted, glaring at Summer. I reached over and opened my cooler, grabbing the first can of hard seltzer my hands touched. Lime. *My favorite.* I cracked it open and took a long sip. Anything to keep me from talking about my sex life.

"Angel." *Fuck.* The word sent shivers down my spine. I glanced over at him, and he glared right back at me. *What the hell is his problem?*

"Well, it sure as hell wasn't as recent as this morning, Summer Potter." I lowered my glasses and shot her a pointed gaze. She merely shrugged.

"I'm a young, feisty, twenty-seven-year-old woman. I'm not looking for my future husband. I'm looking for what's available for the moment."

I rolled my eyes and adjusted my sunglasses. "Exactly. This is a judgement free zone, so stop judging my... extracurricular activities." I settled back into the chair and dug my toes into the warm sand. The crappy weather had done a complete turn-around, and the warm sun was shining down. The sounds of Dierks Bentley's "Beers on Me" filtered through the Bluetooth speakers, mixed with the scattered conversations and squeals of the toddlers playing in the inflatable pool. This was absolute heaven.

"Right, Charlie?" a voice asked, bringing me back to a semi-coherent state.

"Sure, whatever you say," I mumbled back, my eyes remaining closed. I blankly gave a thumbs-up to the group, not caring if I agreed to babysit for a year or gave away my meager life savings. I tuned out their conversation and let the voices dull to a low hum. After a week from hell, I needed a day to unwind and relax. Between my computer crashing with all my research and notes, a massive security breach at the lab, and a broken water heater at the house, I was done with the whole "adulting" thing. I heaved a big sigh and let the heat and breeze lull me to sleep.

"Charlie." Warm breath tickled my ear, as the gravelly voice in my extremely hot dream whispered in my ear.

"Mmmm," I whimpered, turning my face toward his voice. The roughness of his goatee set my body on fire as his lips traced across my cheek and I reached up, wrapping my arms around his neck to pull him closer.

"I love having your arms around me, beautiful, but we may want to keep this family friendly."

My eyes popped open. *Oh, holy fuck.* "Shit!" I untangled my arms from his neck and pushed him away so quickly he landed in the sand. I leapt from the chair, completely flustered. My face burned with embarrassment, as I looked around for potential witnesses. Thankfully, everyone seemed to have already gone inside. The toddler pool was empty and the only people on the beach were Sketch and me.

"Oh God. Sorry about that," I uttered, busying myself with picking up the towel and chairs. "It's been one of those weeks, and I guess my dream was even more realistic than I thought."

"Do you snuggle with everyone who tries to wake you up?"

Humor laced his voice but the look in his molten silver eyes told me differently.

I tried to play it off. "Only when it's a really vivid dream," I said with a fake smile, wiggling my eyebrows to show I was joking. But he didn't take it that way.

"Oh, really? So, it was a hot one, huh? Do tell."

My face fired up hotter than ever and I looked away from his intense gaze. "I didn't say it was a hot dream. Nope, it was just...you know what? They probably need my help in the kitchen. I'm going to clean up..." My voice trailed off as I grabbed the handle of my bag. I winced when the rough fabric scraped against my shoulder. *Damn, I'm probably red as a lobster too.*

He chuckled and took the bag from my shoulder. "It's cool. It's nice to know I'm in yours." I felt the heat from his gaze as his looked me up and down.

"What? No. I thought you were someone else," I blustered, turning away, and looking for something else to carry. There was nothing else to occupy my hands, so I hustled toward the wooden walkway that led from Noah's backyard to the beach and hurried up the deck stairs into the kitchen.

"You're looking a little hot there, Charlie!" Zeke called as I moved past them.

"You know I'm always hot for you, Zeke!" I shot back with a laugh. I made my way through the kitchen and living room, down the narrow hallway to the small guest room I shared with Summer. Thankfully, no one had commandeered the only bathroom with a shower in the house, so I quickly grabbed my clothes and toiletries and staked my claim. Sketch had me all hot and bothered, and I needed to cool down.

After a much-needed cold shower, I threw on old denim shorts and a light pink tank. I debated about not wearing a bra but decided it wasn't worth the attention I'd get. I didn't need to wear a bra. My barely C cup chest wasn't enough to brag about, but my nipple rings didn't need to be showcased when it got colder later.

I left my hair down to air dry and shuffled out to the main living area. The shower had shaken me out of my post-nap fog, and my stomach growled at the scent of Noah's famous BBQ ribs.

"Back to the land of the living?" Kate quipped from the kitchen. Aubrey and Katie were sitting at a toddler sized table, each with a bowl of Cheerios and sliced up bananas in front of them.

"Yeah, for now anyway." I walked over to my beautiful nieces and kissed them both on top of their heads. They paid me no mind, as the food in front of them was more important. Zeke, Sketch, and Shane were putting the wooden picnic tables side-by-side under the massive outdoor tent on the deck, while Megan and Summer chuckled as they brought out the platter of veggies and condiments. I made myself useful and grabbed the caprese salad, along with the basket full of paper plates and plasticware and brought them out to the table off to the side, already loaded down with sides like potato salad, coleslaw, grilled corn, smoked ribs, and Maryland style fried chicken.

"What else do you need me to do?" I asked Kate through the screen.

"Make sure the gate to the stairs is up, because I'm letting them loose." I smiled and ensured the kiddos would be secure on the deck and grabbed a hard seltzer from the ice water filled bucket.

"Why don't you grab me a beer, Angel?" the voice behind me muttered close to my ear. I jumped, as his voice sent shivers down my spine. Damn his effect on me!

With an awkward chuckle, I grabbed the closest bottle to me and turned toward him, flicking the pieces of ice from the glass.

"Here you go." He was so close to me; our bodies were

almost touching. I reached a level of physical awareness that would even make a porn star blush.

Without breaking our gaze, he took the bottle, grazing my fingers with his. The calloused skin sent electricity coursing through me, and it was everything in my power not to moan. His silver eyes darkened. Sketch could see how he was affecting me. And he was enjoying my awkwardness.

"Thanks, Angel." His fingers traced the long, cold neck of his bottle, and picked off the lingering ice. "Tell me, did you get a chance to cool off?"

I nodded, my tongue feeling too thick to speak.

"That's a shame, really. I mean, this ice could do the trick."

The distance between us was so small, he didn't have to reach far. He traced the ice cube over my throat and neckline of my tank. I closed my eyes at the sensation and a whimper escaped from my lips. The cold, wet feeling did the exact opposite of what he said, and it was plain to see it was his intention. He wanted me hot and bothered. And it worked. He held my gaze, his half-lidded eyes full of lust.

"Yo, Sketch! Check the ribs, dude."

The sound of Noah's voice through the screened door broke our trance, and Sketch took a step back. The corners of his lips lifted to a sexy smirk.

"Yeah, dude. I gotcha." He turned from me and nonchalantly walked over to the smoker, and I closed my eyes, heaving a quick sigh. I didn't know what he was doing or why, but damn if I didn't want more. I popped the top of the can in my hand and took a long gulp. Damn him and the way he made me feel.

I placed my drink next to my seat and headed into the kitchen. I needed something to occupy my mind and hands, anything to prevent me from grabbing him and pulling him to me. Something to stop me from climbing him like a tree. Vegetables. I could chop veggies. I pulled the bell peppers, cucumbers, and tomatoes from the bag and grabbed a cutting board and knife. Pulling up a chair at the island, I started chopping. I caught Megan and Kate looking at me expectantly from the corner of my eyes, and I paused, my knife resting on the board.

"What?"

Megan gestured through the kitchen window with wide eyes. The window was right next to the ice bucket. She was looking right at the spot where Sketch and I were standing.

My face flared up and I rolled my eyes, resuming my chopping.

"Oh no, missy. You can't leave us hanging. What the hell was that out there?" Megan whisper yelled.

"Nothing." I shrugged and reached for the carrots. I couldn't answer their question because I didn't know the answer myself.

"That didn't look like nothing," Kate sang. I narrowed my eyes at her. "Oh please, Charlie. You know better. That mean look wouldn't scare a kitten. It sure as hell doesn't work on me."

I stuck out my tongue at her and piled my chopped veggies into a big blue, plastic bowl. I grabbed the bagged lettuce from in front of Kate and ripped it open, dumping the bag in. I ignored their pointed looks and stood, grabbing the salad tongs to mix the salad.

"You like him, Charlie. Why don't you pursue it?" Meg said, pulling out the salad dressing.

"Because I tried to shoot my shot back at Megan's wedding. We had a good time, but afterward? He could barely leave quick enough. He seems interested, but at the same time I'm also getting back-off vibes. Either way, the man makes me hotter than Hades and confuses the fuck out of me at the same time," I muttered.

"Yeah, he's probably trying to figure it out too." Kate smiled knowingly.

I glanced up at my sister and raised my eyebrow. "What do you know?"

"Sketch is complicated. He has a lot of demons he needs to deal with. Normally he's super closed off and all broody and shit. He's different with you. He doesn't treat you like he treats the gym skanks. It's cute how you two dance around each other like middle school teenagers, but good God, you both need to jump in bed and get it done."

My mouth dropped open. "Kate!"

"Charlie!" Kate mocked teasingly. "What did I tell you last weekend? Pull up those big girl panties and take the lead. Grab him by his dick and see how he reacts."

"Do you kiss your daughter with that mouth?" I asked once I picked my jaw off the floor.

"Yeah, and I suck her daddy's dick with it too. What's your point?" she stated bluntly.

I covered my face with my hands. "I can't even with you."

"You know you love me," she said gleefully.

"Only because I have to." I shot her my evilest glare, and she laughed it off.

"What did Kate do now?" a voice said behind me. His scent of smoke, spice, and tobacco permeated the area around me. I felt his body close behind me, and I bit my lip, trying to be anything but stupidly obvious.

"Just sticking her nose in places where it doesn't belong," I muttered, stepping to the side. I grabbed the salad bowl and salad dressing and headed outside. Sketch was confusing me, his closeness told me he wanted me, but his attitude said otherwise. I hated guessing games. Maybe Kate was right. I did need to pull up my big girl undies and tell him what I wanted. Because that's what two consenting adults do, right?

The rest of the crew filed out behind me, and we tucked into a great meal. I made sure to sit between Summer and Benji, but of course, Sketch somehow ended right across from me. I pushed away any awkwardness, determined to enjoy myself. And I did. Laughter and conversation filled the air, and we stuffed our faces with amazing food.

After dinner, Megan's mom came to pick up the toddlers to give Shane and Megan, along with Noah and Kate, a free night. The alcohol flowed freely, and I was grateful Summer and I were spending the night. We took the party to the patio, where the stone fire pit invited more drinking, s'mores, and music. The temperature had taken a dip, so I threw on my hoodie and yoga pants. I tucked my sock-clad toes underneath my legs as I sat as close as possible to the fire. This was the perfect day, I thought, as I sipped the glass of ginger beer and whiskey Megan handed me. It already had me feeling good. Granted, we hadn't stopped drinking since we got here, but this cup had the buzz going full blast.

I glanced around the fire at my friends, my family. Shane leaned against Megan's chair, while she idly ran her fingers through his short hair as he chatted with Benji. Noah and Kate were making out in the chaise lounge chair. And Summer... Summer was missing. So was Zeke. Great. Hopefully, they were hooking up somewhere other than the bed Summer and I were supposed to share.

I inadvertently glanced over at Sketch sitting next to me. I wanted to know what he was thinking. I knew he had demons. I mean, shit, who didn't. But I kind of understood what Kate meant. Sketch's demons were probably more than I could ever comprehend. And I was quite sure he wasn't the person to let anyone in. But then again, maybe I could be that person.

I hopped up and shuffled over to him, sitting at the foot of his chaise lounge. He looked up at me with a raised eyebrow.

"This seat is closer to the fire. I'm freezing," I said simply. His eyes burned into mine, and wordless he spread his legs. He reached over to me and pulled me down to sit between his legs. My body felt alive at his touch, as he wrapped his arms around me. The embrace did more for me than anything else. I felt safe, protected. Warm. Right. As if I was a perfect fit in his arms.

Sketch rested his chin on my shoulder but didn't say a word. Neither did I. We sat in that position, as the conversations flowed around us. Two by two, people started filtering inside as the embers died out. Once my teeth started chattering, I finally relented to the fact we should follow suit. I turned my head and checked on Sketch, who hadn't moved since he first moved me. His beautiful eyes were closed, and with the even breathing, I realized he had fallen sleep.

"Sketch," I whispered, gently stroking his jaw. He didn't wake, but his hold on me tightened.

And so did my heart.

"Sketch, let's go inside," I whispered, shaking his knee. His gray eyes finally opened with a start, and he did a quick look around. "Hey, it's okay. It's super late, we should probably go to bed."

He nodded. I got off the chaise and offered my hand to him. Sketch stared at me for a minute, then gently took my hand as he leveraged himself up. He didn't let go when he guided me inside. He didn't let go of my hand as he led me down to the guest room we were staying in. The door was opened, so who knew where Summer and Zeke ran off to.

He turned on the light and closed the door behind me. His gaze never left mine, sending courses of heat throughout my body. Sketch pulled me into him, wrapping his thick arms around me.

"Just give me this. I don't want to push you. We're not going to fuck, although I'm dying to taste your sweetness. I need to feel you next to me," he murmured, his lips lightly grazing my most sensitive spot under my ear. I shivered, then nodded. He released me, and I took a step back.

Great. Cue the awkwardness.

I turned and grabbed the sleep tank I normally wore and

hurried into the bathroom. I quickly undressed and changed, then glanced at myself in the mirror. My face was flushed from his touch.

"This is not going to be awkward. It's sleep. You need this. He needs this," I whispered. You got this, girl. Pull up those big girl undies.

I splashed cold water on my face and patted it dry with the yellow towel, then shuffled back into the room. He had already removed his shirt, jeans, and shoes, and was under the fluffy floral comforter. I glanced around the room, at the sunny yellow paint and the double bed situated against the wall. The bed would barely be big enough for myself and Summer. But Sketch's massive frame filled the bed. *Oh, this is going to be cozy.*

Sketch's eyes caught mine, and he shuffled over to the side of the bed, away from the wall.

"Don't worry, Charlie. I'll be on my best behavior," he said, his gaze searching my face.

"Who said you have to be?" I replied with a smile. I moved to the foot of the bed and crawled up the mattress, sliding under the cool sheets. His body immediately turned to mine, cocooning mine with his. His arm wrapped around my waist, pulling me close.

"I'm not the guy for you, Charlie," his breath whispered against my hair.

"Why don't you let me decide for myself," I murmured back.

He heaved a heavy sigh and pressed his lips against my head.

"Go to sleep, Charlie."

I smiled in the darkness and scooted closer, his heat enveloping me.

I may not have known where this was going, but I was damn sure I'd enjoy the ride.

8

SKETCH

MY EYES SLOWLY OPENED, AND FOR THE FIRST TIME IN YEARS, I got a decent night's sleep. No nightmares. No dreams. No gasping for air and having my body coated in sweat. I glanced down at the angel beside me. Her strawberry blonde hair splayed over her pillow; her delicate arm wrapped around my torso. Her cupid-bow lips pursed as she slept. She was an angel. An angel didn't need a monster like me tainting her.

I slid out from under the sheets, carefully untangling her legs from mine. I couldn't stop looking at her, warm and soft in the bed. I had no doubt the angel in bed was the reason I slept so well. I felt at peace when she was with me. The demon slept.

I knew she was attracted to me. I sure as hell was into her. She's been stuck in my brain since the night I met her. No other woman does it for me like she does. I had never felt the same magnetic pull with anyone else. But she deserved better. She deserved light and fun times. Not darkness and broody monsters.

I had a choice to make. I could stay with her in bed and address the thick tension between us. Or I could avoid any potential awkwardness and leave before she wakes up. I chickened out. I adjusted the massive morning wood in my running shorts and grabbed my stuff. I followed the aroma of coffee and headed into the kitchen, where Noah, Shane, and Zeke were sitting around the table with mugs in their hands. I nodded in greeting and settled myself down with a mug of my own.

"You good, Sketch?"

I grunted in answer at Noah's question, but Zeke piped in.

"He better be good. Him and Charlie took the guest room, leaving me and Summer to sleep on the couch in the other room. Damn, Noah. You need to get a better mattress for that shit."

Shane looked at me, with his eyebrows raised. "You and Charlie? You better not let Cole find out."

I rolled my eyes. "Cole needs to mind his own business. There's nothing going on between me and his sister."

"Yeah, okay. You're lying through your teeth, man. We see how you're looking at her. She never leaves your sight," Noah scoffed.

I flipped them each the bird and took another swig of my coffee. Thankfully, the conversation took a turn toward work, and I added my input when needed. It's taken me a long time to learn that a "kill-em-all" attitude wasn't always the best approach. But they knew I would be up for anything. The latest intel with Tommy Greene had our blood pulsating. The monster within me was pacing in his cage, wanting to get out. We Skyped with Toren down in the bayou, getting his take on what's going on. Benji, who had left earlier this morning to take care of some errands, joined in the call as well. He grew up down in the swamps and knew the area like the back of his hand. We made plans for Zeke and Benji to meet up with Toren down there.

I heard a noise in the hall and Charlie shuffled in, her messy hair piled on top of her head. Her small frame was decked out in a tank and little cotton shorts. Right away, I could tell she wasn't wearing a bra. My mouth watered, but I wanted to throw one of my hooded sweatshirts over her. I knew Shane and Noah thought of Charlie like a sister, but Zeke was a red-blooded male who wouldn't be immune to the charm Charlie exudes. I caught his eye and gave him a low growl. His smile widened and I knew I showed him my hand.

"Charlie, you look like you slept well," Zeke quipped, wiggling his eyebrows at her. I gave him a not-so-subtle kick under the table, and he cursed loudly.

"I slept amazingly well." Charlie grabbed a mug and poured in the hazelnut creamer Kate was addicted to then made her way to the couch, curling up with her legs tucked under her. Her sleep-laden eyes caught mine and she gave me a sleepy smile. It took everything I had in me to not pick her up and take her back to bed. Preferably the bed at my house, where she belonged.

"So how badly did you wear out Summer?" Charlie asked, taking a sip from her mug.

"A gentleman never sexes and tells," Zeke joked snootily. I laughed out loud. Zeke was the biggest heartbreaker of the group, and while he treated any chick with respect and dignity, he sure as fuck wasn't a gentleman.

"Yeah, okay. Tell it to someone who doesn't know you," Charlie scoffed.

"You wound me with your insensitive words, Miss Charlie." His eyes glimmered with evil before he snuck a quick glance at me. "Why, do you want to find out for yourself?"

That motherfucker is about to get a fist to his throat. A snarl escaped my lips, and my hands were clenched in fists at the same time both Noah and Shane let out shouts of protest. Zeke bounced out of his seat and took the two steps to get to the couch. His long, lean frame flopped down next to her, and he laid his head on her shoulder.

"It's like they know me or something. Reform me, Charlie.

Make me into the good boy I know I can be," Zeke mourned playfully.

"You're so wicked," Charlie said with a laugh, patting the side of his head. The bastard took her smile as a sign to fully snuggle up to her. The fucker gave me a sly grin and the urge to toss him on the beach came on pretty strong.

I didn't find this situation funny at all. I wanted to rip his head from his shoulders for even coming close to her. But I knew it probably wasn't the best way to deal with him. What I needed was a good workout. I muttered some expletives and drained the rest of my coffee. I stood up abruptly and snatched the keys from the table.

"Bring your ass to TR later, Zeke. I'll set you straight," I growled. I whistled for Murray, who was slumbering at Charlie's feet. The traitor looked up at me, then whined softly at her.

"Murray, let's roll dude," I ordered. His long tail thumped quickly, and he heaved himself up. I walked to the door, fully expecting him to follow. But the little bastard had other motives. I heard her musical giggle and an "Ooompf." I glanced over my shoulder, and he had hauled himself onto the couch and used her as a pillow. His massive head was laying on her lap and his tail wagged happily.

"Seriously, dude?" I gave him a stern look, and he nonchalantly closed his eyes and got even more comfortable. That fucker.

"Today is a beautiful day. He can hang out with us downtown. I'll bring him back to your place later." Her eyebrows raised at the suggestion, and my shorts got a little tighter at the thought of having her alone, at my place. *In my bed.*

"Fine. Just text me when he gets to be too much."

I didn't wait around for an answer and let the screen door slam shut behind me. I piled into my Challenger and took off down the road. I put the windows down and turned up the tunes, hoping the sounds of Ice Cube would turn my focus onto something I could control, and not my raging hard on. *A good work out is what I needed to take my mind off Charlie.* Yeah, I was fooling myself. Her sweet, intoxicating scent of vanilla and honeysuckle had completely overtaken my senses and my cock grew heavy as I remembered the feel of her skin next to mine. The warmth of her body. The way she wrapped her legs around mine. How I wanted those legs wrapped around my neck as I tasted her and drank my fill. I was starving, but only for her. Fuck.

Twenty minutes later, I pulled into the empty parking lot of Tactical Redemption. *Thank fuck.* I disengaged the alarm and hustled into the men's locker room. I needed a shower to get the scent of her off my skin. I turned the water on and stepped out of my clothes, my cock heavy with need. Fuck it. I stepped in, not caring about the temperature. The cold-water pin-pricked my hot skin, and I grabbed the base of my cock, tightening my grip as I braced my other arm against the wall. Wishing it was her hand gripping my cock. Wishing it was her warm lips wrapped around it. Wishing it was my hands gripped in her hair as I slid in and out of her tight little body. The tightening in my balls came quickly and with a grunt, I came. I groaned as ribbons of cum painted the walls of the shower, never-ending. I panted with exertion. My cock still throbbed with need, only having taken the edge off. And it would only be satisfied with her.

9

CHARLIE

After waking up a cranky Summer, we leisurely had breakfast with Shane, Megan, Noah, Zeke, and Kate. By midmorning, we were back on the road, only this time, we had an extra passenger.

"Tell me again why we're taking the small horse with us?" Summer said from the passenger seat, gesturing with her thumb behind her. I shot a glance over my right shoulder at the snoring monster and smiled.

"Because he loves me and didn't want to go with Sketch this morning. So, we're going to hang out," I said cheerfully.

"And it gives you an extra excuse to go see the man of your dreams," Summer said with a knowing glance.

I hummed in agreement. Last night, sleeping in his arms, had been wonderful. It felt right, like we fit. Granted, I didn't know what he thought, because I woke up to an empty bed, but I'm sure he felt the connection. It was there. He just needed to acknowledge it.

Summer smiled and nodded approvingly. "Get it, girl. Go after what you want. You deserve it."

I grinned back. "What about you? How was your night with Zeke?"

Summer, who never shied away from talking about her sexual life, blushed.

"Holy shit, Summer. You're blushing. What does that mean?"

"Nothing. It was a great time. I didn't sleep with him. We talked. Kissed a lot, but mostly talked," Summer said with a smile. She turned her face toward the passenger window and chewed on her bottom lip. Her own lying tell.

"Summer? Are you catching the feelings? What happened to 'nobody has time for that?' You really like him! Why don't you try to pursue something with him?" I teased gently.

She pursed her lips and didn't say anything.

"Summer?" I questioned softly. Something was up with her.

"It's nothing. I like how I felt around him. I wasn't some potential notch on his belt, and we really got to talk. Our conversation was hella deep and it clarified the thoughts and feelings I was having toward myself and some others. It's not really feelings for him, per se. But the feeling of someone actually listening." Her murmured voice was low. There was obviously more to this story than she was telling me, but I knew better than to push it.

She changed the subject to something more general. "Hey, do you want to swing by Severn Run Natural Environment Area? I'm dying to get more landscape shots, and it's gorgeous out. I don't want to waste the sun."

I raised my eyebrow. "Are we seriously going to go hiking? Neither one of us have the right gear on."

She shrugged. "It's not like we're going to go deep in the woods. We'll go on the trail that runs with the river."

I glanced back at Murray. As lazy as he was, he loved the water, and we wouldn't be able to keep him out of it. "You know he's going to get soaked. You're giving him a bath when we get home."

"Pfft," she muttered with a wave of her hand. "We have towels. And besides, we'll drop him off with Sketch. He can hose down the horse at his own place."

I chuckled. Worked for me. It had been a while since we went on the trails, and this area was her favorite. I got off the highway and not too long later, we parked. Summer stood on her toes and stretched her calf muscles. She was constantly on the go, and if she went a day without working out, she could be a monster. She grabbed her heavy-duty camera and bag, while I held Murray's leash. He looked at me like, "Really lady? You're going to make me walk?"

"Shush, it's good exercise," I admonished him.

"Who are you trying to convince, you or the miniature pony you have in your hand," Summer said with a laugh. I flipped her the bird, and she took off down the trail in front of me, waving her response right back.

Twenty minutes later, we were laughing at Murray's antics as he splashed in the river. We were walking along the waterfront when my cell phone rang. Thinking it was Sketch checking on his dog, I answered with a laugh.

"Your mutt is walking me, not the other way around," I said with a giggle.

"Charlotte, it's Professor Scott."

"Professor Scott, what's up?" I said, my good mood instantly vanished. The assistant professor of the program never called me, and a feeling of dread filled my stomach.

"Dr. Weber was found dead in his apartment a couple days ago."

"Oh my God. What happened?" I signaled to Summer to stop walking and come closer.

"At first, we thought it was a heart attack, but with everything going on, we had them rush a test for various chemical compounds. Once the federal coroner got a chance to go over him, they found traces of fentanyl on his hands and fingers." His normally reserved voice was filled with panic and doom. Dr. Weber's death was a shock to everyone, but even more proof something more is going on than a simple druggie trying to get his fix.

My stomach dropped.

"Holy shit. What can we do? What did the police say?" I gasped.

"Right now, we're asking everyone to remain calm. But this is dangerous grounds, Charlie. We are all possibly in danger. Do you have a safe place you can lay low?"

"I can find somewhere to go," I whispered.

"That's good. Go there quickly and stay safe." She paused. "And there's more. Nessa is missing."

I gasped. As much as I despised my colleague on the project, I didn't want anything bad to happen to her. "What do you mean, missing?"

"Her father reported her missing last night before we got word about Dr. Weber's cause of death. We're not necessarily positive her disappearance is correlated with Dr. Weber's death, but it doesn't look good. It could possibly mean this is bigger than some drug addict trying to get a fix. It means whoever is behind this, they're starting to target everyone involved with the program."

My heart started beating rapidly and I quickly glanced around, as the feeling of being watch prickled my senses. "But why? We don't have anything that could help them. Everything we have on the project was turned into the feds."

"But do they know that? Plus, you have institutional knowledge. You may not remember the full details, but the bits and pieces you remember, along with the program's prestige, could be beneficial to anyone who wants a piece of the pie."

I cursed softly.

"Just be safe, Charlotte. I'll be in touch."

Right away, my mind went to the worst and my paranoia kicked in. "You too, Professor Scott." We disconnected and I shivered in the warm sun.

Shit had officially hit the fan. But what was I supposed to do? Do I completely make a fool out of myself and panic? Do I run to Sketch or Cole, begging for protection? I felt silly asking them for protection against something that could probably be nothing, but I knew better than to dissuade myself. If it ever got back to Cole and Kate I was potentially in danger and did nothing about it, they'd kick my ass. I surveyed the area around me. Aside from Summer and I, the trail was empty. Nothing screamed, "I'm a dangerous criminal" but duh, no bad guy is ever that obvious.

"What's going on?" Summer asked, lifting her camera to her eye.

"Let's grab Murray and get over to Tactical Redemption. I'll explain it to you in the car," I answered, whistling for Murray.

Summer didn't acknowledge my response. Her gaze in the camera was intently focused on something in the distance.

"Summer? Did you hear me?"

A gunshot went off in the distance, followed by a splash.

"What the hell was that?" I demanded quietly.

"Shit." Her voice of fear had me straightening my spine after I clipped the leash onto the dog. "Run, Charlie, we need to get out of here!"

Fuck.

I gripped Murray's leash in my hand as I took off running after Summer. The thrashing of branches and twigs crashed behind me. They were close and my lungs were burning. I dug in and tried to gain more speed. I felt something touch my bare elbow and I jerked away. Murray growled and tried to attack the person behind me, but I tugged on him, pulling him with me. If I let him go, I knew they'd hurt him.

"Summer, unlock the door!"

I heard the chirp of my alarm and I almost cried with relief. She flew into the driver's seat and Murray hopped into the back while I crashed into the passenger side.

"*Go! Go!*" I screamed.

Summer slammed the Escape into reverse, and we peeled out on the gravel road before I had even shut the door. Murray stood at the back window, growling at the two men who grew smaller as we made tracks out of there.

"What the fuck happened out there, Summer?" I cried, staring at the chasers.

"I saw them, Charlie. I saw them shoot someone and toss them into the river," Summer said grimly.

"Holy hell. We need to call the police!" I scrambled for my phone in my pocket. "Shit. My phone. It must have fallen out!" My life was on my phone. My identity. My numbers. My pictures. And now those creeps had it.

Summer banged her hand on the steering wheel. "Fuck! Okay. Let's think about this. What would Kate do?"

"Call her and Cole," I answered immediately. I thought back to my earlier conversation with Professor Scott and shuddered. "Summer, there is even bigger trouble," I gasped, my eyes widening.

"What the hell are you talking about?" She turned the wheel, taking the exit for 97 at seventy miles an hour.

"Earlier... "

"Oh fuck!"

I could see it coming, but there wasn't anything we could do. A large SUV came off the exit next to us and slammed into the side door. My head bounced against the window at the impact, but Summer kept the Escape upright.

"What the fuck! Go, Summer!" I hollered.

Summer stomped on the gas, but the poor little 4-cylinder engine wasn't enough. The SUV made another hit and

Summer struggled to keep control. She turned the wheel too far and the Escape started leaning. "We're going to crash!" she yelled.

But we didn't crash.

We flipped.

Screams.

Glass shattered.

The groan of metal on metal.

Then silence.

I groaned. A metallic, iron taste was on my lips. Blood. I wearily opened my eyes and turned my head slowly. I looked to my left. Summer was barely hanging on; a massive head wound was bleeding profusely. Her chest wasn't rising, and panic filled my veins.

"Summer. Wake up, babe. Summer?" Nothing. "Oh no no no, Summer. Come on Summer girl, we need to get out of here."

A whine filtered from behind me, and I stretched my neck. "Oh, Murray! You're okay! Let's wake up Summer now, buddy. Come on." Tears filled my eyes as I looked at the gigantic pooch, trapped under my beach chair.

I reached out to Summer, anxious to touch her, when my door was wrenched open. Instinctively, I screamed in terror.

"Charlie, it's me, Kyle. Megan's brother. It's okay, I'm trying to help." I slowly turned my head toward the person speaking. I recognized the familiar blue uniform.

"My friend. Please. You must help her first. She's not okay. She's not breathing," I cried out.

"We'll get her help, but let's get you out of here."

He opened his mouth and while I could tell he was talking, I couldn't understand him thanks to the pounding of blood rushing in my ears. My eyes went back to Summer, and I knew she was gone.

I closed my eyes. And everything went dark.

10

SKETCH

I checked the clock on the wall. A quarter to six. I had left Charlie and the rest of the crew at Noah's house over eight hours ago. I left Charlie.

What the fuck was I thinking? Sleeping with her last night had been everything I had hoped for. And I left her. For what? Because my sick, sadistic side would be too much for her. She didn't know the monster within me. She didn't need the chaos I have created and that lived inside me. There wasn't anything more I could do for her. I couldn't give her the happily-ever-after she deserved. I slammed my fist into the desk, the laminate groaning with my force.

Fuck it. I'll go up to her house, grab the dog and be on my way. Rather take the pussy way out and not even bring up last night, I thought. I was finishing my last input into this stupid accounting system when my cell phone rang.

"Yeah?" I snapped.

"Sketch. Get to my place."

"What the fuck is going on?" I demanded, already snapping the laptop closed. I grabbed my keys and thundered down the stairs.

"There's a situation," Cole said grimly.

"What kind of situation?" I shot back, as I activated the security alarm and automatic locks. I threw open the door to the Challenger and peeled out of the parking lot.

"Charlie." My stomach dropped at the sound of her name.

Fuck. I disconnected the call and threw my phone into the passenger seat. My vision ran red as I picked up speed. My tires screamed as I turned the corner onto Dairy Farm Road and hit the gas on the straightaway. The fifteen miles from the gym to Cole's house was done in less than seven minutes.

My anxiety went through the roof when I spied Toren's jacked up truck parked at an angle on the side of the road. He was supposed to be in Louisiana, monitoring the cartel. *What the fuck is he doing here?* I pushed my way into the house. I slammed open the door and was immediately stopped by Toren.

"Before you get in there, you need to go in there with a cool head," Toren warned softly. *Because obviously something is going to make me lose my shit.*

"Let me through," I said through gritted teeth. I pushed against his massive frame, but the fucker wouldn't budge.

"Seriously Sketch, you can't go stomping in there looking to kill someone. She's okay," he growled. The red lessened a bit, but it didn't help the anxiety flowing through. I took a deep breath and raised my eyebrow.

"Happy now?" I mocked. I shoved him aside and walked into the open family room, where I could see bodies. I knew the names, but the faces were blurred. My focus was solely on Charlie. Her beautiful face was buried in her hands and her shoulders shook. The instinct to kill took over and my hands clenched into fists.

"What. Happened?" I was able to ground out. With a slight gasp, she lifted her head. Her beautiful full cheeks were marred by scratches and blood. A large welt lingered over her perfect lips. And those green eyes. The ones I wanted to never see cry, were filled with tears.

Cole stood up from the couch and came over to me. He bent his head low.

"Charlie was walking in Severn River Run with Summer, who was taking some shots. Summer ended up getting a shot of something someone didn't want photographic evidence of." My stare turned to his. "She got photo evidence of a murder, and what we think was a drug deal gone wrong. They put a bullet in the guy's head and dumped him in to the wetlands. Right afterward, they realized she was there and there was a chase. They ended up flipping the car three times on 97."

"Who was it?" I growled.

"Not sure yet. But the camera didn't miss their face. We sent the images over to Zeke for facial recognition, so we should hear something soon," Kate piped in, her arms wrapped around Charlie's shoulders.

"Good." Thoughts of what to do to those bastards rolled through my head.

"That's not everything," Charlie muttered. I looked over. Her normally strong voice was weak and muddled. I hated seeing her like this. Tears welled up in her eyes again. "We don't know the status of Summer." She covered her face and let out an anguished sob. I looked at Kate for confirmation and she nodded sadly.

"Oh, Angel." My heart ached for her. I went over and gently picked her up, cradling her against my chest. She threw her arms around my neck and buried her face into my chest. I sat in her space on the couch, keeping her curled up in my arms.

"Be careful with her, Sketch. She probably has a nasty concussion. She refused to be seen. We got to the scene as soon as Cole was called," Kate murmured.

I stroked Charlie's back and held her close, my gaze penetrating Cole's.

"There were witnesses. Murray wouldn't let anyone near her until Cole got there. We were able to obtain the camera thanks to Charlie's insistance."

I raised my eyebrows. Witnesses were good. But only if they saw something substantial.

"No plates or IDs, but Charlie says it's the same assholes who are on the pictures."

"Who do we have at state PD that could help us out?" I asked softly, as Charlie's sobs lessened.

"Rick's making some calls. If we can tie this to the cartel or Syndicate, the FBI will be able to take lead over the investigation. But until the faces are ID'd, there's nothing much we can do."

"What about Kyle Connors?" Toren asked, mentioning Megan's brother.

"He's on the Baltimore beat, not state," Cole replied grimly.

"So Sims is all we have. Has she given her statement?" I asked, softly pressing my lips to her forehead.

"Yeah. Thankfully, Kyle was first on the scene. She gave him what he needed, and then we were able to go. Of course, we promised him we would take her for treatment, but once we got her into Cole's truck, she refused. We are doing her a huge disservice by keeping her here at home. She needs to go back for an MRI, make sure there's no major head trauma," Kate bit out.

"I'm fine, Kate," Charlie whispered. "My back hurts and my head is pounding, but I'm fine. There's nothing broken."

"Bullshit, you could have a brain bleed or something. You could be spewing blood into your abdomen but you refused to get treatment," Kate spat out. I knew she wasn't angry at Charlie, but her attitude and tone needed to be adjusted.

"Calm the fuck down, Kate. You know as well as I do she would have been a sitting duck at the hospital."

"We would protect her, Cole! Or we could take her some

place out of the area, to Hopkin's or to Sibley in DC. She would have round the clock care, and we would be with her every single step."

"It doesn't matter. I lost my phone in the park when we were running. I'm sure they grabbed it. They know who I am." Her voice was barely a whisper, but the words carried the weight of a shout.

Fuck.

"The people who were on the project are being targeted," Charlie continued weakly. "Professor Scott called right before everything went nuts to let me know Dr. Weber was found dead with fentyal on his skin." Charlie took in a shuddering breath. "And Nessa Bradshaw is missing."

"They know who she is, regardless," Cole muttered grimly."We have to assume all this events are tied together. She's their number one target now."

"Fuck," I cursed. "We need to get her out of here."

"Exactly. I'd suggest Shane and Megan's farm, but with only one way in and out..."

"And that's putting everyone else in danger," I finished for Cole. That family has been through hell. Shit, we've all been through it one way or another, but they've had the brunt of it. Kate's phone rang, piercing the conversation and she held up her hand to silence us.

"What do you have for me, Sims?" She paused, then her eyes widened. "Are you fucking kidding me? How do they know for sure?" Another pause, then she threw out a string of curses. "Fuck you and the damn protcol, Sims. Keep me updated."

Everyone stared at her as she threw her phone on the couch. "They found blood in the back of Charlie's car. And it didn't match either Summer's or Charlie's," she spat out angerly.

"What the fuck are they talking about?" I growled.

"Charlie's DNA is on file since she's with the Bowen's

program. She had to do all sorts of samples, to include hair follicle and blood. The blood in the trunk of Charlie's Escape matches Nessa's on file, and they want us to bring her in for questioning."

"She isn't going anywhere." My tone turned deadly as I tightened my grip around her waist.

"Sketch, chill the fuck out. We're not going to let her go anywhere."

A knock at the door had us all on alert. Cole palmed his Glock and held it out of view, while he checked the windows.

"It's Trey and Noah." He unlocked the door and let them in, as they staggered under the weight of my almost two hundred pound mastiff.

"How is he?" Charlie looked up from my chest.

"Broken right paw and had to have stitches near his ear, but this beast will live to fight another day," Noah quipped, as he and Trey gently laid Murray on the dog bed next to the fireplace. Cole's pit mix, Jax, whined softly and laid down next to his best buddy.

"What's the plan?" Benji asked, his gaze circling the group.

"What happens to Summer? She's all alone right now," Charlie whimpered. I hugged her back to my chest as tightly as I could without hurting her. The fact that she could have easily been gone was not lost on me. In fact, it scared the shit out of me. It infuriated me. And I'll be damned if I will let it happen.

"We'll take care of Summer. Does she have parents or family we can call?"

"She has family in Towson. Her father is in construction, and her brother has ties to one of the MCs in San Diego. I gave her dad's name and number to Kyle," Kate piped in, her eyes full of sorrow.

"We'll make sure she's taken care of. But first things first. We need to keep you safe," Cole said, coming back into the room. He nodded to me and I rose, gently placing her back on the couch. She grabbed onto my forearms, as if she didn't want me to go.

I cupped her face, treating her like glass. She held on to my hands.

"Don't leave me," she implored, her voice barely a whisper.

"I'm not going anywhere, Angel. I'm right here."

I walked over to Cole and Benji, all the while keeping my eyes on Charlie. That is when I knew, she was never leaving my sights again. Fuck the darkness. The darkness would keep her safe.

"I have a guy that's coming through town tonight. He's a long-haul trucker, so she'll be constantly on the move."

"You're thinking of leaving her with a fucking stranger? Are you out of your damn mind? She needs a damn emergency room," I growled.

Cole glared back at me. "No dickbrain, what kind of brother would I be? I'm leaving you with a stranger. You're both getting out of town for a while. Gage is a good dude and the only one I would trust with this, other than you fools. We were in the same unit back in Afghanistan."

I glared at Kate, who was lightly rubbing Charlie's back. "She's in a bad way. I want to get her seen by a doctor. A real doctor. Not some Marine medic." I shot Benji a shrug. "Nothing against you but…"

Benji shrugged. "I got you. I want her to be seen by a professional as well. An X-ray or even a CT scan would be beneficial and I don't have those at my disposal."

Cole sighed and rubbed his hands over his face. "Yeah I know. But we can't protect her at the hospitals around here. Who knows who they have on the inside. It's not like I can run fingerprint checks and scanners over their belongings. And while I trust Rick and his FBI cronies to get us some of the info we need, there's only so much we can do right now. For the meantime, the mission is clear. Get her out of the area, to some place out of of the way and seen by non-locals. Under a different identity."

"Do we have any idea where Gage is taking us?" Charlie asked quietly.

"We want to get you away from here, but at the same time, we don't want to waste time getting you guys back here if we need you. Benji has a contact in Tennesse and they're doing us a solid. They're going to take care of you guys until we get any updates. They'll be our point of contacts while you're out there," Cole replied, looking at Benji for follow-up.

"How can we trust them?" I demanded. "I am not living our lives in the hands of a one-night stand Benji had in his army days."

"Major Courtney Olliverton was head of my Ops unit back at Fort Bragg. She's also my sister. So yeah, I trust her," Benji shot back at me. I held up his glare and gave him one of my own.

"No, we can't put your sister at risk," Charlie's weak voice came out in protest and my jaw tightened. She was exactly right. The whole reason we were leaving was because we didn't want to put the families in jeopardy.

Benji's eyes softened when he glanced at Charlie. "Don't worry. We're not blood related. We grew up in the same foster home. A whole mess of kids went through the home, so there's no chance anyone will figure out the connection. And if they do, I have no doubt Courtney and her wife can keep you both safe."

"Come on Shortcake, let's get you cleaned up." Kate pulled Charlie into a standing position, and she looked exhausted. With three steps, I had Charlie in my arms, her weak arms wrapped around my neck. I followed Kate back to her old bedroom and softly placed Charlie on the edge of the bed. Kate came in with a couple of warm washcloths and we took care in wiping the blood and dirt from her face. Her expression was numb, as if she couldn't tell we were there, and I glanced at Kate worriedly.

"She'll be okay. She's in shock." Kate gently lifted the hem of Charlie's shirt and pulled it over her head lightly. Goosebumps marked Charlie's battered and bruised skin and the sight of her discolored skin had me wanting to stick my fist in the wall. Kate helped her into a fresh shirt and yoga pants, and while I held her upright, Kate made quick work of the room, gathering items for Charlie into another bag.

"Here's one of my old fake IDs. We look close enough alike, as long as people don't glance too hard. Not having insurance is going to be the tricky factor, but if you bring her into an Urgent Care, she could get an initial diagnosis." She handed me the bag. "These clothes should fit her. There's a hair brush and hair ties, cash, toiletries, and a burner phone for emergencies. They'll hold you over until you get to where you're going. I have a spare number saved and I'll have the phone on me at all times." She carefully slipped a dark hooded sweatshirt over Charlie's head and pulled her strawberry blonde hair into a ponytail, then set a plain black baseball cap over it.

"Once you get on the road, grab some hair dye. I only have bright pink on me, or I'd dye her hair myself. She needs something mundane." Her blue eyes glistened as she looked Charlie over. "I love you, Shortcake," Kate whispered, holding Charlie's hand lightly.

I lifted Charlie in my arms and we followed Kate down the short hall into the family room. Cole and Benji were on the couch, talking strategy. I put her gently on the couch and covered her with the throw blanket.

"Okay, here's the plan. Kate and I are taking your car, Sketch, and we're going to head to the BWI bus station. If someone's watching us, they're going to see someone who resembles Charlie in your car get out and get a bus ticket. While we're gone, Benji is going to load you two up and take you to the warehouse district in Rosedale where my buddy, Gage, is going to be picking up a delivery. We'll sneak you in the back. He's got a bed where Charlie can lay down." He held up the rucksack. "Remember when we were in Vegas, and I got stuck carrying home all the crap? Well, here's your shit."

I took the familiar sack and I rummaged through it. Inside was a fake ID saying my name was Cohen Dupree, along with a couple grand in cash and the encrypted cell phone we use to talk with the teams. My hands landed on a soft-pack at the bottom of the bag. I knew from my days as a SEAL it contained my survival kit with rope, MREs, a multi tool kit, fire-starter kit, fishing line, medical kit, a thermal blanket, and a can opener. A spare magazine and Beretta 9mm were in a holster.

"This been updated recently?" I grunted, going through the bag.

"Yeah, I made sure you got the good MREs. And there's some duct tape and ponchos in the second bag. As soon as she got here, I knew you guys would be bugging out."

"Thanks, bro." I slapped his shoulder.

"Just take care of my baby sister, okay? Then I'll think twice about kicking your ass for canoodling with her last night."

I grunted. "Whatever dude. Take care of Priscilla. She's a pistol." I gave him the keys to my Challenger, and him and Kate kissed Charlie on her head, then they rolled out. I glared at Benji as he twirled his keys on his finger like a dumbass.

Ten minutes later, I was getting antsy.

"How long do we have to wait? Are we going to sit here and twiddle our fucking thumbs? I don't want her around this mess. Let's go."

"Fuck off, Sketch. I'm waiting for the text." A chime came from his pocket. "Let's load up. He just got there and is waiting to get his gear off."

I went and cupped Charlie's face in my massive hands. She looked up at me, her eyes full of sadness and pain. "Angel, I'm going to keep you safe. I promise. I will not let anything happen to you."

Her tiny hand held mine. "I know."

I pressed my lips against hers, knowing this wasn't supposed to be how our first kiss was done, but I couldn't help it. The monster inside me was pacing. He was torn between wanting to go shred the asshole who did this to her, but stand guard and protect her. I wanted to do both. But I knew I wouldn't let her out of my sight.

Benji came back through the door and I straightened. "Kate got a text. The facial profile came back positive on the Russian dudes Toren followed up from New Orleans."

"Obviously he didn't follow them well enough if they got away," I snarled, picking her up. This time, her legs went around my waist and she put her head on my shoulder. Like she fit me perfectly. I tried not to envison another scenario where this would be better, but it was no use. My cock twitched against my shorts and I bit my lip. We crept outside, under Cole's carport and I laid her in the back seat of Benji's truck, sliding in next to her.

"You know the drill. Keep low," he muttered, pulling out of the driveway. I bit my tongue at the smartass response I had and slumped down as far as possible. Thankfully, his windows were blacked out in tint, certainly not legal by Maryland standards. Our ride north along the Baltimore beltway was quiet, and surprisingly quick. Despite the lateness of the hour, the highway was normally known for their constant fuckups. But luck was on our side because we were practically the only ones on the road.

We pulled into Rosedale, a hub of distribution centers and warehouses near the Port of Baltimore. It would be the perfect cover. The area was teeming with semi-trucks, long-haulers, and workers. We pulled around to the farthest location in the back of a dark parking lot, at the same time a dirty black trailer pulled through, pulling up right next to us. I stiffened, hoping this would be the dude Benji knows, but preparing for the worst.

"That's him," came Benji's mutter. He put his truck into park and opened up his door.

"Angel, it's time to go," I whispered, running my finger along her jaw.

She nodded, her eyes shut.

I got out of the cab, and held her hand as she sat up gingerly, her body stiff. The impact of the accident was finally catching up with her. I'm sure her body was crying in agony right now, but the only clue she gave was how carefully she moved.

I went to put my arms around her to carry her, but she held up her hands for me to stop.

"I'm not a fragile invalid, Sketch. I think I can manage to walk to the truck," she whispered.

"You're not fragile, but you're sore. You've had a shit day and you've got to be hurting. Plus, Angel, you're not going to make it into the truck cab all by yourself," I said with a soft chuckle. The cab behind me was massive, and even at six foot six, I would have a hard time getting into it. Not sure how a five-foot one short stuff like Charlie would manage without some help.

She looked up at me, a small smirk coming across her cupid lips. Benji came around the side of the bed, and pulled the two rucksacks out, then took the two steps over to the open cab.

I helped her out, letting her feet touch the ground. A large figure came around the backside of the truck. Dressed in black basketball shorts and a gray muscle shirt, the dude was taller than me and had about thirty pounds of muscle on me. From what I could tell, there wasn't a single inch of skin that wasn't covered in ink.

"All right boys and girls, it's time to roll. The longer we sit here picking our noses, the more attention we're calling to ourselves," he muttered in a low voice. "These my stowaways?"

I stuck my hand out. "Yeah. I'm Sketch and this is Charlie."

"Gage," he said firmly, shaking my hand.

"Charlie," she whispered, sticking out her hand as well. He looked down at her, and I could see he was taking in her injuries. He shook her hand gently and a slight smile appeared on his scarred face. But as quickly as it came, the moment was gone.

"Great. Now that we got the polite bullshit out of the way, we need to go. Travelers or not, I still have to make my deadline." He looked over at me and jerked his thumb behind him. "Why don't you hop in the back, and I'll hand her up to you. There's no way she'll be able to make it up there on her own."

"Works for me." I slapped Benji's outreached hand and brought him in for a half hug. "Keep me in the loop. We got the encrypted. We'll make contact once we get to our location."

"Stay safe. Watch out for him, Smalls," Benji said with a grin, then kissed her on the cheek.

I nodded to Gage and hauled myself into the rear cab of the truck, then bent down as Gage swiftly and as gently as possible, lifted her by the waist. I pulled her up and cringed when she softly cried out in pain.

"I'm sorry, Angel," I whispered in her ear, wrapping my arms around her. I took a step back in the small interior cabin and set her on the bunk behind her. Covered with a light blue blanket, it looked like it doubled as a couch and a sleeping area, with a pull curtain between the living area and the driver portion.

"Where do you want me, Gage?" I said loudly as he started up the diesel engine.

He pulled the curtain closed. "Keep out of sight until we get a few miles down the road. I didn't arrive with a sidekick, so they sure as hell will wonder why the hell I'm leaving with one."

"Roger."

I settled Charlie on to the bed, laying her under the blanket and then sat down beside her. Her small frame trembled under the comforter and her teeth started chattering. I knew shock was settling in. I shucked off my shoes, and somehow managed to contort my bulky frame around her shivering body, tucking the blanket around us both. I pulled her back against my chest, wrapping my arms around her.

"I don't know what's happening to me," she stuttered, shaking uncontrollably.

"It's shock, Angel. Your mind is processing what your body went through. It's okay, I'm here," I said gently, holding her tightly. The wetness on my bare arm told me she was crying, and my heart wrenched. These beautiful eyes should never cry tears of sadness or pain. I kissed the top of her head and breathed her in, wanting nothing more than to take away the pain.

"I got you Charlie, it's okay," I murmured against her ear. I didn't add what my heart wanted me say, I didn't plan on ever letting her go.

We laid on the bed, our bodies molded together, for what felt like minutes, but I knew had to be over hours. Eventually, her body relaxed, and her breathing evened out. I didn't care if my arms fell asleep, or the fact that I barely fit on the mattress. My thoughts were more on her. On how to keep her safe. On how this all fits together.

A few hours had gone by before I gently untangled my arms from her body and pulled away despite every muscle in my being telling me otherwise. I maneuvered my way into the front cab, sliding into the passenger bucket seat of the big rig. Gage gave me a nod, acknowledging my presence but that's it. And it was perfect for me. My thoughts were more than enough to keep me occupied. I knew radio silence was key at this point in time, but the urge to call Kate and Benji was strong. The Syndicate was behind this, despite no rumblings from the underworld. I felt it in my gut. But now it's a matter of keeping three steps ahead of them and ensuring Charlie stays safe. It meant trusting the rest of Tactical Redemption would get to the bottom of it.

We drove in silence for the longest time, with classic rock playing low on the radio. I worried about Charlie's head injury, but she needed the rest.

"How much longer until we have to stop for gas?" My voice was low, but Gage heard me.

"About another seventy-five miles or so. We've made good time and there hasn't been any word about the two of you on the radio."

"For now, anyway," I murmured.

We settled back into silence, both alone in our thoughts. Going into an unknown situation without communication unsettled me. It went against every bone in my body. But there wasn't any more I could do. Trust didn't come easily to me, but Benji seemed to know what the hell we were getting into.

I checked on Charlie frequently. She slept soundly, but I worried. The first order of business was to get her medical attention. The fact she was hurt gutted me. I wanted to destroy the bastards who did this. I wanted to peel the layers of skin off their bodies. Cut their appendages off with my favorite blade. Then, while their tormented souls are dying of agony, I wanted to look them in their eyes, while I lowered them into a barrel full of acid.

A static crackle came through the CB radio, interrupting my plans. Gage cursed and turned down the music.

"Calling all Maryland, D.C., Virginia, and Pennsylvania drivers. A BOLO has been issued for Charlotte Rae Parker, Caucasian female, five foot tall, with reddish blonde hair, green eyes, and tattoos on both arms. Injuries are apparent and she is considered endangered. Last seen with Seth Davis, A. K. A. Sketch, white male, six foot six inches, shaved head, and gray eyes. Noticeable features include full tattoo sleeves on both arms. Considered armed and extremely dangerous." The automated recording paused and then repeated the words.

I slammed my fist into the dash. If they're already issuing a BOLO, that meant the Syndicate didn't buy the fact we got on the bus. Or they had already chased the ruse.

Either way, we were screwed.

"Hey Big Easy, you on this channel?"

Gage shook his head in warning to me to stay quiet and clicked the receiver.

"Big Easy here. What's going on, Larry?"

"Sitting here on 66, trying to get onto Interstate 81. There's about fifteen of us waiting for them to clear the damn weigh station. Cops are all over the place, causing a mess. It's a good forty-five-minute wait to get through."

"Are they doing inspections?"

"Man, it's so freaking random. I can't tell what the hell they're doing. Some are doing the regular inspections; some are hauling everything out of the hold to get a look. I have no clue what they're looking for, but whatever it is, it's going to add extra time to our schedules."

"Roger that."

"Hit me up when you get close. Since it's going to be a while, we might as well grab a burger at the diner across the street."

"Yeah. I'll do that. I owe you some grub anyway," Gage replied. His voice was friendly, but his expression was anything but. I could tell he was calculating the distance in his head, and how much time we had left before hitting the weigh station.

He disconnected the call and looked over at me.

"How long?"

Gage frowned. "We aren't going to make it to Tennessee. At least not going this route, that's for damn sure." He paused, thinking. "We have thirty minutes until we're close. Let me check something real quick."

With his left hand on the steering wheel, he used his right hand to type out a message. After a moment, he dropped his phone into the cup holder.

"Now what?" I demanded. I needed to come up with a plan and quickly. I had no clue where we were, but I knew we weren't near any urban areas. It was mostly rural with an occasional dollar store here and there.

"Trust me," Gage grumbled.

Not two minutes later, the phone dinged with a message.

Barely taking his eyes off the road, Gage read the message and nodded with what looked like satisfaction.

"Here's the deal. Once we get into Ruckersville, we'll stop at a rest stop. Wheels will be waiting for you, with a pre-paid cell phone and an address in the center console. As soon as you get into the car, go east on 64 and then hit redial. You'll be directed to a safe house where you can stay until Charlie is well enough to get to Tennessee to meet with your contact. You'll be on your own from there. I can't risk taking you any further."

"What the hell is going on? Who are we meeting?"

Gage snorted. "I take it Benji didn't tell you what we do?"

I glared at him incredulously. "Nah, we didn't have time for tea and chit chat after all hell broke loose."

"Figured as much. It's a long story and unfortunately, we don't have time. I'll leave it up to Phoebe to fill you in. But trust me when I say she is good people. I trust her with my own life."

Talk about a leap of faith. Putting your life in the hands of strangers is one thing but putting the lives of your loved ones on the line is something totally different. I was out of my comfort zone and it fucking sucked.

"You better be telling the truth. Because I have no problems showing you how well I can play," I growled.

Every mission has contingency plans. The "what-if" scenarios. We would have back up to the back up plans. But it's not the case right now. We have been going by the seat of our pants since the moment we got word of Charlie's accident. We were flying blind with nothing but trust and pixie dust.

I made my way into the back compartment and gently placed my hand on Charlie's shoulder.

"Angel, I need you to wake up," I said as gently as I could.

She rolled over slowly, wincing as her body turned toward me. Her green eyes slowly blinked open. They were clear and focused. That's a good sign.

"Hey, what's going on?" Her voice was hoarse and dry.

"Change of plans, Angel. We're stopping soon and then we're bouncing out of here. How are you feeling?"

She wet her lips with the tip of her tongue. "Like my car flipped over on I-95."

I rolled my eyes. The smartass remark meant she was feeling more like herself. Good. I helped her into a sitting position and placed the baseball hat gently on her head. I hated moving her, but it was necessary. I put my arm around her and softly pulled her close.

"Heads up guys, we're coming up to the rest area. Get ready to roll out," Gage's voice lumbered from the front cabin.

"Thanks for the ride, Gage." She raised her eyes at the burly man in the driver's seat. He caught our gaze in the rearview mirror and gave her a nod.

"Take care of yourself, sweets. Don't take too much of this guy's bullshit."

My eyes narrowed as I glared at him, giving him the middle finger. But Charlie laughed softly.

Charlie leaned into me as we made the turn into the rest area, slowing down as we approached a small brick building.

Once we had parked, I slipped out of the cab, and reached up to help her down. As soon as her toes touched the ground, we hurried into the tree line, under the cover of darkness. While she sunk down to the base of the pine tree, I crept toward the parking, to see what I had to work with.

Gage's Big Easy Big Rig had already driven off. The parking lot was empty, aside from what looked like a busted-up older model sedan. I couldn't tell from my vantage point if the car was supposed to be a silver or if it was covered in dirt, but whatever. If it got us to the safe house, I'd take a tricycle at this point.

I gently led Charlie out of the trees and up to the rest area. When we got closer, we could see the building itself was closed for repairs. There weren't any cameras I could see, so I sat Charlie onto a bench while I tried to break into our latest mode of transportation.

If we were in a time crunch, I would have smashed in the window and jump-started the car, but I needed to look as inconspicuous as possible. I checked the tire wells and felt a bit of relief when my hand clasped around a cool piece of metal. I helped Charlie into the passenger seat and after several starts and stops, the old, rusted piece of junk sputtered to life.

I looked over at Charlie in the passenger seat and I caught her gaze.

"What's the plan?" she asked, her voice soft with weariness.

"Gage hooked us up with a contact and a safe house. We'll bunk there until we're able to get to Tennessee." I opened the center console and pulled out the address and the phone, handing them to her. "Since you're my partner in crime on this adventure, you get to navigate."

Charlie smiled slightly. "Would be glad to if I knew where we were."

I looked over my shoulder. "We're in Staunton with directions that say to head east. So east is where we're headed." I shifted the car into reverse and pulled out of the spot. Once I got on the road, it was a quick turn onto east Route 64.

"Now where do we go?" Charlie asked.

"Go ahead and turn on the phone, then hit redial. Someone should be able to give us directions." My eyes traveled to the mirrors to make sure we didn't pick up any trails. Thankfully, in the dead of the night, we were clear. But no one knows how long it will last.

Charlie voiced a greeting and then went silent, only saying the occasional affirmation. And with a quiet thanks, she hung up.

"Where to, navigator?" I spoke up.

"We follow 64 into Roanoke, and then we go into the Downtown area." She gave me an address on Water Street.

"Okay, Water Street it is." I laced my fingers with hers, and then brought her hand up and kissed the back of her hand.

"I know you're scared. I know you're worried. But I promise you, Angel. I won't let anything happen to you," I muttered.

"I know, Sketch. Despite all this craziness going on, I feel safe. As long as I'm with you, I'm safe. I just want to be able to see my family. I hate putting them in danger," she replied, worry filling her voice.

"Trust me, your family can take care of themselves. They have the rest of Tactical Redemption protecting them."

"Yeah, that's what I'm afraid of. TR isn't only your family, Sketch. They're mine too. I don't want anything to happen to anyone I know."

"It's why they're willing to lay down their lives for you. Because you're one of us. But know this. The world's best team of assassins protects them. The Syndicate or whoever the hell is behind this will face a deadly fight if it comes to it." I cleared my throat. "But right now, let's focus on getting you to safety. Hopefully, this contact of Gage's has medical experience. You need to be checked out."

Charlie mumbled in agreement. We made the hour and a half trek quickly and as Charlie gave directions on how to get to the house, I grew leery. Thankfully, Roanoke was a college town in Virginia. Hopefully, we'd blend in with the rest of the residents and students. I pulled into a residential area, full of townhomes and smaller single-family units. More urban areas gave way to suburban and before we knew it, we were at the address. A small ranch-style home with mature trees in the front yard, with a lone light on in the window.

"The lady on the phone said to pull into the driveway and into the open garage," Charlie instructed. I did what she said and as soon as our back bumper made it inside, the door began to close. Someone must have been watching us closely.

I grabbed both rucksacks and walked over to the passenger side door, helping Charlie out of her seat when the interior garage door opened. A thick, gorgeous woman filled the doorway, her hands on her hips.

"Y'all come on in now and get settled. It's close to midnight and I need to be getting home." The southern twang in her voice was full of no-nonsense bullshit. Immediately, I could tell I would like this woman.

I maneuvered Charlie through the door, and the woman whom I presumed to be Phoebe closed it quickly. We stood in her small, but functional kitchen. With weathered solid wood floors, antiquated brown cabinets, and the smell of a home-cooked meal, this reminded me of home—of my childhood.

"I'm Phoebe. I'll be helping y'all out while you're here," she said, hurrying over to the stove and flicking off the burner.

"Sorry for the impromptu visit, ma'am. But we appreciate the assistance," Charlie said gratefully. "I'm—"

"No, sweetie. We don't exchange names here. Think plausible deniability." Phoebe wiped her hands with a dish towel and came back over to us. Her brown eyes were full of kindness and warmth. "I don't need to know your names or your story. I know when Gage Anderson calls, we jump into action."

"Your help was definitely needed. Thank you." I glanced around the kitchen, and through the archway. "Is there someplace I can put our things?"

"Of course. Go down the hall, and there will be two bedrooms and a single bathroom. You can take either one of those. Once I give you the rules of the house, I'll be on my way." Phoebe glanced at Charlie. "I'll feed her while you're getting settled."

"Will we be able to get medical treatment? She was in a car accident earlier today," I asked, urgency filling my voice.

Concern crossed Phoebe's face. "We have a physician we can call over. It won't be until later when he gets off his shift at the hospital."

I brought Charlie over to the pedestal table and chairs, setting her down as gently as I could, and then made my way down the hall to the two bedrooms. One was fit for children with two twin beds and a box of toys against the wall. The baby blue walls were covered with decals of superheroes. The second room must have been the primary; it only held a queen size bed and a dresser. There were no pictures on the walls, it was the bare essentials, completely different from the children's room.

I walked the short distance back to the kitchen, where Ms. Phoebe had two plates piled high with meatloaf, mashed potatoes, and green beans. She gestured for me to take a seat and she took the seat across from us.

"While y'all fill your bellies, I'll give you the rules. I'm not sure what Gage told you. But he is an honorable and noble man. You see, we run the Rainbow Trail. We relocate women and children caught up in domestic violence and sex trafficking rings. We provide them with safe passage to their final destination. No names are ever exchanged, at most it's an initial.

People don't stay for more than a few days before they're moved on again, until we know they're safe and able to start healing. We have a railroad of people helping, from movers to physicians and counselors, to military operatives. We work with the local and federal agencies to ensure women and children are able to be free."

I looked at her in amazement. We've worked in coordination with the Rainbow Trail before, but never face to face. There was a situation down in Latin America where we worked with them to free seventy children in danger of being auctioned off.

"Well, if we're doing initials, then this is C, and I'm S." I gestured to Charlie and myself.

Phoebe smiled knowingly. "Yes, I know who you are, S. Our organizations have crossed paths before, and I recognized your face. Your reputation within our various organizations spreads wide."

I cleared my throat, hoping she'd keep that information to herself. "What can we do to help?"

"Right now, it's about keeping the two of you safe. The security protocols here are simple. This is a safe space, so no electronic usage is permitted to prevent any geolocating. The house is yours to use for the next couple of days, but please don't make it a point to venture out often. If you need to go out, use the basement door. It's covered by the deck. Our neighbors normally don't pay us any mind, but they're used to seeing random women with small children. Not two grown adults. And with your sudden notoriety, I don't want to expose this house to the media or police."

"I need to get a hold of my team and give them a heads up on what's going on and to alert my point of contact in Tennessee," I mumbled, my mouth full of mashed potatoes.

"I understand. You need to ensure those calls count, and once you're done, turn off the phone."

It would be vital for us to remain in contact with our team, but I understood the potential issues. I nodded and reached for another serving of meatloaf.

"I thought you said you work with the local agencies," Charlie asked, the question on my mind as well.

"We work in conjunction with them; however, they do not know the locations of our homes or the people who work for the organization. It's for everyone's protection. If victim statements are required, we meet at a police station," Phoebe replied, getting up to go to the oven.

"We stocked the pantry and fridge for the next few days, so you should be good to go. The physician should be here shortly. Once he leaves, you'll be on your own until the weekend. Gage briefly told me your next stop, and we will have the people and transportation in place to make it happen." She pulled out a pie from the oven and the smell of cinnamon and peaches wafted over us. I was stuffed, but I knew I wouldn't be able to say no to peach pie.

"What's your security concept like?" I asked, standing to take my plate to the sink.

"We have a security monitoring system, which is twenty-four seven. Perimeter cameras are located on both the exterior and interior of the house, except for the bedrooms and bathrooms. We found it stressed the families more in the presence of in-house armed security, so they are stationed close by if there is any sort of emergency."

"Weapons?" I asked, leaning against the counter, and crossing my arms.

"There are no weapons hidden in the home. I suspect you brought your own?" Phoebe replied, as she put aluminum foil on the leftovers.

I nodded.

"That's good. For the situation you're currently in, I would expect you to." Phoebe turned back to the table when a swift knock came at the door.

I immediately reached for my Glock hidden in my waist pouch, when she held out her hand to stop me. Charlie's green eyes widened, and she limped over to me as quick as her body would let her.

Phoebe held out her hand to calm us. "I assume it's the doctor. Please wait here."

She hurried over to the back door and peeked through the blinds. "Thank you for coming so quickly, Doc."

"Quite all right, Ms. Phoebe. I'm happy to help." An older gentleman, with a portly stomach and silver coiffed hair, bustled into the kitchen carrying an old-fashioned satchel and what looked like a heavy case. I took the three steps needed to take the box off his hands and was surprised the old man could pick up something this heavy.

"That there, son, is a portable X-ray machine. Please plug it into the wall over there. It needs time to warm up, like any old man needs."

"Doc, this is your patient. We call her C," Phoebe replied.

"It's a pleasure to meet you, my dear. Now let's get you situated." Taking Charlie's hand, he led her slowly into the front living room. The room was minimally decorated, but I was pleased to see they had blackout shades over the windows. I took a defensive position against the wall and watched with an eagle eye. This doctor may be discreet and great at what he does, but he had his hands on my heart. I would be damned if anything more happened to her on my watch.

The Doc sat her down onto the denim-colored couch and started working her limbs, stretching and flexing them to see where her pain was. Then X-rayed where it was the worst and gave her the stitches she needed in her temple. After giving her a thorough examination, he wrapped her left knee in a bandage.

"Nothing is broken and there doesn't seem to be any internal bleeding. You, dear girl, are just very banged up. Here are four pills you can use to combat any severe pain. Soak the knee in Epsom salts, and rest. Your body needs to heal." He nodded to Phoebe. "She'll be good to travel in a few days, as long as she stays quiet."

Charlie was about to speak up when I did for her. "I will make sure she rests." I caught her glaring at me from the corner of my eye and I inwardly chuckled.

Doc gave me a smile, like he knew I would have my work cut out for me. He patted Charlie on the arm and nodded his goodbye to Phoebe and walked out into the darkness. I checked my watch and realized it was close to four in the morning.

"Thank you, Ms. Phoebe. I'm so sorry we kept you up this late," Charlie said apologetically.

"Oh sweetheart, I'm up this late regularly. Someone has to look after the broken and redeemed," Phoebe said with a smile.

"Gage said you're good people, Ms. Phoebe. I'm not someone who puts their faith into a lot of people, but you have restored my faith in humanity a little," I said softly.

Phoebe blushed at the compliment. She fussed over us for a few more minutes and showed us the security system before leaving for the night. She told us to not expect anyone else at the home until we were ready to be transported to Tennessee and we agreed to maintain the secrecy of the home and of the program. But I knew, deep down, we would end up working together again.

As soon as the door was closed and secured, I turned to Charlie. She looked like she would fall over in exhaustion.

"Come on, Angel. Let's get you into a shower and into bed," I said, as I walked over to her. She snorted quietly.

"Forget a shower, I want to go to sleep," she mumbled, barely able to keep her eyes open.

"Trust me, you'll feel so much better." I scooped up her tiny frame and held her against my chest, then walked the short distance to the only bathroom in the house. I set her on the toilet and turned on the water. While it warmed, I gently removed her white t-shirt then lifted her up to remove her shorts and panties. I tried my hardest to avert my eyes, but seeing her sun-kissed skin, the swell of her breasts and curve of her hips set my body on fire.

Charlie caught my stare and blushed, then tried to cover herself. I put a firm grip on her wrist.

"No. You don't get to hide this gorgeous body from me." My voice was husky with need, and I couldn't hide my physical reaction. Despite the bumps and bruises, her body was exquisite.

"This isn't how I pictured my first time being naked in front of you," she said, and ducked her head as if she was embarrassed.

"Oh, you pictured this before?" I joked, but it was anything but a joke. My mouth went dry, and my cock hardened even more.

Shakily, she stood, her body close to mine.

"Oh yeah, many times," she said. Her confidence shattered me. I looked down in her eyes and watched as her pupils dilated with lust. The steam from the shower filled the small bathroom, and it mixed with the scent of her need.

"What did you picture?" I was not ashamed to stutter the words, this woman had knocked the wind out of me.

Her luscious full lips curved into a smile.

"One day I'll show you instead." She ran her hand up my arm, wrapping it around my neck. I bent down, closer to her lips. With the faintest brush against mine, my resolve snapped. I wrapped my arms around her waist and crushed her to my chest, crashing my lips to hers. She gasped in pain and instantly, I felt like a dick and pulled back. What the hell was I thinking, kissing her like that? Especially after all the shit she had been through today.

I pulled away, breathless, and rested my forehead against hers. She put her palms on my chest and gently pushed me back a step, then used my bicep to steady herself as she got into the shower.

"Do you want my help?" I knew I was tempting fate by asking, and a good part of my brain, the one that was standing up at attention right now, wanted her to say yes. That she needed me in the shower with her.

I felt a tinge of disappointment when she said no. It was for the best though. Being in the shower with her was the last shred of temptation I needed.

"I'll wait right outside," I muttered as I left the room. I shut the bathroom door to where she could have privacy, but I could rush in if she needed me.

I leaned against the wall and rubbed my hand over my face to chase the lust crowding my thoughts. She absolutely has no clue what she had done. Once I had a taste, it took everything I had not to devour her. This was a bad idea. A terrible idea that could end in flames.

And damn if I didn't want to combust with her.

11

CHARLIE

DESPITE THE THICK SEXUAL TENSION AND ONE HELL OF A KISS, nothing else happened. Sure, there were a few innuendos or some light flirting, but nothing more than a light touch. I caught his glances when he thought I wasn't looking, but Sketch was a consummate professional. He didn't try to touch me at all, other than helping me get up and move around. And as sexually frustrating as it was, I'm glad one of us had a sensible approach.

Three days after we arrived, we got the call. They've noticed a lot of federal agent movement into Tennessee, and they were filling in the gap between us and Tennessee at a rapid clip. We knew they had figured out our endgame. So, the plan had to be switched up. We couldn't stay in Roanoke and risk any exposure for our current safe house or the Rainbow Trail. We had to go on the move again. First, we drove northeast, to Pittsburgh only to have to leave due to getting a tail on our way from the market. Then we headed to West Virginia, to a cabin deep in the woods, only to be chased out by a freaking skunk. The lack of available cell phone reception didn't help, either.

Despite all of it, the cold, icy exterior of his slowly melted bit by bit. Stuck in the car, hour after hour, I got Sketch talking. It started off with the radio, of course. Our tastes in music were similar but we argued over which band was the best of all time. He said it was Lynyrd Skynyrd. I begrudgingly agreed, but still think The Beatles were way better. Food preferences were similar, with a few exceptions. When we stopped off at a country market, he gleefully ate two small bowls of fried chicken livers, much to my disgust.

When we got back into the car with our provisions, I opened the bag of gummy worms & offered him one.

"Nope, I'm good," Sketch replied as we pulled away.

I wrinkled my nose. "You mean to tell me you'll eat a nasty fried chicken liver, but not a gummy worm?"

"I don't do candy."

"Wait, what? For real? No candy? What about chocolate?" I gasped.

"I'm not a fan," he muttered, shaking his head.

"No sweets? At all?" I demanded. Sketch chuckled and rubbed his hands over his three-day old stubble.

"Huh. That explains a lot, actually." I tsked. "You need some sweetness in your life to break down your cold exterior."

Sketch turned to me, with his sexy ass smirk. "That's why I got you."

My eyebrow raised. "Oh, am I supposed to make you all sweet and gooey?"

He smiled as he bit his lower lip and looked me up and down. "That's right. You're all the sweetness I need."

Heat flamed my cheeks and I smirked. "You know I'm here in case you get a craving for something gooey and sweet," I sassed.

His silver eyes turned molten as he licked his lips. "Behave yourself, Charlie."

I smirked and turned my head to the window. At some point, he was going to break. And I couldn't wait until he did.

We needed a landing pad, but no more than a day's drive from Baltimore, in the event his team needed him. Through an encrypted connection and various back door channels, Sketch got in contact with a friend with a vacant apartment for us. After three and half hours driving through the night, we arrived at a small town in Virginia, shortly after two in the morning. Sketch was familiar with the town, so it wasn't a difficult drive. Driving down the main street felt like we were going back in time. It was small and quaint, with a cobblestone road and mom and pop shops filling the storefronts of old buildings. We turned down a side street, and then pulled into a narrow driveway we would have totally missed had Sketch not known to look for it.

"Ready?" Sketch mumbled as we stopped under a weeping willow. He didn't bother waiting for an answer and got out of the car and stretched. His shorts hung low on his hips, and I got a peek of the V muscles. I quickly looked away and got out of the car. The last thing I needed was him seeing me drool. The air was thick with humidity, and I felt the window and looked at our new temporary digs. I couldn't see much, but the three-level brick building looked as if it had been here since the beginning of time.

Palming the car keys, Sketch hustled me over the to the solid wooden door, and we ducked inside. The small foyer was dressed in old dark wood panels and antique furniture. Without speaking, Sketch led me into a narrow stairwell, the stairs creaked with each step. We reached the top and Sketch knocked softly on the door. A woman about our age, with warm, hazel eyes and layered brown hair greeted us with a smile.

"C and S? I'm Brittny. Come on in." She showed us into a one room studio. The original expansive wood flooring and paneling had continued up here. A queen size bed filled up much of the room, with one door I assumed led to the only bathroom. A kitchenette off to the side completed the space.

"Nice to meet you." I reached out my hand to her, but Brittny bypassed that and pulled me into a gentle hug.

"Sorry, I'm a hugger," she joked with a smile on her face and then turned to Sketch. "Except for you. I've heard all about you. I ain't hugging you. You look like you'd break my neck just for touching you. Although I'm sure you're a softy on the inside."

I chuckled, and man did it feel good to laugh. "Yeah, he has an image to uphold." Sketch rolled his eyes and continued to look around.

"I know you're such a conversationalist, but I'm going to have to cut in and tell you about the place," Brittny continued, poking the bear. "Security cameras are up throughout the property and are monitored by a close and trusted source. There is a VPN here, so if you need to make a call, you can. This town is a safe space. Everything closes-up early, except for the grocery stores and restaurants. There's a farmer's market on Saturday and a street fair this Friday evening, which brings in people from the neighboring towns. You don't have to worry about the locals here. It may look like small-town USA, but they keep to themselves for the most part."

"Will the fact that we're infamous on a Bonnie and Clyde level be a factor? Because if it's going to cause issues, we can find a more remote place." Sketch was skeptical, and I could understand why. The last thing we needed was a Good Samaritan, calling us in. But please...no more remote locations. I don't ask for much, except for a hot shower every now and then, and a functioning toilet.

"Well, sorry not sorry to say you're already yesterday's news. Your names haven't been mentioned since the BOLO was released a month ago and Mack didn't post your wanted posters. This is when short attention spans and a deluge of twenty-four-hour information works in our favor."

"Sheriff Mack is good people. I served with him overseas. I'll reach out and let him know we've arrived. He's expecting us."

"We can't say enough about Sheriff Mack. He helps the Rainbow Trail often. Wish we could have more assets like him." Brittny paused, then went on. "I heard about your situation, and trust when I say you couldn't be in better hands."

She put her hands on her hips and looked around. "Well, I think that's everything. Let me know if you have any issues with anything. I don't have anyone else waiting for this space, so please stay as long as you'd like. There is some peanut butter, bread, and jelly in the fridge, along with coffee and creamer. Anything else you need, just hit up the general store down the street."

"Thanks, Brittny. We appreciate it," I said with a small smile.

"Of course." With a squeeze of my hand, she left, and gently shut the door behind her. I shrugged off the bag which carried all my gear, dumping it on the purple loveseat at the foot of the bed.

The lone bed.

As in, we're going to have to do this dance of Sketch refusing to share a bed with me, no matter how many times I tell him nothing will happen. Which will result in me getting pissed at Sketch for his "morals" and him sleeping on the floor in a sleeping bag. Even when we were in a tent in West-By-God West Virginia, we still fought over the sleeping bag. His excuse then was because of my injuries. Well, my injuries are practically healed now, being a month after the car accident. But I'm sure he'll come up with some other reason why he can't sleep in the same bed as me.

Whatever.

It was one of the many things we bickered about. I tried to be helpful but ended up feeling like I was nothing but trouble. I know he was trying to stay on guard. And the sexual tension between us didn't help. I know he was tired of being always on alert. But truth be told, I was tired too. Tired of being on the run. Tired of wondering about our next location. Tired of schlepping our crap to different locations. I was tired of always repacking our car in the morning, in the event we had to make a quick getaway. I was tired of having to look over my shoulder to make sure we weren't being followed. Tired of being so fucking sexually frustrated.

We went into what is now our normal routine. I set up shop on the sole table and loaded up the laptop we bought off a broke college kid in town and got our secure network up and running. Sketch went through the security motions, putting in his standard boobytraps and entry notifications.

"Anything new?" Sketch was too busying glaring out the window to even look at me when he was talking.

I rolled my eyes at one of the few phrases he typically uttered. The man doesn't relax. Obviously with good reason not to, but still.

I childishly stuck my tongue at him behind his back.

"We haven't received any messages, if that's what your two-word question is asking," I snarked back. Yes, Snarky was my middle name.

He let the blinds go and turned toward me, his lips lifting to a smirk.

"You sound tired. You need to get some sleep."

"Sure. Let's call it tired. More like frustrated as hell, but whatever," I mumbled, my eyes intent on the screen in front of me.

"I didn't quite catch that. What did you say, Angel?" He mockingly cupped his ear.

"It's not like you're going to listen to me anyway, so why bother repeating myself?" I snapped. I rose out of the chair so quickly the chair fell back in a clatter. I didn't even check to see if it was broken, stomped over to my travel pack, and got out my toiletry kit. Thank goodness for 24-hour super centers which allowed us to get the necessities like shampoo, conditioner, and ... off the shelf little self-love bullets in the personal hygiene department. Because it was the only way to handle this frustration before I exploded.

He gently grabbed my bicep as I tried to maneuver around his bulking frame.

"What's wrong, Charlie?" Sketch demanded.

I tried to yank my arm out of his grasp. "Nothing I can't take care of myself," I replied, rolling my eyes.

"What? What are you taking care of?"

"Nothing. I'm tired. Frustrated. Just done. But whatever, it's fine. You can let me go," I replied grumbly, not meeting his stare.

"Do you not think I'm frustrated too? Do you think I'm okay with this? Do you think this isn't torturing me?"

"How the fuck is this torture for you?" I asked sarcastically.

"Because being with you is torture, Charlie." I gasped and wrestled with his grip, but he tightened his fingers on my skin. I should be scared, but the fierceness of his stare and the touch of his fingers on my skin sent shock waves through my body, making it harder for me to control the wetness flooding my panties.

He yanked me to his body, and I felt his desire, pressing against my stomach. It took every ounce of self-control I had to not rub myself against him like a cat in heat.

"This is what's torture. Knowing you're so close to me, to feel your skin on mine. I know those panties of yours are soaked. I can smell how aroused you are." He dipped his head, running his nose against my jaw, his thick cock making his presence known between the thin layers of our clothing. "Knowing you're so close, that you're wanting this as much as I do."

"If you want me as badly as I want you, why are you fighting this?" I asked, my voice coming out as a breathless whisper.

"Because I know, once I have you, there's no going back. Once I have your sweet pussy wrapped around my cock, I wouldn't be able to think of anything else. I would constantly crave to be between your legs. To feast on your skin. To watch my cock be sucked between those luscious lips."

My breath hitched and my panties were indeed soaked, my pussy throbbing with need. If his words could get me this hot, the thoughts of him touching me sent me on fire.

"You want that. I can see your pupils dilate. Your pulse is pounding. There's nothing I want to do more than to press you into bed and slide between your slickness."

"You still haven't told me. What's stopping you?" I breathed out, raggedly. Sketch had me wound tighter than I've ever been. I needed him more than I needed my last breath. And I was damn sure to not be the only one frustrated as hell.

"Because, Angel. You don't belong to me. You don't need to be in my world of darkness. Your light is too bright for me," Sketch replied, his voice almost a murmur. He reluctantly let me go and took a step back. I missed the closeness immediately.

"You're wrong, Sketch. I want you so badly I can taste you on my lips. But you're a coward. You are scared we would be so hot we'd light the world on fire. And that terrifies you. Fuck your darkness. You don't belong there any more than I do."

I stared at him for a beat, then took a step back, my legs bumping against the loveseat. I shucked off my socks and sneakers, then pulled the dark gray t-shirt over my head, leaving me in a basic cotton white bra. His eyes darkened, turning into molten silver. The monster of a cock twitched against his belly, under his fitted black shirt.

My mouth watered. I wanted to taste him, just as badly as I wanted him in between my legs.

"Don't do it, Charlie."

"Don't do what, Sketch? Don't give in to what I want the most? What I've wanted for years? To with the man who has consumed my mind and heart?"

His eyes stared at my fingers as they flirted around the edge of my black yoga pants. I shimmied the pants down my legs, my eyes watching his for the slightest hint of reaction. For a response. For an indication this was actually going to happen or if I was going to have to take matters into my own hands. Again.

I kicked my pants off and reached around, unhooked my bra, and let it fall off my shoulders. I stared at him, in nothing but my cotton panties, daring him to make a move.

Within the blink of an eye, he fell to his knees. His thick arms pulled me close and pressed his face right at my stomach.

"You sure you know what you're doing, Angel?" he murmured, his lips dancing across my flesh. "Because once I stop, there's no going back. I will never be able to get enough."

"Please, Sketch." My breathless plea was finally answered. He rose to his feet, catching me underneath my thighs and hoisted me up. My legs wrapped around him, pressing close while my arms went around his neck. His lips attacked mine with raw need and I answered in kind.

The kiss was everything I thought it would be.

Savage. Needing. Plundering and taking.

My core soaked my panties and I ground my pelvis against him. He pressed his cock against my center, and I surged against him in trying to find the friction I so desperately needed.

"I need you." I broke the kiss off with a gasp.

His devilish smile flashed, the hunger shining bright. "Don't worry Angel, you have me."

Sketch brought me over to the bed, laying me down gently, and then reached up to rip the cotton panties from my body. He dove in between my legs, throwing them over his shoulders while he feasted on my core. His tongue lapped at my clit while his fingers thrusted in and out, curling against my G-spot while his other hand pressed on my lower abdomen. I had been riding on the edge for so long, it didn't take much. My muscles tightened around his fingers, and I exploded, my body in a free-fall. I shouted out his name and dug my fingers into the sheets.

"That's my girl," he murmured, lifting his head. His lips were soaked in my juices, and I reveled in it. I have never fallen that hard before. I wanted ... no ... needed... to taste him. I sat up and reached for the waistband of his shorts, but before I could make a move, he gently pushed me back down.

"Angel, I know what you want, and damn if I don't want it too. But I'm so on edge that if your mouth goes anywhere near this cock, I'll explode." Sketch licked his lips and slid off his shorts. His thick, large cock slapped his stomach. A silver barbell ran horizontal to his thick shaft with another barbell pierced at the base, and I about drooled. He crawled over my body, making sure to keep his weight on his forearms.

"Last chance, Angel." His voice struggled with control as his cock teased my entrance.

I wrapped my legs around his waist and pressed myself closer.

"Let's set the world on fire," I whispered.

He crashed his lips on mine in a frenzy. Like he couldn't get enough. With one hand on my throat, he plunged deep. My gasp turned into a moan as my body adjusted to the fullness. Sketch blazed a trail from my mouth to my neck with his tongue while he slowly pulled out, only to impale me once more.

"I'm in fucking heaven," he groaned.

"Sketch, please..." I didn't know what I was begging for, but I needed him.

"Oh Angel, I'm going to take my time and savor this." He

smirked, as he pulled out completely. I whimpered at the emptiness but gasped as his piercing slipped inside me again. I needed more. So desperately, I needed more.

He set the pace, alternating between fast and hard thrusts to deep and slow, while his hand gathered my hair, pulling on it hard. I was barely hanging on and I so wanted to fall off the edge. I gasped his name, and his thrusts faltered, but then quickened.

"Please," I begged without shame.

His control snapped. His thrusts became more frantic and harder. All I could do was hang on. I could feel the orgasm building.

"Come for me, Angel," he groaned. All it took was him to circle my clit twice and I came.

I exploded into a million shattering stars with a scream.

"That's my good girl." Sketch pulled out completely and helped me turn around to my hands and knees. With a push of the hand so my chest was touching the bed and a hard smack to my ass check, he plunged back into me. The angle hit different, and we both moaned. His bruising grip on my hips pushed and pulled against his body. The ache built quickly, quicker than the first.

"I know you have one more..." he growled, his lips tracing the rim of my ear. He reached around and pinched my clit. We detonated, my muscles milking him as he pulsed inside me.

12

SKETCH

WE LIT THE WORLD ON FIRE. SEVERAL TIMES OVER.

And I would watch it burn again just to please her.

I felt her before I opened my eyes. Her heart shaped ass was pressed against my cock, her full and heavy breast cupped in my hand. I pressed my lips to the dip in her neck and suckled gently.

Charlie moaned in appreciation, and wiggled her ass against me even more, her wetness coating my cock. I shifted my body, lifting her leg and slid inside her warmth. Her muscles clamped down, tightening like a vice.

I groaned in pleasure. She rocked back into me, and our rhythm started off slow and sensuous. Soon her arm snaked up and grabbed the back of my neck and her movement became more frantic.

"Let go baby, I got you," I moaned in her ear, as my hand went to her clit, strumming the nub lightly with my thumb.

And she detonated in my arms with a wail.

My thrusts quickened, and I held her hips firmly to my cock. My balls tightened as she let out another wail of ecstasy. I came hard, her tight walls milking my cock dry.

"Fuck me," she mumbled, wiping her sweaty brow.

"I think I did," I joked, sliding out from in between her legs.

"Yeah. You definitely did." Charlie took a deep breath. "But we should probably grab some condoms the next time we're at a store."

My life paused at that exact moment. Shit. She's right. We've had sex twice now where I didn't use a condom and came right inside of her. *But why didn't I feel a sense of panic?* Because the thought of knocking up Charlie and keeping her forever didn't make me feel bad. It brought out the primal caveman in me. I raised my eyebrow and smirked.

"You're absolutely right." I nipped her shoulder. "I'm sorry. I should have been better prepared. Thought through it. But know, I'm clean and I get tested annually. Plus, you're the first person I've ever been with and not used a condom."

She twisted her body to face me and gave me a skeptical look. "Are you serious?"

"Yeah. I wouldn't lie to you, especially about this."

"Huh." She wrapped her arms around my neck. "I'm clean as well. We get regular checkups as part of the internship. I'm also on birth control." She pecked my lips, and the kiss deepened.

"That's good because I don't think I could ever wear condoms after slipping into your pussy without one. It's heaven." I kissed her languidly, savoring every moment while I could.

I pulled away, reluctantly. Her mouth was spellbinding and as much as I wanted to stay under her charm, for the whole day, we did have to look out for other priorities. Like reaching out to the Sheriff.

I checked over her shoulder at the old clock on the dresser. It was close to ten-thirty in the morning.

"We might as well call Mack." I reached for the phone. She groaned and rolled back over. I chuckled and placed the call.

"This is Sheriff Mack."

"We made it."

"Jack's Diner, twenty minutes." I hung up the phone and looked over at Charlie. Her 'freshly fucked look,' with tangled newly dyed dark brown hair, swollen lips, and flushed cheeks had my cock hardening, but I knew she needed to eat. And we needed to get going before we were back under the covers.

"Hope you're hungry," I stated, my eyes raking over her bare body. Her luscious lips lifted in a smirk.

"For?"

"Although I could feast on your body all damn day, we do need to get up to get actual sustenance. We're meeting the sheriff. Let's go."

"Ugh, you're so damn bossy. Fine. I'll jump in the shower, and we can get going." She rolled her beautiful green eyes at me, and as she walked by, swaying her hips, marked with my bite marks, I smacked her ass with a thwack. She let out a curse.

"Don't threaten me with a good time!" she called out, before she closed the bathroom door.

I shook my head and chuckled, but then hustled in after her. Only to dirty her up real quick, then ensuring all the parts were nice and clean.

After we finally dressed, we hopped into the car and drove to the other side of town. We finally pulled into the parking lot of an airstream trailer. Mack had invited me to town when I was on leave years back, and since we were relatively close, I made the trip several times. The first place he took me to was here, Jack's diner. A small, old Air-Stream trailer originally from the 50s with limited seating and a Formica countertop right in front of the griddle. Best breakfast food I have ever had. We walked in, and as usual, most seats were filled. Sheriff Mack was holding court in a corner booth with some locals. I raised my chin and directed Charlie toward the opposite corner.

The smells from the griddle made my mouth water, and I

grabbed the menu as soon we sat down in the narrow booth. A beautiful waitress with curves and curly hair about Charlie's age came over, placing waters down in front of us and filled up our coffee mugs before rushing off.

"What are you getting?" Charlie asked, pouring sugar into her coffee.

"One of everything." I set the menu aside and caught her wide-eyed stare. "What? I'm hungry."

"Obviously," she said with a raised eyebrow, pursuing the menu on her own.

We placed our orders with the same waitress. Charlie broke out in laughter when I gave my order, in fact ordering one of everything.

"I'll take the steak medium rare, the eggs fried, a short stack of blueberry pancakes, corned beef hash, bacon, scrapple, sausage, and can I please have a side of biscuits and gravy?" The skeptical look on the waitress's face was priceless.

"I'm a growing boy," I said with a shrug.

"Can I please have a blueberry short stack with a side of bacon? Provided this fool doesn't clean you out?" Charlie asked with a smile and the waitress hustled off.

"So how long are we staying here?" Charlie asked, sipping her coffee.

I shrugged. "Depends on what Mack tells us. We need to check in with the team and see what we're missing." I hated not being in constant contact, but we tried to limit how often we reach out to them to about twice a week. Unless something critical came up, which they would send a message over our encrypted system.

We sat in silence for ten minutes, listening to the news station playing over the TV, when I looked over Charlie's shoulder and saw Mack making his way toward us. "Slide over here and let Mack have your seat."

I stood and let Charlie slide in next to the window so Mack could take her spot.

"What's the word, Mack?" I reached across the table and shook his hand.

"Sketch. It's been a long time."

"It has been. This is my girl, Charlie."

The young waitress brought our food, greeting the Sheriff again.

"Sheriff, you want another plate of short stacks?" The way Mack looked at the waitress was the same way I looked at Charlie, like he wanted something more than food.

"Hey there, Mia. Yes, and another cup of coffee if you don't mind." Mia nodded and bustled over to the next table. "I see your ways with the ladies hasn't changed," Mack said with a grin and a nod at Charlie. "Always trying to get what's out of your league."

"At least she knows I want her. What about you and Ms. Mia? Does she realize you want to extend the long arm of the law toward her?" I quipped with a smirk.

Charlie groaned and elbowed me in my ribs. "Sketch, that line was so fucking lame," she said, rolling her eyes.

Mack chuckled, only to stop in a cough when Mia came by with his short stack and the carafe of coffee.

"Any news?" I asked, shoveling food into my mouth. Small talk wasn't my forte and Mac knew it. It was time to get down to business.

"Nothing new," Mack muttered, sipping his coffee. "The feds are making a big racket, with the highway closures and ramping down near the border of Virginia and Tennessee, but you already knew that."

"What are your contacts saying?" I growled. Mack had a five-year stint at the FBI, in addition to the military life. The guy had more contacts than the Pentagon, thanks to his many years of service to the country. He made some good friends in some influential places. And it's not always the people at the top. Mack made a point to get to know the observers. The people in the background. They can often tell you more than the people at the top.

"They're trying to connect you both to the explosion at the lab. The fact Charlie worked there, in addition to your ... field experience ... just helps the narrative. Along with the 'evidence' they found in the trunk of her SUV of her missing co-worker. But apparently there is also a lot of pushback going on behind the scenes. Faulty testing with the evidence, protocols not being followed. Not to mention the fact they're treating the body found at the park as a separate incident. The top brass is worried about having another PR shitstorm——especially if there isn't any evidence. They're finally recovering from the Tommy Green debacle, but to add this to their laundry list of shit gone wrong? They're not ready for this kind of fuck up."

"I wonder if Rick is part of the pushback?" Charlie mused. I wondered as well. Rick wasn't our only FBI contact, but I wasn't sure how much weight he truly held.

"Probably not as much as we would need him to. The main question is what to do from here," Mack said with a pointed look. "What exactly is their endgame?"

"From what the intel Kate has learned from Rick, we believe the Syndicate is pissed off Bowen Research is trying to capitalize, or really, profit, off something they're making money from."

"You mean, we're taking away their market share?"

"That's right. At some point, the products Bowen is going to create will be cutting into everyone's profits. What sells the drugs? Their main money draw is providing a product that hooks the buyer. Look at the Opioid crisis, not only have the pharmaceutical companies made a huge profit off it, by providing a legal way of getting people hooked on their shit.

But so have the small-time drug dealers and big cartels. There is a market to this drug, and everyone has a slice of the pie. So, what if we're looking at it the wrong way? What if it's not the Syndicate at play."

"But what if it's another company trying to get the upper hand?" Realization dawned on Charlie's face. "I guess it wouldn't be surprising. But this is extreme, even for the most competitive of companies."

"Is it though? This program is going to be worth billions when it comes to market. Not for the patent itself, but for future business and grants."

"True, this is a cutthroat business. But you're talking about this as if Bowen will be the only one creating these drugs. That won't be the case. Bowen is helping the CDC and NIH with the research, but the Fed will own the patents. The option for production will be there for whichever company wants to fulfill the market demand."

"You hear of businesses price gouging all the time, why would this be any different?"

"Because the fed would require a maximum of exclusivity for a period of six months. After the six months are up, generics could be created, and the price would go down," Charlie replied. "I guess I'm not seeing a good long-term goal for this sort of sabotage."

"Fuck." Well, there went that idea. "At some point, we're going to need to draw whoever is running this shitshow out of hiding."

"What do you mean? Like using someone as bait?" Charlie questioned.

"Not necessarily using someone, but maybe something. We know they're looking for something, because they wouldn't have trashed your place or the lab for no reason." I leaned back in the booth and crossed my arms.

"My gut is telling me there are more players in the mix than you think. Something of this magnitude requires a skill-set not many people have. If they're trying to recreate something, wouldn't they go to the experts?" Mack suggested. His walkie-talkie squawked and Mack looked down quickly.

"I have to run but I'm around, so hit me up if you need anything. Charlie, it was nice to meet you." He shook our hands and threw a twenty down on the table. When we protested, he raised his eyebrow and gave a firm look. "For the tip."

"That's what she said," quipped Charlie, with a laugh. Mack rolled his eyes and rolled out, leaving Charlie's chortles behind.

I threw two additional twenties on the table which more than covered the tab. "You ready?"

Charlie surveyed the empty plates in front of us. All ten of them, with most of them being from me. "Did you get enough to eat?" she questioned saucily.

"For now, I'll be hungry for dessert when we get back." I gave her a wink and pulled her out of the booth. We ambled out of the diner and made our way back to the car. The drive was short and before long, we were back at the apartment, tangled up in the sheets again. Once I had my first taste of Charlie, I couldn't get enough of her.

"You are the best workout," Charlie said with a sigh, wiping her hair off her sweaty brow. I ducked my head and licked the moisture from her collarbone, and shifted my weight, collapsing in a heap next to her. I rolled onto my back and pulled her into my side.

"You can work me out any time," I quipped.

We laid in the peaceful quiet.

She chuckled, then her gaze grew apprehensive. "Question."

"You probably won't like my answer but go ahead," I responded curiously. *This probably won't end well.*

"Why do you call me Angel? Everyone in our circle calls me

Shortcake except for you." Her whispered words danced across my skin. I sucked in my breath and exhaled slowly. I knew the conversation would come eventually, but it didn't make it any easier to discuss.

"Because when I met you the first time, I was in an extremely dark place. I was dead inside. Numb. I was hanging to my humanity by a shred. And then you came into the room with your strawberry blonde hair up in some sort of knot on your head, your curvy ass in some yoga pants, and your glasses on. But the thing I noticed most? Your light. Your smile was a beacon of light and it just . . . filled me with peace. You were the right to my wrong. The light to the never-ending darkness," I murmured, trailing my fingers along her spine.

She propped herself on her forearms. "Why? Why do you believe you're this unfeeling beast that doesn't deserve peace?"

"Because I've done shit no one with a soul could ever comprehend. Because of the amount of blood I've spilled, and I did it with a smile. I took joy in it. But something happened and I knew I had to get out."

"What happened?"

I sighed. The conversation was going to have to happen eventually. Because while I was never going to let her go, she deserved to know who she was in bed with.

"We were in the jungles of South America where we were tracking a cartel through a village. Shit went south quickly, and we took a big loss. There were civilian casualties, a lot of innocent lives were lost. The cartel used civilians as shields. Children were used as soldiers. It was the worst situation a solider ever wanted to be in. You knew they were the enemy, and it was a kill or be killed situation." I let out a heavy sigh then continued as the memories of that day came crashing down.

"We were in the middle of a fire fight, when a little boy, maybe five or six, came out of a hut holding hands with another kid, a small little girl. I had my finger next to the trigger when I first saw movement, but we immediately ceased our fire and tried to get the kids to come over to us."

I closed my eyes, the little girl immediately coming to mind. Her large brown eyes with the tears streaming down her face. "They started running toward us. But the cartel used our humanity as diversion and started firing at us. The kids got caught in the firefight. I broke position and grabbed them. We retreated and rushed them back to the base camp where our medical team was waiting."

"What happened to them?"

"The boy survived, and they brought him to the orphanage. The little girl didn't make it."

"Oh, Sketch." Her beautiful green eyes filled with tears. "That little girl's death is not your fault."

My lips set in a thin line. "Actually, it was. This was my op. I led my team into the jungle on the hunt. Had we not gone in those jungles, they wouldn't have been in the middle of a gun fight."

Charlie sat up and crossed her arms over her chest. "That's bullshit and you know it. You knew they were being held hostage. You pulled back. You lost men in that fight. You didn't kill the little girl in cold blood. You tried to fucking save her."

"I didn't do enough. And I'm going to have to live with it for the rest of my life. And really, would you want that sort of person in your life? I am known as an emotionless dick, and I thrive in the title. I am not compassionate or sensitive to others. I rarely care about the feelings of strangers. My circle is small because I want it to be. I prefer to be on the outside looking in because it's how you don't get hurt. I've seen how someone living the life I lead can affect the family dynamic. I've seen the shit end of people when they feel they're entitled to someone's time, security, or money. And I have seen how weaknesses are used against people. I mean shit, look at Shane and Megan. She was his sole weakness. Same with Kate and

Noah. And going into battle, either on foreign soil or beating down cartels here at home, a weakness will be used against you." I glanced down at her face and saw the disappointment. Fuck.

"Shit. I'm screwing this up." I pulled her back down into the bed and into my arms. "My past is chaotic. I'm not the man you take home to your parents and have the whole storybook life with a picket fence and two point five kids. I have the blood of hundreds of people on my hands, and I don't regret a single drop. I found joy in spilling their blood. It calmed the rage I carry."

I felt her body freeze at those words. I gentle raised her eyes to mine. "I need you to know that. I need you to understand I won't be like Noah and Shane. That I can't put my madness behind me and change who I am. I can't do that. But I meant what I said earlier. There's no going back for me. I've wanted you for so damn long. I may be the monster in the dark, but you're the angel in the light. I've held off from drawing you in, I didn't want to bring you into my world." I traced her jawline with my finger, my eyes penetrating her beautiful green ones.

"You're not a monster," she whispered, her eyes blazing into mine.

"Oh, Angel. How I wish you were right."

"I am right. I see the good in you. I see your light. You have your demons, but fuck, Sketch, you have paid the price. You're pushing back; you're fighting them. You're not letting them win. That's the man I've fallen for. And my parents love you, so we're golden." Her eyes fired with passion and clarity. The heat in my chest bloomed and I attacked her lips. This. This is why I was fighting the darkness. Because of her.

"You can make a man forget his demons," I murmured against her lips.

"Good," she whispered back. I slowed my kiss, and pressed my forehead against hers, breathing as one.

We laid in the quiet, lost in our thoughts, when she spoke up again.

"We needed this." Her fingernails lightly ran up and down my arm.

"Hmm?" I wasn't paying attention, well, not as much as I should.

"We've been on the go for so long. Nothing but running and hiding. We needed some time to be us, to take a pause on this chaotic life we're currently living in."

I traced her jawline with my finger. "And to finally release some of the sexual tension?"

She smirked. "Sexual tension? Try sexual frustration."

"Aw Angel, let me take care of that for you."

I gripped her chin and crushed her lips with my own. She let out a whimper, allowing me to sweep my tongue into hers, caressing her tongue with mine. My hands slid down her waist and I lifted her onto my lap. The slickness of her heat, still dripping with my cum, had my cock hard in an instant.

The piercing rubbed up against her clit as she ground against me. She lifted and positioned my cock right at her entrance, then sank down.

Fucking heaven.

We both moaned at the fullness. Her pussy tightened each time the piercing on the base of my dick rubbed against her clit. She closed her eyes and adjusted to my thickness, her center. Her tight pussy stretched around my cock like a glove, making me feel like a thirteen-year-old boy.

My hands gripped her ass while she rolled her hips, meeting my thrusts at each turn.

"You feel so fucking good," I moaned. I moved my hand from her ass to her throat, squeezing gently. Charlie's green eyes widened and if anything, got wetter.

"Oh, we found a kink. How does that feel, Angel?" I said with a smirk. If even possible, her muscles started to clench around me, which made my thrusts harder. I was already on the edge of release. I sat up and brought my lips to hers.

Fuck. She really is too perfect. I slammed my mouth against hers and devoured her.

"You are fucking mine. Say it, Angel," I breathed against her lips, my hips thrusting up, and hitting the angle I knew she loved.

"I'm yours, Sketch. I've always been yours," she gasped back.

The last remaining string of control snapped, and I flipped her onto her back. Sitting back on my knees, I grabbed her legs and pulled her to me.

"Sketch, please," Charlie begged, her eyes hooded.

I didn't keep my Angel waiting and immediately plunged into her slick heat. She fisted the sheets while I pounded into her pussy. The angle her body was in had the piercing in the head of my cock pressing against her G-spot. That pushed her over the precipice. She fell with a scream on her lips. Once her pussy clenched around my cock, it was all over. After several pumps, I buried myself to the hilt while shouting her name as I came.

I lowered myself to cover her, my forearms keeping my weight off her.

"You're so fucking mine," I said. I buried my face her shoulder, feeling her heartbeat against mine.

Her arms draped around me. "And you're mine."

We laid there, wrapped in each other, before reality set in.

"For a moment, I was able to forget what was going on." She brushed her lips against my shoulder, squeezing me to her before loosening them up.

I sighed deeply. She was right. Of course. This isn't a vacation. It was easy to forget why we were on the run, why we were away from our family and friends. Because, in this room, it was the two of us.

"As much as I'm loving this, we need to check in with the rest of the team," I murmured. I placed a lingering kiss on her luscious lips and moved out from under the sheet. Slipping on my shorts, I grabbed the laptop and dialed into the secure program.

"Anything?" Charlie asked, brushing strands of hair out of her face. I took pride in seeing her bruised lips and the flush on her cheeks. She looked thoroughly fucked and sated, all because of me.

"Nothing in yet." My eyes narrowed and I exhaled in frustration. I knew there wasn't much I could do here, but it pissed me off we weren't any further.

"Look. We've been cooped up in the safe houses for the last month. We only go out for necessities. Why don't we take the evening and check out the festival that's going on in town?" Charlie suggested, running her fingernails gently over my scalp. "I can hear the bands starting up, and Brittny said people from all over come out here. We'll blend in."

My mind raced through all the potential risks. But I could see her point. We needed to breathe for a moment. And while having fun in bed is a great break from the ongoing drama, being able to take Charlie out on a real date and be a normal couple would be nice.

"Let me check in with Mack to make sure he hasn't heard anything new, then yeah, it sounds good."

The smile she gave me lit me up in all the best ways. I lived for her smile.

I picked up the encrypted phone and made the call. After confirming nothing new was in the area, and he hadn't heard of any movements, I rattled off a quick message to the team, with the highlights of the conversation I had with Mack. But mentally, I kept going back to one of the main points we seized on. We needed to narrow down the next possible target. I had eyes on Charlie and one person was already presumed dead. Who else was left?

I posed the question to Charlie while she flicked through the channels on the TV.

"Aside from Doctor Weber? Michael Van Buren was the third competitor on my team. He's the son of the CEO and head scientist at Bowen. There are about twenty other scientists who are on the program, alongside the various other government reps who came and went through the building with other teams."

"I'm not versed in Biotech jargon so give me a rundown on who is what in the grand scheme of things."

"The government has their own scientists embedded with ours. They work in tandem with Bowen's lead researcher and scientists. We frequently have government officials come to the labs to check on the status of projects so they can appear intelligent for when they go before cameras and take credit for what they signed for. It's not a secret what we were working on. It's federally funded by the CDC and the NIH, along with private grants and donations. Any breakthroughs always get the press coverage," Charlie said thoughtfully.

"Your specific project was targeted. No others were. Why? What drug were you replicating?"

"We were trying to create a drug that combines the medicinal elements of cocaine and heroin, but without their addictive properties. Both drugs have a long history of being used in medicine, but they became part of the "War on Drugs campaign" in the eighties, and the federal government labeled them as narcotics. This program would take the best of both drugs, without the bad."

"Who would benefit from using this?" I questioned.

"Anyone in need of it. People with painful disabilities, particularly post-surgical care. I mean, think about it. Heroin comes from morphine, which naturally occurs from the opium poppy and is used in overseas medical centers for pain management. Recreationally, it's used to for the euphoric feeling, but it also has the pain management properties. Same with cocaine. Cocaine is occasionally used in surgeries to stop the bleeding during nasal/ENT surgery, but that use is exceedingly rare. Here in the US, since it's a schedule A narcotic, medical professionals can't use it."

"This would change the entire narrative for the pharmaceutical industry," I surmised.

"Of course it would. Think about how many people are on opioids now, legally. They get the prescription from their doctor, and then get addicted in the current form. Big Pharma is on the hook for knowingly getting people addicted. They're the same as the drug dealers on the streets. Only the stuff dealers sell on the streets is more likely cut with something, like sugar, cornstarch, or borax, which then increases the toxic nature of it," she replied.

"So, you're taking two narcotics and creating a super one?"

"When you put it that way, yes. We're taking the best properties of both and turning it into something considerably harder to abuse." Charlie sat up. "And if you can take it safely without being addicted to it, you're less likely to abuse the drug. And the less abuse . . ."

"The more your body can heal," I muttered softly. My mind raced with the possibilities. "How far along the process are you?"

"Human trials were tentatively scheduled to begin in four months. But I'm almost positive they're now delayed forever." Charlie frowned. She paused in thought and stared blankly at the floor.

"What?" I asked.

"This has turned into a total clusterfuck. Aside from the huge mess at the labs, Dr. Weber told the program the government froze our funding, and we couldn't continue until the investigation is complete. Which makes total sense. It's just odd though. About two weeks before the shit hit the fan, we were pulled into the conference room to discuss the private grant we received from an anonymous donor. This is normally a good thing, but Dr. Weber was more anxious and nervous than normal."

"Did he give any clues as to why his attitude changed?"

"Not really. He kept going on and on about the potential for new growth and what was on the horizon. Something about taking it to the next level. But he didn't give us clarification what was on the horizon."

"That at least tells me they're planning for bigger and better things, which would be normal in their type of market. But you would think he would be happy about it." I may not know Biotech, but I had a little experience with running a business. Planning for future projects and expenditures is pretty standard. Most companies, even small businesses like Tactical Redemption forecast their next set of objectives before the first set is even written in stone.

"You would think so, right? If it were any other situation, we would use the funding to expand our portfolio, our expertise. We'd have additional researchers and a larger objective. But here's the thing—it was super vague. No specific projects. No outline for the future of Bowen Biotech. And right after we were flushed with all the money, the pressure to bring it to market quicker was intense. We suddenly were overwhelmed with fresh faces everywhere. Not the normal interns, either. Suits started coming more often. More people were poking around, taking notes, and observing. They were all supposedly with Bowen, but we never got introduced. There were a lot of hush hush meetings, closed access discussions we weren't privy to. Which was odd because all meetings were normally open door. It was a team type of environment—until it wasn't." Charlie shrugged. "I wish I could be of more help. I mean, I could write down what I remember of the formula, but it wouldn't tell you what you needed to know, would it?"

"Maybe? I don't know any organic chemists who are looking to make the jump to a criminal enterprise, but I'm sure it wouldn't hurt to keep them on our radar." I jotted the reminder down to tell Zeke. "Tell me about Nessa. Why would the police think you would have something to do with her disappearance?"

"Nessa and Michael are my competition, and we don't get along at all. That's the only explanation I could see. We've been in the same program for about three years now, competing for the same slots. And once Bowen announced this internship, the competition pressure increased. Even Michael had to compete for it," Charlie replied, shrugging.

"How were you all competing if the three of you got into the program?" I asked, tapping my pencil on the table.

"The internship with Bowen isn't the endgame. At the end of the program, Bowen will hire the person who made the biggest impact. This is a lucrative position, not only because of the financial aspect but it would elevate the level of prestige in the Biotech world. Bowen is determined to change how the world cures and heals." Charlie pursed her lips thoughtfully. "Whoever gets this position will have a direct impact on the industry as a whole and will be the face of the next new wave of Biotech research."

"That is a big deal for someone who is starting out," I muttered, impressed. She was the entire package, ready to do good in this world. The small voice in the back of my head whispered, *And you'd hold her back.* I mentally pushed back the thought. I couldn't let the demons get in the way. Not this time.

"For someone my age, in their mid-to-late twenties, to have a hand in creating something which will help present and future generations? Oh yeah, this is a big freaking deal."

"Did you work well with Nessa and Michael?"

"Professionally, yes. They're both smart as hell. They know the science. But would I trust them to watch my pet rock? Nope. They come from the same circle, the rich narcissists, who don't care about how the drugs impact the community and are really only looking to make money."

"That's good to know." I put it into the note over to Cole and hit send. "All right Angel, I'm all yours. Let's head on down."

I slapped a faded ball cap over my head and threw on a blue long-sleeved tee with my cargo shorts. Even though it was warm out, I wanted to cover up my noticeable tattoos. I slipped on a pair of my worn sneakers. "You ready?"

"Yeah." Charlie pulled her deep brown hair through the baseball cap and slid her toes into some flip flops. While she looked beautiful with it, I preferred her original strawberry blonde. Her curvy thighs looked delicious in her frayed cut-off shorts and faded gray t-shirt, a souvenir we picked from a bar outside of Richmond. We made our way down the interior stairs, exiting out of the door leading out to the alley, then made the walk over to Main Street.

The fair was already crowded with people, kids in strollers, and dogs. Even goats on leashes were walked like pets. A band played at one end, while vendors selling their wares in pop up tents lined both sides of the streets. Food trucks with the delicious smells wafted through the air, with craft breweries setting up a beer garden area at one of the streets. Hand in hand, we blended into the crowd, meandering our way up and down the street. I kept watch behind my sunglasses, my eyes peeled for any potential threat or danger. We perused the vendors, checking out the local crafts and tasting some of the best craft beers I had in a long time. Little by little, I could see the stress lift from Charlie's shoulders, and I knew coming out was the best thing for her. Well, for us both. Getting out of the safe house and out of our heads for a minute helped clear the jumbled thoughts in my head.

After grabbing cones of freshly made ice cream from a farmer's food truck, we made our way over to a nearby bench under the shade of a tree. Just watching her lick the dripping ice cream made my cock twitch.

"It should be illegal," I muttered.

"Oh, you mean this?" Her eyes twinkled with mischief as she made a low moan and twirled her tongue around the tip of the cone.

"Oh, we'll put that tongue to good use later on."

After filling our bellies with beer and great food, we made our way back to the apartment, after making sure we weren't being followed. Once inside, I pushed Charlie against the door, holding her arms above her head with one hand, while the other was full of her generous breasts. She arched into me; her sigh filled with need. My lips blazed a trail from her mouth down to the sweet spot on her neck and bit down. Charlie's breath hitched, her pelvis grinding into my tented shorts.

I unbuttoned her shorts, letting them fall to her ankles, then yanked off her shirt.

"I want to touch you," Charlie breathed.

"Oh, you're going to be touching something." I let go of her arms and dropped to my knees, hooking a leg over my shoulder as she braced herself against the door. My tongue blazed a trail from her inner thigh to her dripping center. The scent of lavender and honeysuckle had my mouth watering. I gently ran my tongue over her slit and smirked while she shivered. I found my new and only addiction. I lapped at her nub and inserted two fingers into her sheath, stretching her and crooking them in a come-hither motion. Her sharp intake of breath told me I got the right spot.

"Oh God yes." She grasped my head and ground on my face, searching for her release. I feasted like a king and let her essence and scent consume me. I was ravenous and I could live on Charlie. Her muscles tensed and I knew she was close.

Despite her cry of desperation, I stood up and let my shorts drop, my thick cock bouncing off my lower abs.

"I need you to come on my cock. I want to feel your pussy milk me dry." I lifted her up and wrapped her legs around me. Then plunged into her heat. I pounded inside her pussy, like a man without control, groaning when her body clenched mine. I grabbed her jaw and claimed her mouth, letting her taste her deliciousness.

"Come on Angel, I know you got one more in there." I rubbed at her bud, at the same time I buried myself deeper.

"I can't ... I can't..." she wheezed; her eyes shut tightly.

"Baby girl, your pussy is so damn drenched, I think you got one more." My thrusts increased in pace. "Come on, Angel. Come for me."

My balls tightened and I was right on the edge. As soon as her pussy clamped around my cock, I followed with a roar.

I stood there, with her legs wrapped around me and my cock half-hard, and our chests heaving. She is my heaven, pure and simple. I gently let her legs fall to the ground and cleaned us off with my discarded shirt.

I tucked her into my chest, my heart rapidly beating.

"I have to tell you, thank you." Charlie's breathless murmur had me confused.

"Oh Angel, no thank you," I said with a smirk.

She swatted my bicep and rolled her eyes.

"Seriously. Thank you. Thank you for doing all you're doing to keep me safe." She cupped my face her gaze intent on mine. I turned my head and kissed the palm of her hand.

"You don't need to thank me, Angel. I would fight the demons in hell to protect you." *Even if the demons are in me.* I didn't speak those words, but it didn't need to be said. It was the truth.

"I know you would. And I would do the same for you. I

hope you know that." Her green eyes stared at me, showing me everything I needed to know. The trust. The desire.

The alert on my phone pinged, bringing us out of the love haze and into the harsh reality.

"What is it?" Charlie asked.

"It's from Cole, saying we need to check the site for an update." I pried myself away from her warmth and sat down at the computer, typing in my verification codes and authentication factors. Within a few seconds, the information came up.

"Fuck."

The news was grim from all fronts. Three agents were dead, shot after chasing one of the Syndicate members down in Florida. A cargo container of women was found sinking in the Gulf of Mexico, with no survivors. A note was found on the dark web, demanding Charlie's return to the lab. And Kate was down for the count in the ICU, thanks to a gun fight outside Baltimore.

All compliments of the Syndicate.

My blood boiled; rage coursed through me. Not only at the lengths the Syndicate was going to, but at my own incompetence. How could I have been so fucking stupid. I should be there with the team, on the front line, not sitting here playing house with Charlie. We were playing pretend while lives were on the line. We were playing fucking cat and mouse games without an end in sight.

"What's going on?" Charlie wrapped the sheet around her and came to join me at the makeshift table. She read over my shoulder the brief notes Zeke had sent over. Her face paled and I could tell she read about Kate.

"She's okay. She's stable and in the ICU." I tried to reassure her, but my assurance fell flat. It was a lie. She knew it. I knew it.

It was time to get back to reality.

"What can we do?" she whispered.

"We can't do anything here. We're playing fucking house, while those we love are getting torn apart." My words escaped my lips before I could even understand what I said. "Charlie, I—"

She held her hand up. "Nope. It's fine. I get it. I'm not taking what you're saying out of context. I understand. You're right, we are out here living in an essential bubble where we aren't apart of what's going on back at home. But - hold on – I can't have this conversation with you while I'm naked." She dropped the sheet and threw on her clothes from earlier. I looked away, my fingers rapidly moving over the phone's keyboard.

Charlie walked back over, fully dressed. "Okay," she said after taking a cleansing breath. "Where do we go from here?"

"I have no clue. I can't bring you there, but I'm not leaving you here by yourself."

"Use me." The calm declaration set my blood on ice.

"What?" I swung around to look at her. "Are you fucking out of your mind?" I growled.

"No. They want something I can provide. They won't hurt or kill me, until they get what they need. It would give your team time to ramp up." Her demeanor was calm, factual. It was a plausible solution, but one I would never take.

"That's not going to happen," I snarled. "I'm going to reach out to Mack to see if you can hang with him until we get you out of here."

I sent the text over to Mack, then tossed the phone onto the table. I stalked over to my rucksack and started shoving random shit in there. The laptop would stay here with her. I quickly went through my mental list, what needed to be done and who I needed to call. My blood boiled, needing the satisfaction of blood being spilled.

"What the hell are you talking about, Sketch? We're a team. You literally said it wasn't safe, and now you're going to leave me here?"

"Yes, Angel. We aren't going anywhere. You're going to stay put while I head up to check in with TR. I'm going to have you maintain communication through the phone and laptop." After I threw on a t-shirt, I shoved my feet into my shoes.

"Um, wait what? Think again because I'm not staying here without you." Her eyes narrowed and she crossed her arms, but the panic was set in her tone.

"Sorry, Angel, this has to be the way it is." I moved to her side and wrapped my arms around her. I felt her panic rising, but there was no other way to do this. I felt powerless out here.

"I'm not leaving without you!" she demanded. "I'm the only real solution your team has."

"I'm not going to lose you too!" I roared. The beast inside me wanted to scream and tear the world apart at the thought of her doing that.

"I'm not going to lose you either!" she shouted back. Any other person, man or woman, would shrink at me. But no, my woman stands up to me. Damn if it didn't make me love her even more. I yanked her into my arms and held her tightly.

"I can't deal with the idea of bringing you into Hell's circle. If I know you're out of the line of fire, I'll be better equipped to handle what is going on up there. Please stay here," I whispered, my lips pressed against her hair. I knew leaving her here was the right but difficult choice. Thankfully, I didn't have to wait for Mack's reply. I knew he would watch over her.

"Sketch." Her protest died on her lips because I took them with an urgency like never before. I swept her tongue and nipped at her lips, as if I was memorizing them for the last time.

"Don't leave me behind, Sketch. Not now. Please. I'm afraid I'm going to lose you when we finally found each other," she whispered, tears choking her voice.

Fuck. My gut twisted.

"Angel, listen to me. I will be back for you. I promise you.

The phone is right here. The only numbers listed are the burners and the number for Mack. Don't call anyone else." I breathed in her scent one last time, then gently pushed away from her. I took one last look at her tearstained face then walked out the door.

13

CHARLIE

MY GUT TWISTED AND DROPPED AS I WATCHED HIM ROLL OUT. I'll be damned if I let him roll out of here without a plan in mind. I may not have the exact text in front of me, but I know someone is asking for my return in exchange for a cease-fire. Wait. Not asking. Demanding.

I wanted to go after Sketch and put a stop to whatever hell he was about to raise. But figuring out how exactly to do it left me flustered. I plopped down on the loveseat and stared blankly at the door.

Take a deep breath and think. I inhaled deeply through my nose and exhaled through my mouth and tried to calm my mind. Being in the middle of nowhere left me without many options, and while this town was pretty enough, I was pretty sure the town didn't have a ride sharing service that would take me a hundred miles east. What good would it do anyway? I couldn't exactly go running into Tactical Redemption, my laptop blazing. *I'm a scientist, not a bad ass.* But I needed to do something. I couldn't sit here, like a freaking damsel in distress, waiting for her prince to come and save her.

Screw it. I would figure out the details later. All that

mattered now was getting to Tactical Redemption and back to my family. Back to Sketch. Yes, it was reckless and stupid. Yes, I realized my family would kill me if I didn't die in the process. But if there was something I could do that would be of any benefit to the team, then why can't I do it? I have my strengths and weaknesses like any other human. I'm not an adverse risk-taker. I analyze everything to death. I have to; if not, I wouldn't be able to proceed in my work. My life is all about analyzing the data and taking the necessary risks to get to my objective.

And Sketch was worth the risk.

I flew into action, throwing my clothes and laptop back into the knapsack and rummaging through the tangled sheets to find my sneakers.

A shrill ring startled the heck out of me. I grabbed the phone, anxious for it to be Sketch, telling me he was going to turn around and get me.

"Sketch?"

"Not quite." A familiar voice came through the phone, and it took me a minute to place it.

"Michael? How did you get this number?"

He chuckled dryly. "It's time for you to come home, Charlotte."

"How did you get this number?" I demanded, my heart dropping like a stone. If he knew where I was or how to get the number, had they been following us this entire time?

"We know everything. Tell Sketch we appreciate his gesture to try and throw us off course. But wait, he's not there is he? He left you by your lonesome."

"I'm not alone." My voice stood firm when I was anything but.

"Charlotte don't take us for fools. We know you're alone. We have quite enjoyed the show you have put on today." Michael paused. "Understand this. We know everything. We see everything. We know you have a pistol in the black book bag over there. We know your shirt has a bar logo and your toes are painted pink."

Fuck. They were watching me. They were watching us. I felt like I was going to be sick. A bang sounded on the door, startling me.

"Open the door. Or we'll paint this town and the entire Rainbow Trail red."

Fuck. They were seriously here. How the hell did we not see it? How did we miss them?

My hands shook, as I took the pistol out of the backpack.

"Go fuck yourself, Michael." The growl was low, but I would be damned if they were taking me alive.

"You might want to check yourself, you fat bitch." A text message came through. "You may want to see for yourself. We're not to be fucked with."

Trembling, I clicked on the image link and bile brewed up from my stomach. Sketch was laid out in what looked like a van interior. A large blood spot formed on his gray basketball shorts, and he was still struggling with two other men. His face was already pale, probably due to the loss of blood, and I knew his time was limited. Sobs got caught in my throat while tears spilled down my cheeks.

"Say hi to your girlfriend, Sketch," the voice on the video said.

"Get away from her. You got me. That's all you need." His voice was strained and already weak. Fuck. I needed to help him.

"We see everything, Charlie. We know everything. You can't escape us. Now, you have a choice. Come out willingly, and we won't touch your family. Decide not to and we'll have a little fun with your boyfriend. By the way, we also have eyes on your entire family. It would suck for something to happen to your precious niece."

What else could I do? There was no other way out of this

situation. I glanced around the room, looking for something else I could use as a weapon or a stalling technique, but I found nothing.

"You're wasting time, you fucking bitch. Open this door right now."

I inhaled a shuddering breath and exhaled slowly, then opened the large wooden door. A man with the arms the size of tree trunks reached out and grabbed my wrist, yanking me out into the hall. My scream died in my throat as his large hand went around my throat, crushing my windpipe and shoving me against the wall. Immediately, my hands went to his wrists as I struggled to breathe.

Dark spots danced across my eyes.

"I despise waiting for prissy bitches like you," the giant muttered. His nasty breath caused my stomach to revolt in protest. "But we're going to be cool, yeah?" His soulless eyes bore into mine.

"I'M COMING WILLINGLY. Just leave my family alone," I gurgled, struggling against the ogre.

A razor-sharp zap infiltrated my senses, and I dropped the man's arm. Electric pain flooded through me, and a gargled scream came from my lips. I felt my body give away in a free-fall.

And then my world went black.

———

A STINGING SLAP against my cheek brought me out of my stupor. I blinked against the grainy light and moistened my lips as I tried to make sense of my surroundings.

"About time you woke up." The feminine voice filled my ears and I winced at the familiar tone and pitch of her whine.

"Even as a dead person, you're annoying as hell," I grumbled. I glanced around me and tugged on the long leash my ankle was attached to. The room I was in should be familiar territory. A Mag-Spec machine, microscopes, beakers, and a computer placed on a stainless-steel tabletop. The fluorescent light flickered. The walls were blank with whiteboards. A mattress pallet was placed on the floor and a toilet with a sink took up a corner. "Where's Sketch?"

"That psychotic killer is in the room next door. Don't worry, we made sure he's stable." Her snide voice was like nails on a chalkboard.

"Well pardon me for not believing a single word you say, you traitorous twat. I want to see him," I growled.

"You are in no place to make demands." She gestured around her. "For the moment, you'll have to trust in the fact your homicidal boyfriend is in the next room, all stitched up from the gunshot wound in his thigh and is currently in stable condition.

A bit of relief came over me and I glared at Nessa. "What the hell is this place? What, did you look up bad science movies and determine the décor based on those?"

"If you think we'd waste the finer things on you, you're sorely mistaken," she said with a smirk. "This is where you'll be from now on."

"I am going to need more information than that. Why am I here?"

"Because your super smart brain is required. The formulas you created with Nessa and Michael will help solidify the black market and patent for the next generation of illegal narcotics," a booming voice echoed throughout the room, and I winced at the sudden onslaught of nausea. Dressed in a suit with a bald head and a muscular build, the man who walked in was the epitome of what a gangster would look like.

"Who the hell are you and why should I listen?" I wheezed out.

"Charlotte, this is Sebastian Cruz," Nessa said saucily, as if I knew what the hell it was supposed to mean to me.

"Is that supposed to scare me? I suppose you're the big, bad boss who is going to tell me what to do?" I quipped sarcastically. My projection was better than what I originally intended. I couldn't show these people any fear. Even though I was almost one minute away from peeing my pants.

Nessa smirked. "Poor Charlotte. You should fear Sebastian. But he's not going to be the one telling you what to do." She paused, then gestured behind me. "He is."

I made the mistake of turning around and froze in disbelief. Dr. Weber entered through the marked doorway, looking smug. "What the hell is going on here?"

"Charlotte Parker. So glad you could join us." Dr. Weber's polite and almost formal tone had me doing a double take.

"I feel like I'm in the twilight zone. So please, someone enlighten me. This should be the part where you tell me what the hell is going on. Because honestly, I'm confused as hell. Dr. Weber, you're involved with this too? How could you?"

"My dear prodigy, I'm the mastermind behind this. You would think tenure at a university and a board position at a bio-research firm would be enough, but alas, not true. I'm a man of many goals, and this is another stepping-stone of that path," the doctor said magnanimously, as if he was doing the world a grand favor.

"You and I, along with Michael's help, are going to get the formula back on track. With a few tweaks of course," Nessa supplied, all the while studying her notebook.

"Why do you need me?" I asked, my voice low. "Why go through this drama? You know everything I do about the program."

"Because you're the missing link. We tried doing this

without you, but when everything was destroyed in the explosion, we realized we needed your research. I know you pride yourself on remembering the nuances and tiny details of any formula. We need to pick your brain until we have it correct," Michael replied, walking up to Nessa and wrapping his arm around her waist. His sick and twisted smile had me gagging. If I wasn't in such a precarious situation, I would have laughed in his face and mocked his tone. But unfortunately, it wasn't the case now. I had to figure out what my next step was going to be.

"Okay, so the deal is what exactly? I help you tweak the missing pieces to the formula and then what, you let me go?" I scoffed. "I may not be wise to the gangster way of life, but I think I know how this will end up. You're going to kill me as soon as I have this figured out."

Sebastian chuckled, but the vein throbbing in his head said this was anything but a laughing matter.

"You would be correct, Charlotte. However, it will depend on how well you work. Your life could be extended if you choose to be more cooperative."

"So basically, play nice or get out of the sandbox." My sarcasm didn't go unnoticed, and Sebastian's gaze narrowed at me. He opened his mouth to speak but Nessa cut him off.

"Exactly. And to ensure you don't throw some chemicals together, we're going to be using your boyfriend as a test subject."

My stomach dropped and my heart faltered. I covered my mouth in horror. "What do you mean, use him as a test subject? We can't go from formula to test subject! There are too many steps in between to ensure the safety of the drug. Even if we're able to come up with a formula which works, it wouldn't—shouldn't—be ready for human trials until we make sure the cell mapping is correct and the library is in sync."

"Which should incentive you to work with us. To do your job correctly and get the formula accurate so you can save your man. Once we're done with him, we have a whole slew of test subjects." Michael shrugged, as if this was the most natural sequence of events.

"You've got to be kidding me." I paused as my mind raced with potential ways to create the formula and keep Sketch alive and safe at the same time. My heart hurt at the likelihood of that happening. Most likely I would end up killing him or putting him into an overdose.

"I'll do it on one condition." Anger and desperation fueled my tone. I knew they didn't have to agree to any conditions. I was in a situation where it would be fruitless to fight. They had me at their will, and I knew to keep Sketch alive, I needed to do what they said.

"This should be golden," Michael sneered.

"Go fuck yourself, Michael, I'm not even listening to whatever small-dick energy you're spewing," I spat at him and looked straight at Sebastian, the man in charge. "I will remain in your service, doing whatever you need me to do. I will do my damnedest to replicate the formula and I will make sure it works on Sketch. But I implore you, as soon as he's healed and we know the formula works, please let him go. Leave my family alone."

Sebastian arched his eyebrow and scoffed. "You have the balls to bargain with us? We are not fools, Charlotte. We know the monster that lies in the bed next door. The moment he gets out of our facilities, he'll be attempting to avenge his 'Angel.' He will never leave this place. But we can ensure he lives and continues to be a test subject for us. And ... to show we're not as horrible as you make us out to be, your family will be left alone."

"There's a bit of an issue with your madness. What exactly are we going to use for the chemical make up? They have regulated the hell out of the necessary ingredients for this very reason. Do you have a shipment of the solvents and potassium permanganate? Because all that went kaboom when your dumbasses blew up the lab." I knew I was grasping at straws, but I was desperate.

Nessa rolled her eyes. "Of course we do. Did you think we'd blow up our supply of ingredients?"

"But why the explosion? Why destroy everything only to redo it? It makes no sense."

Nessa groaned and pushed away from the table. "Seriously, you are not this stupid. Do I need to spell it out for you? Who would own the patent rights for the formulas? The fed. But Bowen Research would be doing the work and making the product. We needed the fed to fund our little operation so we could get started. To them, the project itself was a risky investment. But they don't know they basically funded the Syndicate's next product line."

An indigent gasp escaped my lips. I had been basically working for a drug cartel. What the actual fuck? They used the government, along with all the red-tape and political nonsense, to fuel their next drug.

"And what exactly is this new product line?" I whispered.

"A purer, more addictive version of the original. We create the synthetic version with a higher price point while marketing it as less addictive, when in reality it's the opposite. We already have the East Coast and Southern markets. The next step would be is taking over the Global market," Michael said with a smug grin.

"You don't think the line between Bowen and the Syndicate will be found? Are you confident in your ability to obscure the evidence that everything won't blow up in your faces?"

"Enough, Nessa. We don't need to share all the details with the hostage." Sebastian's cruel grin had my blood run cold. "All you have to know is we hold all the cards. Whether the government eventually figures out the line between the Syndicate and their research doesn't matter nor will it help you in this current situation. You have the necessary equipment and supplies to continue your research. You have a viable test subject that will ensure your results are applicable. Anything else is inconsequential and will very much lead to a disappointing result for your friend and the family you claim to hold so dear."

"That's right. Don't screw us over, do the good work, and your family will be spared. Your lover will live while you're here. Or at least until you accidentally kill him by overdose. And the longer you work with us, the longer you live." Nessa stepped closer to me, to where we were practically nose to nose. "But please, keep being a bitch and I'll be happy to cut your life short."

I made a kissy face back at her and she snarled, her arm extended for a punch. I readied myself for a blow, but Michael grabbed her arm at the last possible second.

"Shut her down, Michael," barked Sebastian. He stalked over to me with murder in his eyes. "Your laptop is over there. You have the next twenty-four hours to work on your portion of the formula. I expect some sort of tangible progress. You may not care about your own life, but you do care about your family. And you seem to have a fondness for a certain tattooed mercenary in the room next door. Don't disappoint me, Charlotte. You won't like the consequences."

The lack of soul in his eyes scared me more than his words. I knew it wasn't blather or nonsense he was spewing. It was absolute truth.

If I didn't do this, the people I love would die.

14

CHARLIE

A WEEK AND A HALF INTO THIS MADNESS. I'VE TRIED DRAGGING my feet. I've tried lying. I've tried to create a compound which could make him heal faster or would make him sleep longer. But Nessa and Michael were right behind me and ensured I followed their instructions. They locked up the materials each night, only giving me a composition book and pencil to work with at night when they closed the lab down. Thankfully, I was able to drag the mattress pallet into the room where Sketch slept. I knew they were watching us and monitoring his vitals remotely, because they would ask questions when they would come in the next morning.

The lab they set up was almost exactly the same as the one they blew up. Thankfully, they had the correct protective equipment. Working with volatile chemical compounds was one thing. Working with them while tied to a support beam and testing them on the man who had my heart was totally different.

The varying formulas they wanted me to create have worked, by computer standards. We have yet to test them on

Sketch and I tried my hardest to delay it. But the Syndicate wouldn't be swayed.

"Please, let me use this on mice. You know what the outcome will be if it's not correct. If it's wrong, we could lose him. And then who would we have to test it on?" I pleaded. I knew it was a long shot, but maybe if I appealed to their scientific senses, Dr. Weber and the others may actually be reasonable.

Sebastian, on the other hand, was not.

"Test it on him, or we'll bring your niece in here and test it on her."

Fuck.

With angry tears in my eyes, I managed my way to his bed and decreased the propofol and morphine that had been keeping him stable and pain free while in a drug-induced coma. The Syndicate's trauma doc gave me a crash course in pulmonology and showed me how to pull out the endotracheal tube and turn off the ventilator he had been on since the shooting. I held my breath as he had held his, and I was relieved when he started breathing on his own.

"Any time today, Ms. Parker." The voice came from overhead. The reminder someone was always watching my every move.

"For fuck's sake. He's not conscious yet, Cruz. I could shoot him up with this cocktail, but you won't know how it works if he's not awake. Hold your fucking horses," I snapped, my glare going to the camera in the corner.

"Do you think you're in any position to test me? Wake him the fuck up."

I knew, reluctantly, if everything went as it was supposed to, Sketch would wake up within the next hour. If everything went as it should, I would be able to inject him with this toxic cocktail in the next few hours. He would be coherent until I did. After that, who knows what would happen.

"What the fuck is supposed to happen once he gets injected?"

"We'll observe him."

"You're putting three of the most potent and aggressive drugs into this man, and you're going to let him go batshit crazy? His behavior and reaction will be unpredictable. There's no way to guarantee his safety, or mine for that matter."

"That's not our concern. Mr. Davis will be one of many test subjects. If he chooses to rage out or have an unanticipated reaction, we'll have to move on to the rest. Consider this stage one of the testing panel."

Those fucking bastards.

I sat back onto the mattress pallets and waited. What I waited for; I don't know. The monitors for his vitals were watched remotely, so there wasn't anything telling me about his heart rate, brain activity, or pulse rate. I had a simple stethoscope and could take his blood pressure that way. But nothing would give me a sign that he was in distress.

The second his eyes opened, I exhaled deeply. He let out a groan and I was right at his side. Sketch licked his cracked lips. "Angel."

Relief flooded through me. At this moment in time, I knew he was okay.

"Hey there," I whispered. I held the straw and plastic cup against his lips and let him slowly sip the cool water.

"What the hell happened?" he groaned.

"You were shot in the thigh, and we were brought here. It was a bit dicey, but you're healing great." I felt so fake saying this, and I knew he could tell I was lying. His molten silver eyes held mine.

"Are you okay? Did they touch you?" Sketch raised his hands and lightly traced my chin. Knowing the faded bruise looked better than before, I leaned into his touch.

"They tried to. But I gave it back just as good," I murmured.

"Where are we?" His eyes became more focused, and he did a quick glance around the room. "This doesn't look like a regular hospital."

My lower lip trembled. "Because we're at some Syndicate lab. We've been here for the last two weeks."

Sketch's jaw clenched and his eyes hardened. "I'm assuming since it's just us in here, they have us monitored?" I nodded, unable to speak.

"Fuck." He rubbed his face with his massive palm. "We'll figure a way out of here, Angel. I promise."

"That's highly improbable, Mr. Davis, as you're going to be Ms. Parker's test subject for the foreseeable future. The only way to get out of here will be in a pine box." The voice overhead toned emotionlessly above us.

Sketch lifted his chin and glared at the speaker. "Are you such a big pussy that you can't take care of me yourself?"

"Of course not. However, we're not the ones creating the products needed. That would be your 'Angel.' You should really think about updating her nickname to 'Angel of Death.' Because with her new formula, more and more people will be addicted and fall prey to her drug."

The guilt overwhelmed me, and tears started falling. Sebastian said everything I had feared. I was going to be a murderer either way. If my formula didn't kill Sketch, they would certainly kill others who were already down the wrong path.

"Who is it?" Sketch muttered, his eyes looking at the camera.

"Sebastian Cruz. Apparently, he's a pretty big deal," I whispered with a shrug. "Dr. Weber, Michael, and Nessa are involved as well. This was their plan all along, to have the government fund the research, then create the product to be sold on the black market. But they're not looking to make it less addictive. They're hoping to hook more people on it without having people overdose."

"Essentially expanding their customer base?"

"Yeah. They are going to have the market cornered. Bowen Biotech will be both the hero and villain. While Bowen Biotech receives more investment money and grants to come up with another solution, they're also selling their own drugs on the streets. They're playing both sides of the game."

Sketch closed his eyes and sighed. "What are they having you work on?"

"They had me work with Nessa and Michael to continue the first batch and ensure the formula was optimized for alteration."

"And they want you to test it on me." It wasn't a statement requiring a response. He knew, as well as I did, we weren't going to get out of it.

"They have close access to Aubrey, my parents, and the rest of the team," I whispered. "They were going to let you die. I didn't know what to do." I choked back a sob and pleaded for... I didn't know. Forgiveness? Understanding? Redemption?

"Oh, Angel." Sketch sat up with a grimace and took my face into his massive hands. "You got dragged into something that is not your fault. We'll figure this out. We'll get out of here, I promise." His murmur was almost too low, but it was for my ears only.

"Since you're properly reunited, can we please continue?" Dr. Weber's voice echoed in the room. Sketch snarled at the intrusion; his expression feral. I knew once he was strong enough, he would destroy whoever was in his path. But they wanted to keep him pliant and subdued. Hence the push to start the testing.

"What are we working with today?" Sketch asked softly.

"Today is a mix of cocaine and MDMA. A few components of each," I replied grimly.

"Not going easy on me, are you?" He chuckled, like we were discussing a recipe for dinner, not a mixture of chemicals that would probably kill him. I turned away, and he grasped my chin. "Hey. Look at me." My gaze melted into his calm and collected one.

"I'm going to be okay. Don't forget, I'm pretty familiar with odd mixes of narcotics getting stuck in my arm. I told you heroin was my drug of choice after I left the team. I was able to get through it once. I will fight through it again. And I will sure as hell fight it to get back to you."

"I tried to dilute it as much as I could," I insisted, the tears spilling down my cheeks.

"I know you did. I know this isn't you doing this. You're in survival mode. And I probably would have made the same choice," Sketch whispered gently. He lied. We both knew it. He pulled me in for a soft kiss. A kiss of future promises.

"Now!" the voice roared. I startled and jumped back.

Shaking, I picked up the syringe and wiped a spot on his best vein on the inside of his elbow. Old track scars dotted the veins, and I knew he had fought these demons before.

Before I put the needle to skin, he paused my hand.

"Whatever I do or say while I'm not myself, please forgive me." Instead of being scared or angry, he was worried. Worried about what he would say while I was pumping drugs into his system.

"I'm so sorry, Sketch," I whispered for forgiveness. His face flinched, but he kept his eyes on me the entire time, as I depressed the syringe, emptying the toxic cocktail. All melted down into a solution, each ingredient on its own was deadly. However, with the ingredients combined, meant it was extremely dangerous. There was no telling what Sketch would be like when the drugs took hold.

15

CHARLIE

His legs twitched, softly at first. Then Sketch aggressively kicked off his blankets, as if something heavy sat on his legs. Sweat beaded on his forehead. Sketch's massive body barely fit into the hospital bed, but it seemed as he grew more agitated, the larger he grew.

I expected something like this. The cocktail mix had effects for every sadist. And the combination of the three put them all into a blender.

"Sketch?" I crossed over to his side and wiped his forehead with a cold rag. I went to turn to get more water when a hand grasped my hand on his forehead. His gray eyes shot open, the pupils in his eyes becoming larger than the iris itself.

He let out a deep exhale. And then looked directly into my eyes.

"Angel," he breathed. His lips parted with a sigh. Sketch's arms, once loosely against his side, tightened and clenched into fists.

"What the fuck is all over me?" Sketch thrashed on the bed, letting out an animalistic roar, tossing off the blanket that had covered his legs. He gasped out, jumping out of his bed, and ripped off his shirt. A move that without the drug cocktail, he wouldn't have been able to do. I stumbled back, only because I knew he was unpredictable.

"Sketch. It's just me. It's Charlie. You're okay, I promise." The lie slipped through my lips like water. As if there was something I could do to make him better.

"God... I need..." he panted, his hand running across his bare abs and then down his thighs, grazing his bandaged wound. He hissed in pain.

"Hey, why don't we sit back down? I don't want you to hurt yourself. You're healing," I soothed, taking a small step toward him.

"Ah fuck," he snarled. He tore the IV port out of the vein on his hand. His body was metabolizing the drugs quicker than I had anticipated. I scrambled back hitting the wall as he stalked toward me.

"Hey, it's okay. I'm right here. I got you, Sketch." The lies kept coming, I didn't know what I was doing, let alone how to help him without the help of Narcan or something similar.

His eyes closed and he took a deep breath.

"Angel."

His voice, dark and seductive, gave me a double take. His hand slid down his abdomen and gripped his thick bulging cock through the sweatpants he was wearing. As soon as his fingertips brushed the tip, he groaned loudly with his head thrown back. He lowered his pants and I whimpered. *Fuck it all.* Because I knew this wasn't right. I knew it was the drugs that were making him this way. But damn if it wasn't hot.

His eyes popped open, and he looked at me, with hunger in his eyes. I was his prey, and he was the predator.

"Get out," he growled.

"I can't," I wailed, shaking my head. "I'm stuck here, like you."

"You need to get out. Get her out of here," Sketch bellowed

at the ceiling. "Don't let her face your sins. Face the devil yourself, you bastards."

"Talk to me, Sketch. How are you feeling? What's going on in your head?" I asked, trying to divert his attention to get him to focus on something other than sex.

"I feel like a fucking God, Angel. I don't know what will happen if you get near me. I feel like I need to fuck but also kill. Stay away from me," Sketch grunted out, grimacing in both agony and rage.

I wanted to go to him, let him take his anguish out on me. I could take his destruction, his fire.

The battle waged within him. He stalked and paced the room like a caged lion. I saw the moment his control was fringing. Sketch stalked toward me, his silver orbs now glittering like mercury.

"Fuck, Angel. I'm trying my hardest. But it's like I can't control myself. I'm going to hurt you." Sketch grasped my bicep, his fingertips pressing into the thickness of my arm.

"You're not going to hurt me." I searched his face for the trace of Sketch I long had feelings for. I could see him right there, under the surface. Sketch would never do anything to hurt me, willingly.

He stroked his pierced cock, running a hand up and down his length.

"I'm not going to be gentle," he warned.

"It's okay." I gave him a small smile.

"I hate that they're watching. But I can't hold back," he groaned. He picked me up in his arms and yanked my pants and underwear down to my ankles. With no warning or foreplay, he wrapped my legs around his waist and slammed into me. I cried out, but not in pain. Sketch pressed me up against the wall, showing my pussy no mercy as he pounded into me. I didn't have time to adjust to his thickness when I exploded the first time. The first one melted right into the second. It was never-ending.

"That's right Angel, keep going." He left one hand squeezing my ass cheek while bringing the other to my throat. The pressure was harder than ever before. I momentarily panicked as black dots began to flutter under my eyelids, only to gasp for air when he let go. He moved his hand up to my jaw and turned my head to the side. Sketch buried his face at the base of my neck, biting lightly and licking my skin.

He rubbed my ultra-sensitive clit even more and the stars shattered as I screamed his name. My pussy clenched his cock like a glove. "I hate that they're watching this, hearing you scream for me. It's supposed to be for my ears only." His lips and teeth tugged at the spot between my neck and shoulder. My muscles clinched in response and Sketch groaned.

"Your pussy feels like a fucking vice. It's the best feeling," he moaned.

"Sketch, you have my screams. You have my soul." I raised my hands to his jaw and attacked his lips with mine. Our tongues danced and teeth mashed as he wrung more pleasure out of my weary and sated body.

"I'm never going to let you go. You could get tired of me; you're going to get mad at me. I'm going to be an asshole some-times and you may even hate me. But know this, Angel. You're fucking mine. You will always be mine. Whoever tries to get in between us will suffer by my hands," he panted, his chest heaving as he claimed me in front of the Syndicate.

"I'm yours. I'm yours," I chanted, as he hammered into me. "I'm yours."

He gripped my throat tighter as his rhythm quickened, his thrusts hard and unforgiving. With one final thrust, he found bliss. His eyes closed and a look of euphoria came over him. His cock continued to pulse through me, branding me as his from the inside out. I milked every drop out of him. My chest heaved with exertion, and we were covered with sweat. He pulled out slowly, causing me to wince. Sketch pressed his lips against mine.

"Stay here," he murmured in my ear. I kept my face neutral, but I wondered what the plan was. I didn't have to wait long, as he tucked his half-hard cock into his joggers and rushed the door on the other side of the lab.

Oh fuck. He's going to take the door off. The two security guards outside the lab drew their weapons, their steely gazes taking in the situation and ready for if, or when, Sketch ripped the door open.

"You got your fucking show, now let us leave," he growled, his chest heaving. His fists were clenched and every vein in his arms were evident. Sketch was trying to hold it together, but he was hanging on by a thread. He pulled on the door again, and it gave a bit.

The maniacal smile grew on his face and for the first time since meeting him, a small bit of fear went through me. I wasn't afraid for me. I was more afraid for whoever was on the other side of the wall. Sketch pulled the door harder, giving it all he had. It was slowly inching open, as he was bending the frame. I yanked on my clothes quickly, only freezing when I heard a loud noise. A bullet had penetrated the glass window but didn't cause it to break. *Bulletproof windows.* That's helpful. As he continued to pull the door from the hinge, a voice came over the loudspeaker.

"Step away from the door, Seth Davis. Or Charlie will become test subject number two."

Suddenly the door between the recovery room and the lab slammed shut, separating us entirely.

"No! Charlie!" he bellowed, running over to the door, desperately trying to open it.

"Sketch!" I cried, trying to find the latch or an escape lever, or something. Anything to get to Sketch.

Sketch stood up sluggishly, his eyes heavy. "Angel." His voice was weak and slurred.

"No! What did you do? What did you do? Sketch! Look at me, stay with me. Fight this, Sketch. You got to fight this!" I screamed. Tears ran down my face as my once strong beast crumpled to the ground unconscious.

As soon as the threat against them was gone, the doors unlocked. I flew to his side and checked his pulse. It was there, but weak.

I coughed at the sweet air that was pumped into the room. Chloroform. "You fucking bastards. You got what you wanted. You saw the results. Now let him go," I yelled at the ceiling.

I didn't get a response. I didn't expect one. In the depths of my heart, I knew they would never let us go. Defeat weighed down on me and I felt hopeless. I grabbed the sleeping mat over to where Sketch was, and struggled to get him on there, so he would be comfortable, then checked his wounds. The outburst had aggravated the stiches in his leg, but thankfully nothing I couldn't take care of. I changed his bandages and gave him another injection of antibiotic. Once he was taken care of, I laid down next to him, with my head on his chest, and pulled the blanket over us.

And for the first time since being taken, I sobbed.

16

SKETCH

THE PAIN RADIATING IN MY LEG BROUGHT ME OUT OF WHATEVER spell I was under. Even though I wasn't fully there, the pain made its presence known.

"Fuck..." The groan escaped my lips before my eyes snapped open. The stiff bed and bright, sterile environment told me it was a medical facility, but not one I would associate with a hospital. The metallic taste of antibiotics filled my mouth. I gagged and fought against puking. I tried to raise my hands and stopped when I felt the tug of metal against my skin. My arms were tethered to the rails of the bed. I tested my legs, and found they weren't cuffed. That's more than what I anticipated, but until I got out of these belts, I was completely trapped in the bed.

Instead of panicking, I focused on my other senses. The glare of the white lights showed it was an empty room with one door, one bed, and an IV drip attached to my hand. I felt the stickiness of the cordless monitoring sensors attached to my torso. There was a large mirror, one that reminded me of a one-way window often found in interrogation rooms.

I tried to walk back through what happened. The last thing I remember was tasting Charlie's lips and walking out the door. I made it down the stairs and bumped into a local. Or what I figured was a local. Whoever it was, put a pistol to my thigh, and shot at point blank range.

Fuck! Charlie. I needed to get to her. Make sure she was okay. I yanked at the tethers furiously, testing the strength I had left. My muscles screamed at the movement, but I pushed through, the need to see Charlie greater than any other pain. God helped whoever took my Angel because the beast will be raining hell fire down upon them.

"That's enough, Mr. Davis. At this point, you're not doing anything more than stressing yourself out. And we would prefer our test subjects be whole prior to testing." The voice came from above, but I glared at the mirror off to the side, where I was sure the voice would be standing.

"Show yourself," I growled.

"In due time," the distorted voice continued. "You've been out for a while, but your vitals look good. I'll be sending her in shortly."

My jaw tightened and my hands rolled into fists. I glared at the mirror while my brain tried to get out of the fog it was in. How long was 'a while'? The door opened and I readied myself to unleash fury on whoever walked through there. But my heart stuttered when a short woman walked in. Her frame had lost some of the curves I loved holding on to. Her green eyes had dulled and the bags under her eyes were darker than my oversized t-shirt she was wearing.

"Angel," I gasped. Her eyes widened and filled with tears as she rushed over, throwing herself onto my chest. I groaned in pain but tried desperately to hold her to me. She felt like home.

"I am so glad you're awake." Her murmur was whispered against the thin material of the shirt I was encased in.

"You're definitely something I want to see when I first open my eyes. Hey, look at me," I muttered. Her eyes lifted to mine and as she wiped her eyes, her face hardened. "Give me the rundown. What's going on?"

"Do you ... do you remember anything? At all?" Her gaze searched my eyes, looking for something I guess could give her a clue.

"No. All I remember is getting shot in the leg by an old woman. How long has it been?" My voice sounded like I had smoked a carton of cigarettes in under an hour. Charlie frowned and reached next to me for a plastic cup with a straw sticking out. She touched it to my lips, and I took a small sip, and once the water hit my lips, I took longer swallows.

She put it down after I finished the cup and pushed away a lock of dingy brown hair. "So, timeline-wise, we've been here for two weeks. You've been either unconscious or knocked out for almost the entire time. They're keeping you sedated, constantly, unless they're ready for another reaction test."

Two weeks is a lot of time. Knowing my team, they were going nuts searching for us. "I've been out?" I asked, again testing my strength against the ties that bonded me to the bed. Since my muscles were weak, it made sense.

"Pretty much. They did surgery to fix your leg and you were out for a couple days. But you've been either tested on or put into a drug induced sleep. We wake you up periodically, but I haven't figured out a way to keep you awake all the time." She took a breath. "The Syndicate is working with Bowen Research. They're taking the funding and equipment provided by the fed to create a new product line."

I saw the fear in her eyes and my heart dropped. "Tell me what's going on, Angel."

Charlie bit her lower lip when it trembled. "They wanted to tweak the original formula to make it even more addictive. Completely opposite of what the original intent was. They needed my help. To encourage my help, they're using you as a test subject. And our families as collateral."

The rage flew through my veins quicky. I wanted to break out and destroy them. To inject them with their own poison and watch them suffer. To put their families through hell.

"How many of them are there?"

"There are about five to seven guards and they're heavily armed. This room, along with the lab, is being watched remotely by the rest of the Syndicate. And I can't move further than right here." She lifted the rope that was attached to her ankle. A heavy-duty nylon rope I remember using when I was working the fishing boats. The type that doesn't fray or cut easily.

"What's the rope tied to?"

"A support beam in the middle of the next room. It looks like a stripper pole to be honest." She shrugged, playing off the fear. "I mean, I know I wanted to try some kinky-ish stuff with you, but this isn't the type of kinky fuckery I had in mind." Charlie was scared out of her mind, but the little bit of sass showed me she was still in there.

"We'll have to figure out our own brand of 'kinky fuckery' once we get out of here," I said with a half grin. With my mind clearer, I took a better glance around the room. The cameras Charlie mentioned were in every corner and a microphone and speaker were in the middle of the room. There was a small toilet and sink located on the far wall. And next to me stood the IV pole. There was nothing else. No monitors, no other equipment, nothing could be used as a weapon or an escape device. I couldn't see into the other room, but I guessed it would be similar.

"I'm the human guinea pig. What have been my side effects?" I asked. My previous incoherent states were extremely dangerous, and I knew the type of drugs they were concocting weren't ones that turned me into a giggly schoolgirl. No. These drugs brought out the dangerous side.

"You tried to rip the doors off the hinges, so they had to gas you with Chloroform. Your rage was for everyone." She paused. "Everyone except for me."

Fuck.

My eyes washed over her, really looking at her, and that's when I noticed the handprints around her neck. The purple bruise forming under her jaw. I closed my eyes and breathed through the anger.

"Was that from me?" I growled. Charlie instinctively stepped back but my hand snapped out and grabbed her wrist. "Answer me, Charlie. Did I do that to you?"

"You weren't you, Sketch. You were under the influence of a mix of heavy-duty narcotics. No, it wasn't you."

"Don't make excuses for me, Charlie," I snapped.

"No. You don't get to take the blame for this bullshit, Sketch. You literally had no choice. I was the one pumping the drugs into your system. The fact you're even coherent now is a surprise because I was scared I killed you. So, don't. You're the fucking victim of this mess. And guess what? Even though I hated the fact you weren't in your right frame of mind, I quite enjoyed it. I feel guilty about that too, like I took advantage of you. Maybe I did and it's something we're going to have to deal with after all this. But it doesn't matter. Now the big question is how the fuck do we get out of here?" she spat out harshly. She was right. There would be time to get through the aftermath.

Huh. Angel enjoyed the monster. I knew there was a bit of devil in that pure soul. "Don't worry, we're going to circle back on your little rant once we get out of here." I flexed my legs and joints, to see how bad it really was. My leg felt tight, and I had a lot of muscle weakness, but nothing too alarming.

"Of course, that would be what you're focusing on. Okay, let's get serious. How are you feeling now?" Charlie murmured, as she changed the dressing on my leg. Her head was down low, and I could barely hear her.

"Like my brain is in a fog. What's the latest you know?" I whispered.

Charlie nodded, strands of her hair hiding her green eyes from me. "That's to be expected. They're giving you a larger mixed dose of Propofol, and Fentanyl than normally prescribed to keep you sedated." She fixed the bandage and looked up. "I found when people are talking near the vents, their voices travel this way. Today is Saturday. I heard two men talking about some big meeting Dr. Weber is going to be having with the board of directors at Bowen later today. They were discussing catering options. Sebastian should be there as a 'silent investor'." Her eyes widened at the implication.

"They're coming here. Is there another Bowen research facility?" If that was the case, it was never in our reports or our documentation.

Charlie shrugged. "I don't know. As far as I can tell, Bowen has only one research campus. But they do partner with other companies for manufacturing and distribution. We could be at one of their locations. But I haven't been able to see what we're dealing with outside this room."

Then they were right under the fed's noses all along. "Do you have any idea of the location or the set up?"

"It's close enough to the research campus. I know Dr. Weber would go there for meetings and he would return relatively quickly."

I closed my eyes at the beginning of a major fucking headache. "Is there a way to get a message to the teams?"

Charlie shook her head. "Not really," she murmured. "All communication has been blocked. I tried to add a message with Cole's phone number to the shared cloud account, but I'm not sure if it went through or if anyone was able to see it."

"They're looking for us. You're doing great. Hopefully,

someone is checking the cloud." My thumb rubbed the back of her hand. "How are you feeling? Have they hurt you?"

Charlie shook her head. "Aside from making me test drugs on you? I've been peachy," she said dryly. She pursed her lips and thought aloud. "If we can cause a big enough of a distraction, we could swipe a phone from the guards and get word to Tactical Redemption."

I raised my eyebrow at her. "What do you have in mind?"

"I think it would be our only chance. Our window of time is pretty short. They tend to drone on and on, but I have a feeling Sebastian won't want the board to stay longer than absolutely necessary. The ropes would be our setback."

I gave her a smirk. "They may be cut proof, but they're not fireproof."

Charlie thought it over and softly replied. "True. And we're using a small Bunsen burner to create the chemical mixture we need. If there was a big enough distraction, I could probably create a chemical explosion." She bit down on her bottom lip. "I couldn't do it before because I don't have the needed upper body strength to carry you."

"Listen to me, Angel. You are doing everything you can. And now that I'm coherent enough, we're going to get through this mess together. Now, if there was a fire, would it be a big enough distraction to bring the guards down?"

Charlie's face grew serious. "I'm not sure. They're literally the brawn but not the brains in this whole shebang. I have no clue if they understand the nuances of what chemical reactions look like. I checked around, and like other places, there is a sprinkler system set up in the event of a fire. If the guards do come, I'm hoping they'll come running and check it out before letting Sebastian know."

I nodded. "What's the plan?"

She took the used gauze, bandage wrappers, and ointment over to the trash. Out of the corner of my eye, I could see she slipped a piece of gauze into her pocket and added a couple more rolls to boot. When she was done, she made her way back to my side. She took out her pen light and proceeded to pretend to check my eyes.

Charlie shrugged and bent down close, her lips brushing my ear. "We're going to light the world on fire."

17

CHARLIE

THE GUARD BROUGHT DOWN MY MEAL AND INCLUDED ONE FOR Sketch as well. A baloney and cheese sandwich on dry white bread, applesauce, and a bottle of water. My lip curled in disgust. I may not be a world class chef, and I may over-boil my spaghetti noodles and burn my grilled cheeses. But even I knew a sandwich needs at least mustard or mayo.

I brought Sketch his food and arranged for him to sit up.

"What's on the menu?" he murmured.

I straightened up and looked at him carefully, knowing full well he wasn't talking about what was on his tray. "They wanted a tweaked version of what I gave you last time."

"Is it ready?" He took a spoonful of applesauce and looked at me expectantly, like we were discussing dinner recipes.

"Pretty much. I've been holding off testing until they get back. It's mostly cocaine with barely any MDMA." I narrowed my eyes and glared at him once the realization hit me. "No."

"Angel—" he started.

"Don't 'Angel' me. Are you fucking out of your mind? You were shot, Sketch. And yes, you're healing really well, but you haven't moved other than trips to the toilet. Your muscle mass is weak. And besides that, I'm not going to push a cocktail this unpredictable into you while we try to get the fuck out of here," I hissed.

"Angel," he soothed. "That's why I need you to do this. You know this is the right thing to do. It's the only way I'll be able to get out of here on my own two feet. You're not going to be able to carry me out of here and defend yourself."

Fuck. He was right. Not necessarily about the cocktail, but about the whole carrying him out. That was the only part of the plan I hadn't been able find a solution to.

"Ugh. I hate this. Fine. You're right. Be ready. We're going to have to do this quickly," I muttered. This must be timed perfectly. I hustled over to the table, with the rope dragging behind me.

Thankfully, the rope they have me tied with was long. If I got far enough away, I could singe the rope apart. I pulled my hair back into a rat's nest on top of my head and sat down in front of the lab and started jotting down notes, looking as if I was dutifully fulfilling my duties. But in reality, I was doing the equations which could create the biggest boom for the least amount of damage.

With Sketch sequestered in the other room, it would be easy to close off his space with the vacuum lock, sealing the aerosol chemicals into this room alone. The sensors would alert the guards, but if we were ready, hopefully we could knock them right out. I was hoping the alarm was attached to the main fire sensor in the building, so when one went off, it would create a domino effect and immediately alert emergency services. That was a big hope.

But how to get it to explode when I'm not close by?

I set to work filling a syringe with the cocktail mixture that would hopefully help get Sketch moving. Slipping the one for Sketch into my right pocket, I pulled on my gas mask and closed the door to Sketch's side of the room. I would have to hurry if I was going to seal off his section in time.

Taking the bottle of melted sodium permanganate, I mixed it in with the phencyclidine I had left over from the last injection I gave. I took two syringes and filled them to the brim, to use as a weapon. With my back to the cameras, I reined in the rope, shorting it up length so I could lift it up to the burner. I held up the nylon rope to the flame. Often nylon releases toxic materials when put to elevated temperatures, and the black smoke emitted rose quickly.

With only a second, the rope snapped, and I was free from the pole. I measured out a length and burnt off another end. I put the beaker of cocktail mix with one end of the rope next to the Bunsen burner and used the rope as a bridge between the two.

As soon as the one end caught on fire, I scrambled to the other side of the room. I managed to sneak inside the other room and close the door before the explosion shook the room. I dropped to my knees and covered my ears. But we were safe. For this second.

Alarms screamed and smoked filled the lab. I hurried to check on Sketch, who was trying to sit up on his own.

"Shoot me up, Angel, and let's get out of here," he muttered, as he dropped his feet to the ground. I helped him stand up and he held out his arm.

I hesitated.

"Angel, we don't have much time," he said with a grimace.

"I hate myself for doing this." I inserted the syringe with the cocktail into his vein. I dropped the empty needle and pulled the extra gas mask over his head. "Do not take this off until we get upstairs."

We heard shouts from beyond the door and maneuvered around the flames to get close. The second the door slid open, Sketch smashed his way through, destroying everyone who got in his path. Once they were down, he picked up the dropped weapons and handed one to me.

"I don't see any windows, so we must be in the basement," I said, my voice muffled by the mask.

"Then we go up." Sketch grabbed my hand and hurried me down the hall, looking for a stairwell.

"Here we go." He pushed open a door. I supported his weight as we limped up the stairs. The alarms continued to blare, and I knew it was only a matter of time before re-enforcements came. We came to a door marked L, and I slowly opened the door to peek out. The hallway was crowded, but everyone was so in a rush to get out of the building, they didn't pay attention.

"Let's go." I braced the door opened and Sketch powered through. With his arm over my shoulder and bracing his weight, we made it a few steps down the hall, slipping in with the mob to the exit.

We were going to make it. I didn't know what we'd do when we got out, but I was sure we'd be able to steal a car or get a ride. We'd be able to get somewhere public or at least touch base with his team.

A sharp bang exploded above us. Screams and shrieks filled the hallway as people ducked and ran in panic. A hand snatched my wrist and yanked me back, severing my hold with Sketch. Three large men moved in, grabbing Sketch by the shoulders, and forcing him down to his knees. Fury crossed his face, and I knew it was only a matter of time before he exploded.

"Did you truly forget our deal, Ms. Parker? Your expertise for your families' lives." The metal blunt end of a gun pressed against my temple. Sebastian's dark words filled my heart with terror. I shot a wide-eye gaze at Sketch. His body turned to stone, and a low growl came from his lips.

"You have about five minutes before this place is crawling

with feds. The alarms are all connected to a separate service which can't be disarmed or disabled. It will notify all emergency services as well as the CDC. If you stick around, you're going to be caught," I said firmly, my voice more confident than I felt. But Sketch watched every move I made. Every tremor in my hand and wobble in my tone. Murder filled his eyes.

"Then we should be going." He took a step back, pulling me back with him.

"Let her fucking go." Sketch's voice was low but rang out through the empty corridor like a bomb.

"You aren't going to be able to stop me." Sebastian motioned with the gun to someone, and it was the break in focus I was looking for. I jammed my elbow into his groin and threw my head back at the same time, reaching up to pull the gun from his hands. Like most men, he underestimated me and my strength and stumbled back. I landed a kick to Sebastian's chin, and he went down. At the same time, Sketch stood up with a roar, grabbing one man and quickly twisting his neck. He grabbed the man's gun and quickly laid out two shots, hitting each man in black with a bullet to the forehead. I quickly flicked off the safety and pointed the gun at Sebastian. I backed up to Sketch, his firm chest giving me the strength I didn't know I needed.

"You think this is it? You think you fucking won? You won't fucking pull the trigger," Sebastian sneered, rising to his feet. His nose was smeared with blood, and I took a bit of satisfaction in knowing I was responsible for his nose job.

"She doesn't have to."

Bang. Bang Bang.

I jumped back at the same time Sketch's arm wrapped around my chest, holding me against him. A bloom of red flowered in the middle of Sebastian's forehead as he hit the ground. Two more red circles grew on his chest and stomach.

Don't scream, don't scream. My eyes bugged out as my chest started heaving. Trying to breathe.

Sketch's body shook and I wasn't sure if it was due to exhaustion or adrenaline, but he grabbed the guns laying at our feet.

"Come on, Angel, we need to get out of here," he urged quietly, trying to pull me away.

But I stood stock still.

"But... why? Why can't ...? Why can't we wait for the police....?" I stammered.

"Police ask way too many questions, and we can't justify killing four men. Let's go." He pulled me out of the emergency exit. The fresh air cleared the fog in my head, and I was able to push the events into a little box to deal with later. Thankfully, it appeared the rest of the occupants were on the other side of the building. We pressed on, hurrying over to the tree line beyond the parking lot. With blood splattering our clothes & skin, he was right. We didn't want to answer any questions.

"We need to find a phone or a car. Preferably both," he muttered once we got out of sight. I maneuvered him to sit against a tree.

I glanced down at myself. "I'll go and see what I can come up with. Don't move."

He rolled his beautiful silver eyes at me. "You're such a comedian," he said dryly.

The combination of the drugs I gave him plus his pain meds were at war with each other, and both were wearing off. I needed to get him expert medical attention.

I hurried back down to the parking lot, trying to use my short stature for good. I ducked along the line of cars, testing each door to see if we would luck out. Thankfully, the door to a Lexus did open. I climbed in, and searched to see if there were keys, a fob, tablet, or anything that could be used to get us the help we needed.

Jackpot. After searching the trunk, I came up with a cell phone and a gym bag with a bunch of hockey equipment. They even had a kit for sports injuries. Someone's forgetfulness was our gain. I grabbed the phone, the kit, and the extra set of men's clothes and hustled back over to the trees.

My heart faltered as I took him in. Leaning against the tree, Sketch's face was ashen and covered in sweat.

"Shit. You probably strained your leg." I rummaged through the kit and found an instant ice pack. I cracked and twisted it, before helping Sketch shimmy his pants down.

"Keep the ice pack against your leg. Hopefully, this phone doesn't have a passcode." I pressed the on button and held my breath, silently thanking the Gods there wasn't one. "We're good. I'll call Cole."

Thankfully, Cole's number has remained the same since he was a teenager, so I dialed it by memory and crossed my fingers it wasn't tapped by the Syndicate.

"What."

A sob caught in my throat, and I smiled, hearing his voice.

"Cole."

"Charlie? Thank God. Are you okay? Where the hell are you? Is Sketch with you?"

"We got away, but they have eyes on everyone else. You need to keep them safe," I gasped out. With everything, I didn't even think of the ramifications of what would happen with my family.

"We got them secure. There's no way the Syndicate has eyes on them. Where are you?"

I let out the breath I had been holding. "I don't know." I looked around the area we were in. "We blew up a lab. Check the scanners and your contacts with the FBI. There should have been alarms going all over the place."

"Check the fucking scanners and get Sims on the phone," he yelled to someone. Pause. "A storm of federal agents are about to rain down on a town outside Westminster. That's probably you. Sims is already in route and ten minutes away. We're rolling out now and will meet you at Tactical Redemption. Keep low and keep the phone on. Zeke is tracking your coordinates now and he'll meet you right there. We got you, sis."

Tears of relief streamed down my cheeks. "Bring medical. Sketch isn't looking too good."

"I still look better than he does," Sketch mumbled.

"I heard that. The fucker. We're on our way."

I disconnected the call and moved over to Sketch. He was shivering so I helped him into the sweatshirt, then settled in next to him, wrapping my arms around him.

"Just try to stay awake, Seth," I murmured, rubbing up and down his arms.

"I like it when you call me that." His voice started to slur, and my panic raised.

"Yeah? How did you get the name Sketch?" I needed to keep him talking.

"When we were overseas, there was a lot of downtime. So, I sketched. I sketched out my sleeves, tattoo ideas for other guys, even drawings for kids in the villages we were in." He sighed. "I sketched a lot of death. Graphic ways to kill those who we were fighting against."

"It's an outlet for you."

"It's more conducive than slitting the throats of pedos and drug lords." He ran his thumb against the back of my hand.

"Did you sketch in rehab?"

"Yeah. For a bit. Although my drawings for a bit were too macabre for the doctors there. I was in there for a voluntary thirty-day hold. I'd like to say I wasn't an addict, but I was too damn close to becoming one." Sketch lifted his head off my chest and gazed into my eyes. "That's all your brother, by the way."

My eyes widened. "Yeah? He took you to rehab?"

"Yeah. Said the only way I could build Tactical Redemption is if I was clean. He wouldn't be business partners with a junkie. He needed to know I had his back when missions went south."

"Is that where your mom is?" I asked gently.

"No. She's in upstate New York. She has a sister and aunt up there. Since she won't take my calls, I needed to be able to have someone keep an eye on her."

"That's good she has them. And she knows you're there for her too, when she's ready," I said softly, running my fingernails gently against his scalp.

"Angel, if you don't want me to fall asleep, you better stop." I heard the grin in his voice and smiled.

"Yeah, we need you coherent when the team gets here."

A pair of headlights pulled into the parking lot. Unlike the others who migrated over to the building, this one pulled in closer to the trees. As if they were looking for someone. Just then, the phone chimed with a text.

"Cole texted and said Sims is here." I adjusted Sketch off my body and rose to my feet. Pulling up a six-foot-six man who weighed over two-hundred fifty pounds was a bit difficult, but thankfully he managed to shift his weight. A dark large SUV pulled up and a familiar build got out.

"You know, I don't get paid enough for this shit," Rick grumbled, as he ambled into the trees.

"Fuck no, pretty boy. They don't pay you nearly enough to do the amount of ass kissing you do," Sketch snarked.

"You're lucky I like Charlie, or I'd leave your ass here." He wrapped Sketch's arm over his shoulders and together we were able to bring him to the SUV and lay him in the back seat. I hopped in behind the passenger seat and adjusted Sketch's head on my lap while Sims got behind the wheel. Within minutes, we were on the highway. I called Cole to check in.

"Hey, Sketch needs medical. Well, more medical than I can give him. Do you have someone on hand?"

"Maybe he finally needed to have some sense knocked into him."

"Ha. He has as much sense as you do. Seriously, what's the plan?" My fingers ran over Sketch's scalp. Sketch heaved a heavy sigh as I felt a bit of tension roll off him.

"Sims knows where he's going, and don't worry. We'll take good care of him. Well, maybe not too good of care since he's into my baby sister and all." Cole's voice gave a bit of violence, and I rolled my eyes.

"Give me a break. You didn't do this whole caveman big brother routine to Kate."

"Ask Noah next time what happened when he came to my house after him and Kate broke up. Boy almost met the end of my rifle."

"Whatever. I'll smack you upside the head when I see you."

"Love you, Shortcake." His voice was low and gruff.

"Love you too, dork."

Sims handed me a bottle of water. "We're about twenty out from TR. Before they bombard you with questions, I need to ask if there's anything you can give the feds. I'll keep it anonymous."

I knew he understood what my brothers and TR were up to. They made no secret about the tactics they're willing to take since the Syndicate had made this personal. I glanced down at Sketch, who shook his head.

"Plausible deniability," Sketch muttered.

"Fuck!" Rick banged on the steering wheel. "You have to give me more than that. It's bullshit and you know it. This can't be vigilante fucking justice. We need to do this shit by the book. That way we keep this from getting bigger. We need evidence and leads to actually shut this shit down."

I bit my bottom lip. "Angel," Sketch warned, his eyebrow arching.

"If we can't trust Sims, then we're fucking screwed anyway, Sketch," I shot back. Sketch groaned and rubbed his face.

"Fine."

"Bowen Biotech is partnered with the Syndicate. With the fed's help, Bowen is getting the research and the patents. The Syndicate is taking those patents and making stronger, more lethal concoctions altering the chemical reactions in the user's head. It's getting them hooked faster and for longer."

"And why did they want you?" Rick demanded.

"Because I helped create the formula and chemical library. I was the missing piece." I shrugged weakly.

"This makes total sense." Rick rubbed his forehead with his fingers and groaned.

"What do you mean?"

Rick peered into the rearview, first glancing at me and then gestured to Sketch. "I'll explain fully when we get to TR."

That didn't bode well.

I looked down at Sketch, whose eyes were closed. "Sketch?"

"Yes, Angel?"

"Don't die on me," I warned. He grabbed my hand from his head, kissed my palm, then placed it on his chest.

"I just got you. You can't get rid of me that easily."

18

SKETCH

ONCE WE GOT TO TACTICAL REDEMPTION, IT WAS PURE CHAOS. A plan was in motion and a location had been found. We knew where they were. All we needed to do was to get ready and hit them when they least expected it.

Thankfully, Kate wasn't injured. Somehow, they got into our system and were able to mimic the IP and created a fake video. Kate wasn't even in the area. She had been coordinating with Cole and Summer's brother on securing the families and any other innocents from the cartel. Summer survived the crash and made the necessary introductions between us and her brother's MC. Wayne "Hercules" Murphy and his club, Red Scorpions, came out from San Diego to provide security and keep the families secure in a safe house in St. Mary's.

The Red Scorpions took Charlie back to the safe house once they dropped off their crew with us. Unlike before, she didn't fight me on leaving. But, of course, that's when she dropped a bomb. I carried her to the car and strapped her in. She pulled me down and gave me a hard kiss.

. . .

"Go do your thing and come back to me," she whispered, as she gripped the front of my shirt. I smirked and crashed my lips to her lips, my hands cupping her jaw. Her soft lips tasted like the strawberries she was eating earlier. My tongue swept hers and she let out a low moan. I could kiss this woman all day every day, and I was already regretting the idea of her leaving. I slowed my kisses and broke apart, pressing my forehead to hers, our breath as one.

"I'll get you as soon as I can," I rumbled. I took one more kiss, then stepped back and shut the door. She put the window down as I walked back to the warehouse.

"Oh, and Sketch?" I turned at her voice. "No pressure or anything, but I've been in love with you for the last two years. So, you better be safe and come back to me."

My jaw dropped and I almost tripped over my feet. "We're going to have to talk about your little statement when this whole shitshow is over. But yeah, Angel, I love you too." Her beautiful smile lit up my darkness and I watched her leave until I couldn't see the lights anymore.

As soon as I walked back into the warehouse, Noah called my name.

"If you have any friends you want to bring out to play, call them now. Shit is about to get real," Noah said in a grim greeting.

I smirked and pulled out my phone, scrolling to the one person I knew who would be up for something at this level.

I rattled off the address for Tactical Redemption and gave him an hour of a window and hung up without another word. Knowing the distance he was going to have to travel, an hour was going to make his deadline pretty tight, but I figured if anyone could put the pedal to the metal, it would be Jones.

Forty minutes later, I was outside smoking a cigarette and Jones's lifted tank of a truck pulled in right in. He got out and flicked his cigarette to the ground.

Jones looked the same as he did when we parted ways five years ago. He stood at six-three, with a mane of long black hair and deep brown skin, could easily bench me in a deadlift. He was an enemy to all and a friend to few. I had met him in the jungles in Latin America, when our groups had crossed paths on a drug cartel raid. Jones's method of madness gelled easily with mine. We took pride in our work, and I was happy to call him a brother in arms.

"Glad to see you," I said, walking over to him. I shook his hand and gave him a half hug. "You ready to get this show started?" I received a nod in response and led him into the building. Burger and Otis, two of our guards, stood waiting in the alcove, ready to prevent anyone who didn't have the proper access from gaining entrance. I gave them both a nod and I walked toward the back of the warehouse. The rest of the crews were either getting the equipment ready or looking at the maps.

"Jones, meet everyone. Everyone, meet Jones," I said, gesturing widely as I made my way over to Noah in the corner.

"I've got a few acquaintances who want to join in the fun. They've got some personal beef with Elias Cruz," Jones mentioned. "I'll hit them with the coordinates once we are on our way."

"I think everyone has personal beef with that psychopath," Toren replied, tossing comm gear into a bag. "Even though those fights are off the books, he does every dirty fucking deed there is to make sure they don't get up."

"Oh, it sounds like I would have a wonderful time with him." The idea of beating the shit out of someone so vile made me smile.

"You're just as fucked up as he is," Jones scoffed, and I shrugged. I mean, he wasn't wrong.

"You good?" Noah asked quietly.

I shrugged. Benji stitched up the hole in my leg and I was given a nice painkiller. It barely took the edge off, but I couldn't think about it anymore. It was past time to put bodies on the ground. Exhaustion was taking hold, but I knew the prep work needed to be done. Zeke walked up and threw down a packet of paper.

"What's this?" I asked, sliding my knife over the tab to open it.

"Stock receipts. Shares of Bowen Biotech went through the roof today. They're buying all the stock up before they announce the drug to the world," Zeke replied. He slunk in his chair and pulled off his glasses, rubbing his eyes.

"You good?" I asked. I did care, but we were going through the paces, and I didn't want to have to call for a medic if I didn't have to.

"Your concern overwhelms me," he replied, giving me the middle finger. He glanced over at Charlie across the room. "Nessa Bradshaw and Michael Van Buren were found dead with bullet holes in their brains. Dr. Weber is missing. Along with Sebastian Cruz."

"Wait? What? No. I shot the motherfucker in the head myself. He can't be alive," I shot back, my mind retracing everything we did.

"The guy you shot in the hall was a man named Drac Cruz. They're cousins, but him and Sebastian are practically twins. He was put in place as a stand-in for Sebastian whenever the need arises." Zeke pointed to the image on the top page. "This was taken last night, at some fancy gala in Helsinki."

"Geez, how many Cruzes are going to be coming out of the woodwork?" Benji asked, as he read over the paper. He flipped through the rest of the pictures and information.

"What the fuck?" he whispered as his face paled.

"What's up?" Cole ambled over and took a look over Benji's shoulder.

He pointed to a woman in the corner of an image. Even though it was a side profile, the image was plain as day. A woman we all knew well. I looked over at Cole and watched the myriad of emotions cross his face.

"Could she have been undercover, doing a bust?" Benji suggested. He was the one who always thought of the silver linings but there's no way you could put a positive spin on this.

"She's a bounty hunter with no jurisdiction overseas. She wouldn't be laughing it up in a dress at a fucking party overseas, when she was supposed to be in Atlanta." He looked at the picture one last time, then turned to Zeke. "I want her location and ETA on where she's going next."

Zeke nodded once and got to work on his computer. After a few clicks, he looked up.

"She's on the road, headed this way," Zeke replied, checking the monitors from the speed cameras.

"Anyone following?" asked Noah. He shoved the cartridge of ammo into his pocket.

"Negative," Zeke replied.

"Cole, help me out. Do you believe she is a danger?" Noah replied intently.

Cole shook his head and shrugged. "I have no fucking clue. I don't know anything about her anymore," he replied grimly.

"Hey, we have more company coming," Zeke called out.

"You just said negative on the company," Toren snapped.

"That was before she passed Waugh Chapel. Now she has a tail," Zeke replied. His fingers flew across keyboards and his monitors brought up the cameras from the church on the corner two miles away.

"How many are we looking at?" Noah barked.

"Five cars deep."

"Cole, I love you brother, but this is now a bigger threat." I hustled over to the weapons locker. "Arm up, we got incoming," I bellowed.

The rest of the guys shot into motion. I loaded ammo into my AK and shoved extra magazines into my pocket. After I secured my knives to my body, I grabbed one of the guns and headed up to the roof. Unless they already had the drop on us, we would know when Tracie and the Syndicate were close.

"She's coming in hot, ETA, ninety seconds," Zeke's voice came through on comms.

Tactical Redemption was the only building on this road for a reason. I didn't need strangers or thrill seekers trying to be a hot shot. We had motion sensors on the roads, the same ones I put on the road leading to the Turner's compound. There were no other reasons for vehicles to be traveling down this road.

I laid on my stomach and got into position. I had the perfect vantage point to take anyone out. Looking through the night vision scope, a familiar blue Corvette spun into the parking lot, kicking up the gravel as she came through. Tracie lunged out of the car, but her seat belt tangled around her, slowing her down.

"Cole!" she screeched. She struggled with the seat belt before she was able to get loose. She ran up to the door and started banging. "Please let me in! They're coming for you; they know where you are." I heard the door open.

"What the fuck are you doing, Trace?" He said it slowly with no emotion.

"I'm here to warn you. The Syndicate is out for blood," she panted. I couldn't see much from my lookout, but I could tell by Cole's attitude he wasn't having it.

"How do you know what they're planning or doing?" His voice took on the tone very few get to hear. Cole normally keeps it under lock and key, until he unleashes it on someone who deserves it.

"Let me in. I can explain," she panted.

"No." The single word had immediate impact and Tracie crumbled to her knees.

"They have my mom, Cole. They were holding her hostage in a nursing home," she said weakly.

"What did you do, Tracie?" Cole demanded.

"I didn't have a choice!" she cried out.

Cole got right in her face. "For the last fucking time. What. The. Fuck. Did. You. *Do?*"

The hair on the back of my neck bristled and I turned to look. No cars, no drones. But wait....?

Shit. I whistled loudly. Cole jerked his head and yanked Tracie into the building. "We got movement coming from the field," I whispered into the comms.

"How many?"

"About ten. Nope, make it twelve." Suddenly, the area to the west of us, the pasture for the farm behind my property, lit up. Multiple SUVs and trucks were flying across the pasture at a high rate of speed.

"Shit. Multiple vehicles heading in from the west. Here we go." This was going to be a bloodbath. I was looking forward to it.

19

SKETCH

Looking through my night-vision goggles, I started popping the vehicles, first through the windshield and then for the engine compartment. I took three vehicles out, getting direct shots and taking out the drivers.

The rest of the team had taken up in the shadows, with Neil from Alpha team on the opposite side of the roof.

Despite the shots from the roof, the influx of cars didn't stop. We picked them off one by one. A shadow on the roof caught my eye. Before he could do anything, I raised my gun and shot the intruder in the leg. He fell in agony, writhing in pain.

"Stop being a pussy." I walked over and put him in a hog-tie before cuffing him with zip ties, grabbing the lone weapon he had, a Glock. "That will keep you from doing anything stupid." I rummaged through his pockets to find any other weapons, but only found half of a blunt and a gum wrapper.

"You don't pack well for an ambush, do you?" I quipped and I kicked him in the stomach.

"Fuck you," he spat. His beady brown eyes were full of hate.

"Oh, I'm going to have fun with you tonight," I said with a smile, smacking him on the cheek.

I ran over to the ledge of the roof and looked down through my scope, hitting those I knew weren't friendly. Once the outside had been secured, I hustled inside toward the rear of the facility while Neil watched our backs on the roof. A large behemoth lumbered toward me, too close for me to shoot. I ducked down and threw my weight into a punch to his junk. He stumbled and when I rose, I took my knife and sliced his neck in an upward motion. I caught movement out of the corner of my eye and grabbed the neck of another man. Palming the handle, I slashed the blade across his jugular, enjoying the splatter of blood. The heavy weight of the body dropped, and I glanced up to see three figures in the shadows of the gym, trying to get into our weapons vault.

I saw red and picked up my AK. I fired off three rounds, hitting two of the three men.

The third man turned around, with his hands in the air.

"I have answers. I'll tell you everything," he whimpered. *Finally, someone useful.*

He dropped his gun and slid it over to us. I stalked toward him and jerked his wrists around his back, cuffing him with zip ties. I nodded at Trey, who hauled the loser away.

"I think he's the last of them. We have another up on the roof. They both can go in the playroom." I looked over at Cole. "Do we have an ID on these asshats?"

Cole didn't answer, his eyes glued to the camera monitor in horror.

"Cole?" I went over to the monitor to see what caught his attention and immediately cursed.

"Everyone at the front. Now!" I demanded into the mic of our comms. I reached out and clasped Cole's shoulder. "We got her, man. Don't worry."

We rushed to the other side of the warehouse toward the

front door. If we could take this fight outside, it could give us leverage.

We were thirty yards away from the front door, when it opened. Without a care in the world, an older man with a wrinkly face, bald head, and swollen hands waltzed into the front door of our facility, dragging Tracie in behind him. Ten more men broke out behind them. How the hell did they get her when she was already inside?

"I was wondering where you went off to," Cole said roughly, his finger barely resting on the trigger of his Glock. "You know this isn't going to work out the way you hoped it would."

"This young lady was nice enough to come out and escort me in," the man with no neck answered, in a genteel way.

Tracie kept her gaze downward as tears ran down her cheeks. Guilt and shame weighed on her shoulders heavily. She was defeated and resigned to whatever was about to happen.

"Mind telling me why you have your fat mitts on our friend?" I asked, aiming my gun. The team around me did the same. I snuck a glance at Cole. His anger and malice rolled off his body in waves.

"I figure we could make a deal, seeing as how I have something you may want." The voice next to hers had an accent, but I couldn't place the country.

"Who the fuck are you?" Noah demanded.

"You can call me John. I'm an emissary of the Syndicate. I'm here to bring a peace offering, of sorts." He gestured to Tracie. "But I must let you know. This gift is a bit tainted. You see, we are so close to success, and it's all thanks to this lovely lady." He looked down at Tracie with an evil smile. "But we have no use for her any longer. We'd like to exchange her for another."

My gut tightened. Betrayal rocked our team before and to have it done yet again, and by someone we considered family, was even worse. I checked Cole out of the corner of my eye and saw he came to the realization at the same time. His grip tightened on the Glock in his hand.

"What do you want in return?" Cole growled.

"The girl for this one." John dragged Tracie in front of him, holding on to her wrist. Only then did she look up and face us briefly before her gaze returned to the ground.

There was only one girl they could want and that would happen over my dead body.

I growled, my grip tightening on the handle of the gun and my finger resting on the trigger. "No fucking deal."

"That wasn't a request. We could keep both. To make the deal more palatable, we can guarantee no harm would come to the girl Thomas is looking to bring on. Your families would remain untouched."

"Well, John. Tell your boss we said no fucking deal." Cole's cold response had a bite and Tracie jerked, like she was stabbed in the heart. He refused to look at her and stared directly at the man with no neck.

She momentarily lifted her head to look at us. With eyes full of sorrow and pleads for forgiveness, she mouthed, "I'm sorry."

Tracie raised her chin and threw her head back, smashing his jaw with her head. Her hands were no longer restrained so she swung around and with everything she had, she jammed the heel of her hand into the man's nose.

"You fucking bitch!" he sputtered as blood dripped down his face. His hands flew to his nose, and he let Tracie go. She flew out of his reach and scrambled to cross the distance between us.

As soon as Tracie was out of his way, Cole raised his gun and pulled the trigger twice, with both bullets lodging in John's forehead. Bullets started flying as our team pushed forward, while we exchanged gunfire, using the pillars and equipment as cover. The other side were sitting ducks with nothing to save them.

I looked over and saw a body laying between us and them.

"Fuck!" Cole shouted. I gave cover while he scrambled to where Tracie fell, then dragged her behind a wall. As soon as the shooting started, it ended. The silence was deafening.

Bodies littered the floor and blood was all over the place.

Cole frantically ripped apart her thin shirt covered in blood and found the wound, right below her collarbone. "What the hell did you do, Trace?" he muttered as he held the shirt to her wound. Benji skidded back to their side with the medical kit in hand.

"I'm sorry," she gasped, clenching her jaw.

"You're not going to die on me so tell the truth. What the fuck did you do?" Cole gritted out, putting pressure on her chest.

Tracie closed her eyes. "I downloaded a tracker onto your encrypted phone so they could find the location of any calls you made. That's how they were able to find them."

"That bullet better not kill you because I'm going to," I growled. Rage filled me and fury colored my vision. This entire shitshow was her fault.

"When?" Cole seethed. He sat back on his knees and stared at her like he didn't recognize her. And he didn't. I don't think anyone knew her at all.

"The day after they left your house, after the accident. You made a call then got into the shower. It was the only time your phone was left unlocked," Tracie whispered.

"Motherfucker!" Cole shouted. He jumped up and stalked away, leaving Tracie in Benji's hands. He turned back around. "What the fuck did you do that for? My family took you in, made you a part of us. They loved you. I fucking loved you. And this is how you pay them back? By putting my sister in the hands of a fucking cartel!" he thundered, pacing back and forth.

Tracie's body started shaking with sobs. "I'm sorry. Baby, I am so sorry. Really. They had my mother, and it was the only thing I could do. I thought they would be safe because Sketch wouldn't let anything happen to your sister," she bawled.

"Hey man, we need to get her to the hospital," Benji spoke up calmly. His voice was what Cole needed to break through his veil of rage.

"She's going to live, right Benji?" Cole demanded.

Benji continued to pack her wound while he assessed the damage. "Shit. I don't know. We need to get her to an ER quickly."

Cole shook his head. "Gunshot wounds automatically call for a police investigation."

"Please take me to the ER, Cole. I swear I won't say anything," Tracie pleaded. She grimaced in pain.

Cole knelt down and got into her face. "No."

Tracie opened her mouth to speak but Cole cut her off. "I'm going to let you suffer the way you made us suffer, you fucking bitch," Cole snarled. "Toren, call Sims and tell him we have bodies and one severely injured. He can take the grifter to get medical treatment. I don't fucking care if she lives or dies."

Noah warned, "Cole..."

"Fuck off, Noah," Cole growled, as he stormed out.

Noah sighed. The pain for his teammate and brother was evident but as our leader, he had to do the right thing. He nodded to me and Zeke, and it was time to get our new guests in their right spots.

But first.

I knelt to Tracie and put my face close to hers. I gripped her chin painfully and forced her to look at me. Tracie's body trembled and eyes widened. Not from shock or pain. But from fear.

"Do you want to know what I do with people who try to

harm what's mine?" My tone may have been soft, but the violence and malice were there. Her body froze at my words and a cold smile grew on my face and the pressure I put on her jaw tightened. "You probably don't, since they're not around to talk about all the fun games we play. You may have thought you knew us. But you really haven't met me, have you?" The urge to crush her jaw consumed me and I wanted to give in. "You don't deserve to live. You deserve to be in my basement with the other fools who tried to go after mine."

I opened my mouth to say more, but lucky for her, Toren came over.

"Sims was notified and is on his way here to get the traitor," Toren said. His deep brown eyes narrowed, and he gestured to Tracie. "Consider yourself warned. Cole has a decent heart and won't let Sketch play with you. You're lucky. You fucked up. If it had been any other person, lover or not, you can bet your ass you would never be found."

I smiled widely and pushed her chin away, then stood up. Her shoulders shook with sobs and regret.

"Sketch, get with Zeke and bring the visitors down to the basement," Noah called from the door.

I smirked, looking in Tracie's eyes. Terror came across her face. I'm sure she figured out my nasty little hobby. I looked around at those who were left. Zeke already had brought two of our new friends down to the subbasement. I picked up the last one who was semi-coherent and threw him over my shoulder.

"You piss on me, and I'll make you drink from your own dick," I growled and made my way to the stairs. The guy on my shoulder squirmed and twisted, but he was a fool if he thought he could get away. That I would show mercy to him like I did to Tracie. That's not going to happen.

Once on the sub-level, Zeke lowered the three meat hooks from the ceiling and helped me put our friends on each one.

The florescent lights and the ceramic tile made the room ultra-bright and sterile.

"Do you have everything you need?" Zeke asked. I grunted in the affirmative, and he jogged up the stairs and slammed the door shut. While Zeke was no pussy, he wasn't a fan of my methods. Taking my time, I slipped on my hazmat suit and stepped over to the wood chipper, turning it on. The chipper was a good motivational tool. People tend to talk when they're given a choice.

All three men were gagged, struggling with the zip ties. While I despised talking, it was unavoidable.

"Fucker one, two, and three. Let's get started." I grabbed the shirt of fucker one, yanked him forward and pulled the gag out of his mouth. "Who ordered the raid?"

"I... I..." he stuttered. The sound of liquid began hitting the floor. *Fucking hell.* I rolled my eyes.

"YOU'RE PATHETIC." I walked over to the stainless-steel table and picked up a sledgehammer. Without any lead-up or banter, I swung the hammer and smashed it into his right knee as hard as I could. The sound of bones breaking mixed in with his agonizing screams. I took a step to the left and did the same thing against the other knee. The fucker screamed, his molten face turning purple while his legs arched awkwardly inwards. Almost too easy, but he needed to be the incentive for the others to talk.

I stepped over to fucker one and watched him dangle from the hook, his screaming diminished to groans and whimpers. I gave the look that normally strikes the fear in others, with the exception of a certain strawberry-shortcake.

"Last chance."

"Bu—" Fucker one stammered.

"Fuck it. You're not worth my time." With two hands, I

swung the hammer and crashed it against his temple. Brain matter, teeth, and blood went flying. I tossed the dirty tool down onto the floor and looked at the other two.

"Who's next?"

Fucker three started blabbing against his gag. *See? They just needed incentive.*

I snatched off his gag and he couldn't hold his words in.

"We don't get names; we got the orders through John. Lately, we're getting mixed messages when it comes to orders being carried out. There is a lot of infighting too. It's not only the low-level bosses either. It's the leaders of the Syndicate and the Cruz cartel. The Cruz cartel oversees the distribution and sales for North America. Your girl was supposed to put their business back in the black."

"You mean put the super drugs on the streets." My eyebrow raised.

The man nodded vigorously, thinking any good answer would get him out of his current predicament. "I heard the cartel wanted a larger piece of the drug cut. Thomas Cruz was not too happy with the Syndicate getting in their way. Thomas was moving into another cartel's territory, and he was supposed to give a good faith gift, better merchandise for a larger percentage of the share. A good portion of whatever the girl made was supposed to go to Columbia to another cartel, one Thomas is trying to take over. But since it didn't get through, Thomas looked like a fool and was on the hook for over three hundred million dollars." Spittle came out of his mouth and his receding hairline was soaked in sweat.

I kept my face blank, but this information was gold. Any fracture from within would only benefit us. I raised my chin at the last fucker remaining. "This the truth?"

The other guy shrugged. "I wasn't a part of the drug area. I just moved deals with John."

"The bloated blob upstairs?"

"Yeah," he mumbled, and his eyes shot over to his partner.

"Fuck this. Time's up." I grabbed my machete with the carbon blade, and before he could make a protest, made a deep slice across fucker two's swollen stomach. I'm not sure which sounded better. The screams or the sound of someone's innards slopping to the ground. But either way, I was here for it. It only lasted a second and then his voice went quiet.

I glanced over at the last one. He shook his head. "Please, don't. I'm a good asset to have. I can get more information," he babbled, his words tripping over each other.

"What more information do you have for me?" I gave no reaction, but I was skeptical. His information so far has been decent, but I haven't had the chance to verify it yet. For all I know, he could be blowing smoke up my ass just to keep himself alive.

"I know where all the hideouts are, and where they're making the product. And where they have the product stashed."

I raised my eyebrows expectantly.

"Oh...yeah...I guess. Wait. You know there are three different types of products they sell. Guns, drugs, and people. They're all spread out, so if one gets busted, the others are okay. I know they have an incubation place with babies and moms who are pregnant. That's off I-81, near the West VA/Kentucky state line in a cabin, near George Washington Forest."

"What about the drugs?"

"I don't know," he mumbled. I sighed and stepped toward him. "Wait. I think it's in the south somewhere. Texas or Vegas maybe? They were making it up here, but their primary location was near the Southern border."

Huh. Good to know. "Anything else you want to add?" I tapped the machete blade against the steel table.

"Um...Um..."

Time to get this over with. He didn't have any information.

"I'm going to do something I rarely do. I'm going to give you the choice. I can either kill you now or after you watch your friend get chopped and diced into pig food."

His eyes widened and he started stuttering but couldn't answer the question. His face turned a lovely shade of green at the thought of watching his friend going into the chipper.

"Thanks for the info, fucker three. It's been real fun." I took the machete and did a vertical cut, from the man's throat to his flaccid cock. It didn't kill him, but he passed out from the pain. *Sigh.* Normally, I'd take my time and enjoy this. But now it feels like it's dragging on. *Maybe I'm losing my edge?* Who knows?

I decided to hurry fucker three's demise and cut his carotid artery with the antique knife. While he was bleeding out, I turned on the chipper and started slicing up the appendages of the previous two, beginning with the feet and making my way up. Each limb and piece were tossed into the industrial size chipper. The output went directly into a steel hazmat barrel full of lye. Less mess and clean up that way. Except heads. Heads went right into the tub.

I pushed play on my playlist and let Killswitch Engage overtake the sounds of the chipper going. I normally took my time, but I was exhausted, and I wanted to see my girl.

After our guests were thoroughly taken care of and the bin of lye was set aside, I pulled down the hose and sprayed the entire room and chipper with bleach. Since there was a drain in the middle of the room, all water and solutions flowed down into the sewers. The barrel of lye will be transported to the farm behind this property, where it can be disposed of.

After everything was cleaned and I was disinfected, I made my way up the stairs. The majority of the crew had left, and all that remained were Jones, Toren, Cole, and Noah.

"Did the guys in blue show up?" I asked Noah, coming up to his side.

"Yeah. They just left," Noah muttered. He turned to me. "Did you get anything from our visitors?"

I relayed the info I received. Not much we didn't already know, but it was something more.

"We'll take the Southern border. I'm meeting a crew down there in a few days, but we'll add this to the to-do list," Jones stated. He pulled me into a half hug and said, "I'll touch base when we get something good."

"Thanks for helping out. If you and your team need anything, we'll be there," Noah said, shaking Jones's hand.

"Oh, Sketch knows. I always collect my debts." His scarred, weathered face broke out in a grin.

Fuck. I'm sure whatever it is, it'll be nuts. I walked with Jones out to the parking lot and lit up a cigarette.

"You good, homie?" he asked, not even looking in my direction.

I took a deep drag and exhaled the smoke slowly. "Yeah, Jonesy. I am." He smacked my chest with his bit mitts.

"Good." He paused, gazing out into the darkness of the fields. "I'm going to call in that favor."

My eyebrows shot up. "Fuck. You didn't even give me a tug first," I replied.

"You wish. I have some girls needing transport back over the border," he said quietly.

"Back into Mexico or back into the States?" I questioned.

"From Guadalajara to Vancouver."

I let out a low whistle. "That's three thousand miles."

Jonesy turned my way, and I swore I saw the devil in his eyes. "Yep."

"Your retrievals are normally of the powder and pill variety. Not flesh and bone."

"Yeah. Well. Sometimes you have to deviate from the usual bullshit," he mused. Jones's face hardened and his jaw clenched. Just how this situation was personal for me, this retrieval is definitely personal for him.

I clasped him on his shoulder. "Whatever you need, I got you. Let me get my girl settled first."

Jones chuckled. "Yeah. Meet me at the field in Bowie on Saturday. We'll ride out then."

I nodded my head as Noah and Toren walked out.

Jones said his goodbyes to them, then I watched as he got into his heavy-duty truck and peeled out.

"He's interesting," Noah said softly.

I made a noncommittal noise. Jones was...something all right. "He called me in on the trip he's taking down South. Wheels up on Saturday for about three weeks." Noah barely reacted, but I saw his lower jaw tic.

"You going?"

I rubbed the back of my neck and grimaced at the pain. The adrenaline was wearing off and now every ache and bruise came back with a vengeance. "Yeah. As much as I want to take a break, the need to bleed their skulls dry is more intense. I need to see this through."

"I get it. And I'm sure I don't have to tell you that if you break her heart, Kate will kill you without remorse," Noah replied. I snorted. Kate could threaten me all she wanted, but she didn't have to worry, now that I have Charlie, I'm sure as shit not letting her go.

"Everything is locked up. Weapons room is alarmed & locked," Toren rumbled, the keys to his black Indian Scout motorcycle in hand.

"Wrap up briefing tomorrow at ten. Get some rest," Noah called out. Toren responded by giving him the finger and reviving the engine before kicking up the dust and gravel and driving away.

"You're going to make us come in tomorrow?" I gave the

side-eye. It was already three in the morning, and we were all wiped.

Noah snorted. "Uh yeah. I don't care you're banged up and got a trip to plan for. We need to hot wash this while this is fresh in our minds."

"What happened with Cole?" I asked, shoving my hands into the pouch of my hoodie.

"Cole bounced. I don't expect to see him for a while, but hopefully he'll show his face for the wedding. He'll break Kate's heart if he doesn't. I'm going to check in with him in a day or so, see where his mind's at," Noah said grimly.

"He'll be there," I said confidently. Cole needed to get his shit straight before coming home and dealing with the aftermath. Tracie really did a number on him. "While I'm gone and Cole's not around, call Shane if you need help with TR, especially with the business part of it at least."

Noah smirked. "Yes, Dad. Sheesh, it's like you're leaving your kid for the first time."

I rolled my eyes and smacked him in the stomach. "With Cole MIA and me down south, you're damned right I'm going to be like a motherfucking hen." I paused as the image of beautiful green eyes flashed. "Whose got Charlie?"

"I've been in contact with Kate and we're working on the arrangements now. I'd like for her to stay with us; it would make everything easier. At least until we're able to control the situation and have a plan in place," Noah replied. "Kate is going to bring Jax back to our place. Do you want us to take Murray too?"

"Yeah. I'll bring him on Saturday before I hit the field." I limped over to the truck, the muscle in my thigh screaming in pain. "Now take me back to my place so I can go get my girl."

20

CHARLIE

Apparently, I was not a fan of something called downtime. I hated it. I fully blamed the bastards at Bowen Biotech. Because of them and their shady as fuck business dealings, I didn't have a job. The career I worked my ass off for was in limbo. While the federal investigations are going on, no one wanted to hire a potential employee with this sort of baggage. Oh yes, I was the blackmailed chemist who was kidnapped by a large organization of kingpins and warlords. *That would look so awesome on my resume.*

Since I didn't have a job, I didn't have the money to pay rent. Which worked out for the best, because Summer and Casey finally realized what was in their face the entire time. Once the MC brought everyone back from their safe house, Summer ran right into his arms. I was so happy for them, and I knew they'd be good for each other.

For better or worse, our lives changed. Living in that small row house with Summer didn't feel right anymore, so I packed up my stuff and moved into Sketch's private sanctuary on the hill. Cole checked in from the west coast where he had hunted down some leads. We should see him in a month, since he promised Kate he'd be home in time for her wedding. Cole's dog, Jax, had made himself right at home and became Murray's best bud. They have been great bodyguards and snuggle bunnies, but nothing compared to the man I was waiting for.

After the craziness that was the fight at TR, Sketch drove two hours to the small town where our safe house was located. It was a good thing the guys in the MC knew Sketch, because he barged into the house hell-bent on finding something. Well, to find me. As soon as he appeared, we crashed into each other. His lips ravaged mine, and he wouldn't let me go. He picked me up and wrapped my legs around his waist. With a nod to the guy out front but not a single word spoken, he waltzed me out of the front and put me in the front seat of his Challenger. He hurried over to the driver's side and pulled me to his side. We pulled out of the driveway quickly, his hand gripping the inside of my thigh. The simple gesture made my core ache.

Not three minutes on the road, Sketch yanked the steering wheel to the right and pulled onto some dirt road, surrounded by trees. My seat belt was unbuckled, and I was straddling his lap within seconds. Our lips fused together, only separating for a moment while he tore my shirt over my head. Sketch's need to touch me was as bad as mine was. I needed to feel him. To taste him. We couldn't keep our hands off each other.

"Fuck, I need to be inside you," he moaned, his lips tracing a path down my neck. His greedy bites shot hot flashes to my core and I shamelessly ground against him, needing the friction.

I leaned toward him as he somehow slipped off my shorts, all the while I was frantically trying to finagle his shirt off him. It was frantic and rushed, but the second I lined him up with my center and sank down, it was fucking perfection. His large hands squeezed my hips as I bounced up and down on his dick, the friction I needed so badly before was growing higher. Gasps and groans mixed with the sounds of our bodies slapping together. Sketch kissed his way up my neck, then his one hand rested against my throat, squeezing tightly. His other hand played and tugged on my nipple rings. The delicious pain shot through my body.

"Oh God, please. Yes," I gasped. The power of his punishing thrusts danced on the delicate line of pleasure and pain. Sketch sucked and pulled on the rings, and the last line of control broke. I couldn't hold off anymore.

"Come for me, baby. I got you," Sketch groaned, burying his face in my chest, his large hands pinning my waist to his. "Oh God. You feel so damn good."

His thrusts faltered then he slammed into me one final time, causing both of us to shatter. His thick cock pulsed inside me, while my pussy quivered with aftershocks. We sat there, our chests heaving against each other. Sketch's beautiful silver eyes opened, and I saw the world in them. His strength, his love. His light. It was then when I truly understood how much I loved him.

WE HAD TWO DAYS TOGETHER. Two beautiful and glorious days. We didn't leave the bedroom except for food and letting the dogs out. Then he had a mission. What was supposed to be three weeks turned into two months. I knew his job was dangerous but having no contact with him for months was horrible for my anxiety. But I pushed through. I had a life to get back to, and even though I was a scientist with a black stain against her, life still went on. I helped the FBI and DEA with what I could, as limited as it was. Bowen quietly gave me a decent amount of money as thanks for my assistance, when in reality, it was to buy my silence. The scandal and backlash were still ongoing, especially when it turned out Michael's father had a deal made with not only the Syndicate, but with other organized crime operations. The web they wove, how they tried to pit one group against another, was weirdly fascinating but alarming as hell.

It didn't mean this whole thing was over. Not even by a little bit. But thankfully it seemed they were more worried about what was going on inside their own groups, instead of the nerdy chemist who had tattoos and read smutty romance novels.

The scratching at the door and eager barking shook me out of my thoughts. I opened the door and both pups came bounding in. I wouldn't have believed Murray broke his paw a few months back. Both dogs had a ton of energy. I was glad I made the decision to stay here, instead of at Cole's or at Kate's, but it took a while for Kate and Noah to feel it was safe enough. It allowed me to feel closer to him, as weird as it sounds. Being here felt like home.

All of a sudden, the dogs froze. Their ears perked up and they formed a protective stance at the entryway to the kitchen where I was sitting. The low growl in Jax's throat had me rising and reaching for the long chef's knife in the drawer.

The door kicked open and the dogs flew. I rounded the corner, knife in my hand. Then dropped it in shock.

Both dogs sat obediently next to the sexy man on his knees. My hand flew to my mouth in shock and my eyes filled with tears. *Oh my God.*

"Angel. I don't deserve you. But I'm a selfish bastard and don't care about that. I want to keep you all to myself. I need to keep you. You're my light. I'm not on one knee to ask for your hand. I'm on both knees, begging and pleading for you to be mine. Wholly, in everything, forever," his rough voice rumbled. I could always see the truth in his eyes, and right now, I only saw love.

My body quaked from holding back any and all emotion. Emotion had been building up since we last held each other. I rushed the short distance between us and threw my arms around him. On his knees, he came to my chest. His favorite pillows, he once told me. He wrapped his arms around me tightly.

"I'm missed you so much," I breathed as the tears ran down my face. He stood up so I had to tilt my head back. He cupped my jaw and stared into my eyes intently.

"I'll always come home to you." Sketch's lips crashed into mine, as he crushed me to him. He broke the kiss. "You know, you didn't answer my question."

I bit the corner of my lip. "Well. How about this? I'll answer yours if you answer one of mine?"

Sketch narrowed his eyes and tilted his head. "Sure. I'll answer whatever you want. But know this. As soon as I get my answer, you're not going to be able to walk for a week."

I smiled, all the while my heart fluttered, and my nerves were on edge.

"How do you feel about kids?"

"Um, fine I guess..." he said, momentarily confused. "Wait. Are you...?" His eyes widened and his gaze went right to my stomach.

"Yes." I nodded. My anxiety was climbing. I didn't know what I would do if this wasn't what he wanted. If this would be the line he didn't want to cross.

"Fuck, Angel," he breathed. Sketch's big hands gently encircled my waist and pulled me close, his lips pressed against my forehead.

"What do you think? Are you happy?" I asked weakly.

"I'm the luckiest son-of-a-bitch in the world. Yes, I am happy." He tilted my chin up so he could look me in the eyes. "What's wrong? Are you okay with this?"

I let out a breath and my knees went weak. "Yes, I'm more than okay with this. It's that we really haven't had the big 'future' chat yet, you know with the shooting and running away and whatever..." I babbled.

"Angel, I got on my knees the second I got home, to ask you to be mine forever. Your future is our future. If you're happy then I'm fucking over the moon. And if it includes a house full of rug rats, then even better." He kissed me gently on my lips. "But you didn't answer mine. Are you going to be mine forever?"

"Yes." The single word ignited the spark. He picked me up and wrapped my legs around his waist.

AND HE KEPT HIS PROMISE.

I DIDN'T WALK NORMALLY for the rest of that week.

EPILOGUE

The scent of fear and gasoline lingered in the air. The blood was spilled. It covered the ground in puddles, while splattered all over the walls. All that was left from the fight were the bodies that littered the ground. A lone figure walked with purpose around the corpses. He didn't care whose blood it was nor the reason why. He understood the art of the game, and he was determined to be the winner.

Once he cleared the entryway, he looked back. The carnage was everywhere. He smiled, his yellowing teeth showing widely. In his mind, it was beautiful. The delicate appendages, like noses and ears, floating haphazardly in the river that ran between the bodies. The garments saturated in the color crimson. This was how the game was played.

Too bad it couldn't stay like this.

He turned around and snapped his fingers, moving toward the exit. A strike of a match flicked into the river of blood immediately engulfing it into flames.

With a final look at the fire, the figure left his latest funhouse and got into the waiting luxury town car. He settled into the leather seat and adjusted his cufflinks. The privacy partition lowered.

"Where to next, Mr. Cruz?" the driver asked, as he put the car into drive.

A sinister grin crossed his face. "It's time to take a trip, Cedric. This area seems to have..." A large burst of fire exploded out of the roof behind them. "Gone downhill. Get me to the airport and call for a pilot. I have an appointment to make."

Broken Trust (name tentative)
will be released in 2023.

IF YOU NEED HELP

Please take care of yourself.

SAMHSA's National Helpline, 1-800-662-HELP (4357) (also known as the Treatment Referral Routing Service), or TTY: 1-800-487-4889 is a confidential, free, 24-hour-a-day, 365-day-a-year, information service, in English and Spanish, for individuals and family members facing mental and/or substance use disorders.

To report a tip or get help, the confidential National Human Trafficking Hotline is 1 (888) 373-7888. The hotline is available trouble 24/7 and in more than 200 languages.

ABOUT THE AUTHOR
MELISSA HUIE

Creating Sexy Twists at Every Turn.

Melissa was born & raised in Maryland, where her favorite memories took place by the Chesapeake Bay. Now she raises her family in Virginia, and loves bringing her hometown favorites into her sexy, twisted stories. When she's not trying to burn dinner or chasing after her zoo, she can be found at the local coffee shops or breweries with her favorite people.

Melissa can be reached at ...
   Email: AuthorMelissaHuie@gmail.com
   Tiktok: @authormelissahuie
   Facebook: facebook.com/melissadhuie
   Instagram:author_melissa_huie

ACKNOWLEDGMENTS

Seriously....

A HUGE thank you to:

My husband and kiddos – Thank you for making me go write and giving me the ability to hide in my office with my gummy bears, cookies, tacos, and wine. You guys are the best support system I could ever want. I love you so much.

My amazing Editor Amy Briggs – Thank you for reminding me to choose a fucking tense already (ha!) and having the patience to deal with my dramatic lack of confidence.

My awesome Proofer Virginia Tesi Carey - Thank you for being super sweet and having the patience to go over my drafts with a fine-tooth comb.

Reggie Deanching & Bryan Snell. Thank you so much for the amazing cover. It's crazy how an impromptu meeting at a book event in Columbia, SC, led to the most perfect image for this book. You captured Sketch perfectly.

The Jens (aka Jen Scott & Jen Lum) – Thank you for being my sounding board, my smack of reality, the bestest brunch pals, and my road trip partners in crime.

KD Michaels - Thank you for letting your MC Red Scorpions hang out with my crew at Tactical Redemption. I truly appreciate it!

And to everyone else in my life – the readers, fellow authors, friends, family, coworkers - I couldn't have pushed through this book without everyone's support and encouragement. It's because of all of you. Thank you.

www.ingramcontent.com/pod-product-compliance
Lightning Source LLC
Chambersburg PA
CBHW060422180626
46817CB00007B/2628